THE WHITE CONQUERORS

THE CLASSICAL LIBRARY

BY KIRK MUNROE

THE WHITE CONQUERORS

FÉNIX

PRESS

The White Conquerors, Kirk Munroe,
first published by Charles Scribner's Sons,1908.

Republished by Fénix Press,
Jordan Station, ON. L0R 1S0, Canada

Book Design: Steven R. Martins

Library & Archives Canada
ISBN 978-1-7774816-5-0

Table of Contents

Preface

The Classical Library is a collection compiled by Fénix Press of literary classics that should be read, studied, and enjoyed by every home, student, and teacher, whether in the context of the homeschool, elementary, highschool, college, university, or in the most informal and casual of settings.

Fénix Press is proud to republish these literary classics, bringing to the forefront the excellence and masterfulness of these literary contributions. In an age of "nostalgia", with most looking back at the years prior to the 2000s, what better occasion to revisit these classics and to reflect on what made these stories great.

There are arguably four characteristics that make a literary composition a "classic", regardless of the genre. These are: (1) Quality; (2) Longevity; (3) Appeal; and (4) Influence.

As it concerns Quality, classical literature can be appreciated for its structural composition and its commendable artistic features. It would have been highly venerated, or respected by its readers, when it was first published, and this was for the most part because of its masterful artistic quality. And though classics may not be the best-selling books of today, mainly because of their dated language and pacing, they are nonetheless the foundation upon which our Western literary tradition is built. If you are looking for quality that does not disappoint, turn to the classics.

In regard to Longevity, classical literature is known for being representative of its times. The reason many books are considered "classics" today is because they have stood the test of time. That is to say that it was not only read in its time, but it was read well *after* its time, and it *continues* to be read today. In other words, in order for a book to become a "classic", it must live well beyond the life of its author, and that means finding a home in subsequent generations. If it has achieved this longevity, then the work must receive recognition, and that recognition is the designation of being a "classic."

In regard to Appeal, classical literature touches the heart of almost every reader. Most often it is because classics weave different themes within their own narratives, and these themes — whether they be, for example, love, hate, death, life, or faith — draw in readers from a wide range of backgrounds and experiences. As readers have attested, in spite of the fact that they originate from different time periods, the characters and their situations of these "classics" are highly relatable. If they were not, then they could not have stood the test of time.

And finally, in regard to Influence. Classics often

reveal the influence that other writers have had on their general composition. As any avid reader of the classics can attest to, classics are nearly always informed by the history of ideas and literature, and in turn, they inform the great works that follow after them. They are, in other words, the product of influence, and an influence themselves.

Altogether, classical literature is an expression of life, truth, and beauty. Or put differently, an expression of the human soul, reflecting both the human condition, and the remnants of the divine image man bears. Enjoy this republication by Fénix Press for the common good of man, *bonum commune hominis.*

1

A CAPTIVE WARRIOR

NIGHT HAD FALLEN on the island-city of Tenochtitlan, the capital of Anahuac, and the splendid metropolis of the Western world. The evening air was heavy with the scent of myriads of flowers which the Aztec people loved so well, and which their religion bade them cultivate in lavish profusion. From every quarter came the sounds of feasting, of laughter, and of music. The numerous canals of salt-water from the broad lake that washed the foundations of the city on all sides, were alive with darting canoes filled with gay parties of light-hearted revellers. In each canoe burned a torch of sweet-scented wood, that danced and flickered with the motions of the frail craft, its reflection broken by the ripples from hundreds of dipping paddles. Even far out on the placid bosom of the lake, amid the fairylike chinampas, or tiny floating islands, the twinkling canoe-lights flitted like gorgeous fire-flies, paling the silver reflection of the stars with their more ruddy glow.

In the streets of the city the dancing feet of flower-wreathed youths and maidens tripped noiselessly over the smooth cemented pavements; while their elders watched them, with approving smiles, from their curtained doorways, or the flat flower-gardened roofs, of their houses. Above all these scenes of peaceful merriment rose the gloomy pyramids of many temples, ever-present reminders of the cruel and bloody religion with which the whole fair land was cursed.

Before the hideous idols, to which each of these was consecrated, lay offerings of human hearts, torn from the living bodies of that day's victims, and from the summit of each streamed the lurid flames of never-dying altar fires. By night and day they burned, supplied with fuel by an army of slaves who brought it on their backs over the long causeways that connected the island-city with the mainland and its distant forests. These pillars of smoke by day, and ill-omened banners of flame by night, were regarded with fear and hatred by many a dweller in the mountains surrounding the Mexican valley. They were the symbols of a power against which these had struggled in vain, of a tyranny so oppressive that it not only devoted them to lives of toil, hopeless of reward, but to deaths of ignominy and torture whenever fresh victims were demanded for its reeking altars. But while hatred thus burned, fierce and deep-seated, none dared openly to express it, for the power of the all-conquering Aztec was supreme. Far across the lofty mountains, to the great Mexican Gulf on the east, and westward to the broad Pacific; from the parched deserts of the cliff-dwelling tribes on the north, to the impenetrable Mayan forests on the south, the Aztec sway extended, and none might withstand the Aztec arms. If the imperial city demanded tribute it must be promptly given, though nakedness and hunger should result. If its priests demanded victims for their blood-stained altars, these must be yielded without a murmur, that the lives of whole tribes might not be sacrificed. Only one little mountain republic still held out, and defied the armies of the Aztec king, but of it we shall learn more hereafter.

So the mighty city of the lake drew to itself the best of all things from all quarters of the Western world, and was filled to overflowing with the wealth of conquered peoples. Hither came all the gold and silver and precious stones, the richest fabrics, and the first-fruits of the soil. To its markets were driven long caravans of slaves, captured from distant provinces, and condemned to perform such menial tasks as the haughty Aztec disdained to undertake.

During the brilliant reign of the last Montezuma, the royal city attained the summit of its greatness, and defied the world. Blinded by the glitter of its conquests, and secure in the protection of its invincible gods, it feared naught in the future, for what enemy

3

could harm it?

The evening with which this story opens was one of unusual rejoicing in Tenochtitlan, for the morrow was to mark one of the most notable events of Montezuma's reign. The great Aztec calendar stone, the result of years of ceaseless labor, had at length reached the inner court of the principal temple. On the following day it was to be bathed in the blood of victims, and dedicated by the priests. This huge mass of shining porphyry, weighing more than fifty tons, and quarried from the distant mountains beyond the lake of Chalco, had been subjected to the unremitting labors of the most famous astronomers and skilled artisans for so long, that the king had almost despaired of living to witness its completion. Finally, polished like a mirror and cunningly engraved with a countless but orderly array of hieroglyphics, it started on its journey to the city, drawn by the united efforts of ten thousand slaves. Inch by inch, slowly and painfully, costing a thousand lives for every mile of progress, it traversed leagues of rugged country. Even on the great causeway, when it had nearly reached its destination, where the iron-wood rollers ran smoothly and all difficulties seemed at an end, it had broken through a bridge and plunged into the lake, crushing a score of human beings beneath it. With infinite toil and human suffering it had been recovered from the waters, and, as the straining slaves cringed under the biting lashes of their drivers, its triumphal progress was resumed.

At length the huge stone had reached the end of its weary journey, and the morrow was to witness the closing scenes of this great national undertaking. The feasting had already been kept up for a week, or ever since the mighty monolith entered the city. Scores of victims had been sacrificed on the temple altars to insure the favor of the gods during those last days of its progress. But all this was as nothing compared with what would be witnessed on the morrow. For that day the bravest warriors taken in battle had been reserved, and the most beautiful captives. The former would be made to fight against each other under false promises that the lives of the victors should be spared. The latter—handsome youths, delicate maidens, and even little children—would dance a dance of death with wild beasts and deadly serpents, many cages of which had been brought from distant parts for the purpose. Oh! it was truly to be a rare and enjoyable festival, and the hearts of the dwellers in Tenochtitlan thrilled high in anticipation of its pleasures.

And yet, despite the universal joy that reigned in every quarter of the crowded city, it contained at least two hearts that were heavy with the forebodings of sorrow. One was that of its mighty ruler, the priest-warrior, Montezuma, and the other beat in the breast of one even more redoubtable as a warrior than the king himself, who, as a captive, was destined to fight for his life against overwhelming odds on the morrow.

In all that land of warriors there was none so famed

as Tlahuicol. To all men he was known as the Tlas-calan; but ever to himself and to Huetzin, his son, he whispered that he was Tlahuicol the Toltec. For years he had been the dreaded war-chief of the dauntless lit-tle mountain republic of Tlascala, which, alone of all those now occupying the land of Anahuac, had resisted the all-conquering Aztec arms, and retained its free-dom. In spite of this he was not a Tlascalan, but had joined them in one of their times of sorest need, when it seemed as though their surrender to the swarming legions of Montezuma was inevitable. Their army had been defeated, its leaders killed or taken captive, and another day must have witnessed the overthrow of the republic. That night Tlahuicol appeared among them, a young warrior in the first flush of manhood, and addressed them with such fervid eloquence that their sinking spirits were again inflamed, and they gathered courage for one more desperate effort.

In the morning the young stranger led them to an attack against the Aztecs, whose vigilance was relaxed in anticipation of an easy triumph over their enemies. So marvelous was his strength, so admirable his skill, and so reckless his bravery, that the signal victory gained by the Tlascalans that day was afterward said to have been won by Tlahuicol alone. In their excess of gratitude and admiration his brave, but superstitious, followers hailed him as a god, declaring that never in mortal were combined the qualities shown by him that day. From that time forth the fortunes of this stranger were linked with those of the Tlascalans, and all the honors at the disposal of the simple republic were showered upon him. The position of war-chief was accorded to him without question, and for more than a score of years he led his hardy mountaineers to victory in every battle that they fought against the cruel Aztecs. Very early in his new career he was wedded to a beautiful Tlascalan maiden, an only daughter of the noble house of Titcala, the chief of which was the acknowledged head of the republic. The fruits of this marriage were two children: Huetzin, who inherited his father's indomitable bravery, and Tiata, who, even as a child, gave promise that all of her mother's great beauty was to be hers.

As the years rolled on Tlahuicol lost none of his popularity with his troops nor with the people at large; only with the priests was he ever at enmity. He abhorred their bloody human sacrifices, and strove by every means in his power to have them abated. In return, the priests continually strove for his overthrow and to wean the affections of his soldiers from him. For many years their efforts were in vain, but finally their subtle craft gained them a few malcontent adherents. In the very heat of a fierce battle with an Aztec army, commanded by Montezuma in person, a cowardly blow, struck from behind, stretched the Tlascalan war-chief senseless on the ground. When he recovered consciousness he was a prisoner and being hurried toward the Aztec capital. Thither his devoted wife and her children followed him, resigning themselves to a willing captivity, that might even result in death, for the sake of sharing his fortunes.

For more than a year, though every avenue of escape was closely guarded, the noble prisoner was treated with the utmost consideration, and every effort was made to induce him to renounce his allegiance to Tlascala. Honors and riches were promised him if he would devote his sword to the service of the Aztec monarch; but every offer was disdainfully refused, and at length Montezuma reluctantly yielded to the cruel clamor of the priests, and condemned him to sacrifice.

2

"REMEMBER THAT THOU ART A TOLTEC"

Knowing the cruelty of his Aztec captors as well as he did, Tlahuicol had hoped for no mercy from the first. He even attempted to hasten the fate that he foresaw was inevitable, by bitter denunciations of the Aztec priesthood and their horrid rites. Even Topil, the chief priest, whom Montezuma sent to the prisoner with the hope that his awful threats might terrify the bold warrior into an acceptance of his terms, was treated with such scornful contempt, that when he returned to his royal master the priest's dark face was livid with rage. Under penalty of the wrath of the gods, which should be called down upon the whole nation in case his request was not granted, Topil then and there demanded that not only the impious warrior, but his family as well, should be delivered to him for sacrifice.

To this the monarch granted a reluctant consent, only stipulating that they should be reserved for the greatest and most important feasts of the year, and that their fate should not be announced to them until the very hour of sacrifice. Although Topil agreed to these terms, he had no intention of keeping his word. The opportunity of prolonging his enemies› sufferings by anticipation was too precious to be neglected. So he caused the information to be conveyed to Tlahuicol's wife that her husband was doomed to death by torture. At the same time it was intimated, with equal secrecy, to the brave warrior himself, that unless he held himself in readiness to put to death with his own hands a number of Tlascalan captives then awaiting their doom in the dungeons of the great temple, and to lead an Aztec army against the mountain republic, his wife and children should die on the altars of Huitzil. With these cruel threats hanging over them the several members of this unfortunate family were kept apart, and no communication was allowed to pass between them.

Although the stern warrior continued in his defiant attitude, and refused to be moved by either threats or promises, he fell into a state of settled melancholy. This was soon afterward deepened by the sad news that the loving wife, who had shared his captivity as cheerfully as she had his former triumphs, was dead. Of his children he could learn nothing. It was of them that he was thinking, with a heart well-nigh breaking from its weight of sorrow, on the night of rejoicing that preceded the festival of the great calendar stone.

In pursuance of his policy of kindness, by which he hoped to win this redoubtable warrior to his own service, Montezuma had caused Tlahuicol to be lodged in one of the numerous dwellings that formed part of the royal establishment. These buildings, which were occupied by Aztec nobles in attendance upon the king, and by royal hostages from conquered nations, stood with the palace in an immense walled enclosure, hard by the great temple. They were surrounded by gardens planted with a wealth of tropical trees, shrubs, and flowers, traversed by a labyrinth of shaded paths and cool grottoes, watered by canals, lakes, and fountains, and containing immense aviaries of every bird known to the kingdom, as well as cages of serpents and wild animals. Ten large tanks, some filled with salt-water, and others with fresh, were stocked with every procurable variety of fish and marine animal; while for the care of these creatures, whose habits the king was never tired of studying, an army of attendant slaves was maintained. Besides these features of the royal museum, there was a building containing every form of warlike weapon and defensive armor known to the Aztecs, another for rare fabrics, and one for exquisitely wrought vessels of gold, silver, and the prized pottery of Cholula. There was also an establishment for dwarfs and other human monstrosities, which the monarch took pleasure in collecting from all parts of his kingdom.

In this place of beauty, and surrounded by all

that royalty could command of things best calculated to interest and amuse, Tlahuicol chafed at his captivity, and dreamed of his home in the distant mountains. If he could but once more lead his trusty troops to battle against the hated Aztec, how gladly would he pay for the privilege with his life! He was allowed the freedom of the gardens, though always under guard, and sometimes he would stroll to the training-field where the king's sons and other noble youth vied with each other in feats of arms. As he watched them his lip would curl with scorn at their puny efforts, and a fierce desire to show them what a mountain warrior could do with those same weapons would seize upon him. But no weapon was allowed within his reach, and with an air of disgust he would turn and walk back to his own quarters, always closely followed by his watchful guards.

On the evening preceding the day of the great feast, Tlahuicol sat moodily just outside the door of the house in which he was lodged, and which, beautiful as it was, still seemed to him the most hateful of prisons. Two motionless guards, armed with keen-edged maquahuitls, or Aztec swords, stood close at hand at either side, with their eyes fixed upon him. Should he escape, or should he even do himself bodily harm, their lives would be forfeit, and with this knowledge their vigilance was never relaxed.

Tlahuicol sat with downcast eyes and listened to the sounds of revelry that came faintly to him from the city. Clearly he understood their meaning, and wondered if on the morrow he was to meet the doom that he believed to be in store for him. He thought of the wife who was gone from him, and of the son and daughter concerning whose fate he had long been kept in ignorance. From these thoughts he was roused by the sound of approaching footsteps, and at once rose to his feet. In a moment the king, followed at a short distance by armed torch-bearers, stood before him.

Abruptly, and in a tone that proved him to be greatly agitated, Montezuma said:

"Tlahuicol, I am come to thee once again as a friend. As such I would serve thee, and as such I claim thy service."

"Thy friendship I reject, O king, and my service thou shalt never have," returned the other, proudly.

"Hear me to the end," replied the king, calmly; "for many days I have known what thou hast had no means of learning, but which will interest thee. An army of strange beings, white-skinned and bearded, but whether gods or men cannot be determined, have come out of the eastern sea, and landed on our coast. Since their earliest appearance my spies have noted their every movement, and brought me hourly word concerning them. I had hoped they would depart in peace, but was disappointed in the hope. Even now is word brought me that they have attacked and captured my city of Cempoalla, destroyed its gods, and are preparing to advance into the interior. If they be gods my power may not prevail against them. If they be men, as I hope, then will I fight them until they are swept from the face of the earth, and their hearts smoke upon the altars of Huitzil. In such a fight all other feuds should be forgotten, and all the nations of Anahuac united. It is in this service that I would have thy aid. With thy word that thou wilt enlist thy Tlascalans against this common foe, and lead them to battle as of old, both thou and thy children are free. Refuse it, and thy heart shall lie on Huitzil's altar ere the setting of the morrow's sun."

In spite of this startling intelligence, in spite of the tempting offer thus made, and in spite of the terrible threat by which it was accompanied, Tlahuicol's voice, as he answered the king, was as calm as though he was discussing some topic of ordinary interest.

"O king," he said, "know what I have told no man ere now, that I am no Tlascalan, but am a Toltec of the Toltecs. For many generations have my ancestors dwelt in the country of the Mayas. From there I came to this land to battle against thy accursed gods. Since the day that I left the Mayan people have I ever been in communication with them. Thus did I learn long since of strange and terrible beings, white-skinned and bearded as thou dost describe, who had landed on the Mayan coast. I was told much concerning them, and one thing I learned that thou wouldst give half thy kingdom to know for a certainty."

"Tell it me then, I command thee?" cried the king.

"I will tell it," answered Tlahuicol, "upon condition

that thou first grant me a few minutes private converse with my children."

"Thy daughter is removed from here, but thy son is at hand. In return for thy secret, I will grant thee a single minute with him, but no more."

"It is all I ask," replied the prisoner.

The king gave an order to one of the guards and handed him his signet. The soldier departed. In a few minutes he returned accompanied by a tall, finely proportioned youth, of noble bearing, just entering upon manhood. It was Huetzin, who, at sight of his father, whom he had feared was dead, sprang into Tlahuicol's arms, and was enfolded in a close embrace. Quickly releasing himself, the elder man said hurriedly, but in too low a tone for the bystanders to hear:

"Huetzin, my son, by tomorrow's set of sun I may be with thy mother, therefore do thou take these as my latest words. Remember always that thou art a Toltec, that the Aztecs and the Aztec gods are mortal enemies of thy gods and thy people. If thou art spared, as I feel thou wilt be, devote thy life to their overthrow. The white conquerors, of whom I have so often spoken to thee, are even now in the land. If thou canst escape from this den of murderers, make thy way to them, join thyself to them, and lead them to this place. As for little Tiata, I trust thee——"

"Thy time is ended!" interrupted the stern voice of the king; "and now for thy secret?"

There was one more straining embrace between father and son, then the latter, exclaiming, "I will never forget!" was roughly dragged away and disappeared in the darkness.

Folding his arms, and turning grandly to the king, Tlahuicol said: "The secret that thou wouldst hear, O Montezuma, is that the strange beings who trouble thee are not gods, but men. At the same time they be men possessed of powers so terrible that they will sweep thee and thy false gods from the face of the earth, as the breath of the north wind scattereth chaff. Know, too, that sooner than lift hand to stay their coming, I will pray for their success with my latest breath."

"Thy prayers will be few and short, then," answered the king, in a tone of suppressed rage, as he turned away; "for on the morrow thy false heart shall be torn from thy body, and the wild fowls of the air shall feast upon thy carcass."

3

IN THE MARKET-PLACE
OF TENOCHTITLAN

ON THE MORNING of the last and greatest day of the festival by which the mighty calendar stone was dedicated, the rising sun shone from an unclouded sky upon the fair city of Tenochtitlan. All night long a thousand slaves had been busy sweeping and watering its streets, until now their smooth pavements of cement fairly shone with cleanliness. As there were no horses nor other beasts of burden in all the land, as all heavy traffic of the city was carried on in boats by means of the numerous intersecting canals, and as water was everywhere abundant, the cleansing of the ancient city of Tenochtitlan was a much easier task than is that of Mexico, its modern successor.

From earliest dawn troops of country people had thronged the three great causeways leading from the mainland, and poured over them into the city. Fleets of canoes from Tezcuco, on the opposite side of the lake, and from various smaller cities and villages on its border, were constantly arriving laden with parties of expectant sight-seers. Thus the avenues, streets, and squares, as well as the enclosures of the six hundred teocallis or temples of the city, were filled, soon after sunrise, by an eager and joyous multitude.

Especially animated was the scene in the tinguez, or great market-place, of Tlateloco. Here, displaying their wares in its shaded porticos, under booths of green leaves, or beneath awnings of gayly-striped cloth, were gathered traders from all parts of the kingdom, each in the quarter allotted to his particular class of goods. Among them were the goldsmiths of Azapozalco, the potters of Cholula, the weavers of Tezcuco, the stone-carvers of Tenojocan, the hunters of Xilotepec, the fishermen of Cuitlahuac, the mat and chair makers of Quauhtitlan, the florists of Iztapalapan, the fruit-dealers of the tierra templada, and the skilled artisans in feather-work of Xochimilco. Here were armorers displaying arrows, darts, and javelins, headed with an alloy of copper and tin as hard as steel, and tougher, heavy maquahuitls, resembling somewhat both a battle-axe and a sword, with keen blades of glistening itztli or obsidian. Escaupils, or doublets of quilted cotton which no arrow might penetrate, fierce-looking casques, fashioned like the grinning heads of wild animals, and shirts of golden mail, which only nobles might wear.

In other places were quantities of meat, poultry, bread of maize, cakes, pastry, confectionery, smoking bowls of chocolate, flavored with vanilla, which, with the intoxicating pulque, shared the name of national beverage. Barber-shops, and booths for the sale of drugs and herbs abounded. Nor were book-stalls wanting, though the books displayed in them bore slight resemblance to those of modern times. They were formed of broad sheets of cotton cloth, parchment, or a paper made from the leaves of the agave, folded in the shape of fans, and covered with the minute colored pictures by means of which the Aztecs, ignorant of letters, reproduced their ideas on paper. Thus all Aztec writers were artists, and in the education of youth drawing was taught instead of reading and writing. To name all the commodities offered for sale in this vast market-place would be a tedious task, for in all Tenochtitlan were no stores, nor shops, nor places for trade, save this. The money used was in the shape of quills of gold-dust, small bags of cacao beans, and rudely stamped bits of tin.

Besides being a market-place, the tinguez was the centre where all news was exchanged, and to it came all those who wished to hear or tell some new thing. On this particular day two subjects of intense interest agitated the multitude who thronged it, to the exclusion of all other topics. One was the appearance on the coast of the white strangers, who were invariably spoken of as gods, and the other was the spectacle with which the great festival was to conclude that afternoon.

"They do say," exclaimed one portly individual, clad in a flowing tilmatli, or robe of purple cotton cloth, belted at his waist with a broad yellow sash, to the armorer whose store of obsidian daggers he was inspecting, «that the white gods are coming this way, and have even now set forth from Cempoalla."

"So I have heard," replied the other, "but I care not. If the king so wills, they may come. If he forbids, they may not."

"But," continued he of the purple robe, "they do say that the king has already forbidden their advance, and that the strangers pay no heed to his words."

"Then will Huitzil, the all-powerful, awake, and destroy them with a breath."

"But they do say that some of them are gods mighty and terrible in themselves, having the forms both of men and beasts greater and more frightful than ever were seen. And they do say," he almost whispered in his earnestness, "that they breathe fire and smoke like Popocatepetl himself, and that their weapons are thunderbolts."

"Aye, and they do say truly," interrupted a book-seller who had overheard these remarks, "for here it is pictured out in detail, a copy made from one of the reports sent to the king himself."

With this the new-comer unfolded a fan-like sheet of parchment, on which were drawn likenesses of white men in armor, some on horseback and others on foot, of cannon belching forth fire and smoke, and of many other things so strange and wonderful to Aztec eyes that in a few moments the trio were surrounded by a gaping crowd, eagerly pushing and struggling for a glimpse of the marvelous pictures.

Amid the excitement caused by these evidences that the rumors of the white gods, busily circulated for many months, were only too true, the armorer remained calm and self-possessed. He even expressed a contempt for the strange beings who, he declared, were but sea-monsters, after all.

"Can such creatures harm the children of the sun so long as Huitzil, the god of gods, watches over them from his seat above the clouds?" he cried. "Not that he will be called upon to so much as lift a finger; for is not Montezuma, our lord and the lord of lords, able of his own might to drive them into the sea, whence they came? Shall he who overcame Tlahuicol, the greatest warrior of the age, forbid the advance of men, monsters, fire-breathing beasts, or even of gods, in vain? Shame on you for thus belittling your own gods and your king! Alas! that I, in my poverty, am compelled to forge weapons for such as you!"

"They do say," here interposed he of the purple robe, anxious to change the subject, "that Tlahuicol the Tlascalan, who is doomed to sacrifice this day, has demanded the privilege of a warrior who has never turned back to foe, and that the king has granted it."

"Not the battle of despair?" exclaimed the armorer.

"Even so," nodded the other.

"Then will I at once put away my wares, and hasten to secure a place within the serpent wall, for if he meet with worthy foemen the sight of this battle will be worth all the other sights of earth, and I would not miss it, though with my right hand I was forced to pay for admission within the sacred wall."

It was even so. Tlahuicol was to lend a crowning glory to the great festival of his enemies by fighting, for their entertainment, the battle of despair. This was the poor privilege granted to any captive warrior who had never turned back to foe, of fighting for his life and liberty, with a single weapon, and with one foot tethered, against any six who might challenge him, and who might attack him singly or in couples, as they chose. In all Aztec history no captive had ever gained his freedom in this manner, and even so famous a warrior as Tlahuicol was not supposed to have the slightest chance of victory in so unequal a contest. It was well known that he had been out of practice, and had taken almost no exercise for a year. Thus it was held by many that he was now no more than equal to a warrior of ordinary attainments. As to his overcoming six, selected from the throng of young Aztec nobles who eagerly sought this opportunity for acquiring fame and the order of knighthood, which would be conferred upon him who should deal a fatal blow to the redoubtable Tlascalan, the idea was unworthy of consideration.

Nevertheless all agreed that Tlahuicol would make a pretty fight, and even to witness the death-struggle of the warrior whose name had so long been a terror to Aztec ears, was deemed so great a privilege that, hours before the time set for the battle, every inch of available space in the amphitheatre adjoining the great temple was occupied by the eager populace.

This amphitheatre was but a small portion of the vast area reserved in the heart of the city, and enclosed by a stone wall eight feet high, called the Coatapantli, or wall of serpents, for the temple of Huitzil, the war-god. Here were the dwellings of thousands of priests, and quarters for ten thousand troops, granaries, arsenals, seminaries for the priestly education of youth of both sexes, and numerous monuments, the most notable of which was that constructed of one hundred thousand human skulls of victims sacrificed on Huitzil's altars. In the exact centre of the whole towered the great temple, a lofty pyramid of masonry rising in five terraces, which were gained by as many flights of stairs. Each of these gave access to a single terrace, and they were so arranged that from the top of one the entire circuit of the pyramid must be made ere the next flight could be reached.

The top of this mighty pyramid presented a flat surface of nearly an acre in extent. On it, rising to a height of sixty feet, was a shrine sheltering a hideous image of the god and its bloody altar, on which was laid daily offerings of human hearts torn from living bodies. Outside of the shrine stood another altar, on which burned the never-dying fire. It was commonly believed that if by any chance this should be extinguished some dire calamity would overtake the nation. Near by stood the great war-drum of serpents' skins, which was only struck in times of emergency, when the awe-inspiring sound of its hollow boomings could be heard for leagues.

The only other object on the broad level space was a large block of jasper, slightly convex on its upper side. It was the stone of sacrifice, across which victims were laid for the greater convenience of the priests in cutting open their breasts and tearing out the still palpitating hearts in which the blood-loving god delighted. The whole place bore the aspect of a shambles, and was pervaded by a sickening stench. The priests who officiated here, and of whom Topil was the chief, were blood-besmeared from head to foot, and allowed their long hair, also clotted with blood, to hang in elf-locks over their shoulders. Thus their appearance was more savage and terrible than can well be imagined.

4

TLAHUICOL'S
LAST BATTLE

THE AMPHITHEATRE in which Tlahuicol was to make so desperate a fight for his life was enclosed on three sides by low buildings, having terraced roofs on which a vast number of spectators could be accommodated. In its centre was an immense circular stone, like a gigantic mill-stone, on the flat surface of which were fought all gladiatorial combats. Late in the afternoon of the day of feasting, when the thousands of spectators were weary of the brutal games by which until that time they had been entertained, an expectant murmur suddenly swept over the vast assemblage, and then broke into a roar of applause. Six warriors of noble birth, wearing on their heads golden casques in the likenesses of a dog, a fox, a wolf, a bear, an ocelot, and a mountain-lion, with a carriage that bespoke their martial training, had entered the amphitheatre, and were marching slowly around the outer edge of the great stone. When they reached the point nearest the pavilion in which, beneath a canopy of royal green, reclined the king, surrounded by his attendant nobles, the six warriors prostrated themselves until their foreheads touched the pavement. Then they continued their measured march until they reached the side of the amphitheatre opposite that by which they had entered.

Now, to the barbaric music of drums, attabals, and shells, there entered a single figure between a double file of soldiers, and the hurricane of applause by which he was greeted would have proclaimed his identity even had not his name been heard on all sides.

"Tlahuicol the ocelot!" "Tlahuicol the wolf!" "Tlahuicol the mountain-lion!" "Tlahuicol the terrible!" shouted the spectators, and the eyes of the great warrior lighted with a momentary gleam of triumph at these tributes from his enemies. He was conducted directly to the centre of the great stone, where one of his ankles was tethered by a short chain to a ring-bolt let into the unyielding rock. Then one of his guards stripped the tilmatli from his shoulders, disclosing the fact that he was naked, save for a cloth about his loins, and unprotected by armor of any kind. At the same moment another soldier handed the prisoner the maquahuitl with which he was to defend his life.

Tlahuicol balanced it for a moment in his hand, then suddenly snapped its tough staff in two without apparent effort, and disdainfully flung the pieces from him. Turning toward the king he cried, in a loud voice:

"It was but a toy! A child's plaything, and yet it was given me for the defense of my life! Let me, I pray thee, O king, have my own good sword. Then will I show thee a fight that may prove of interest."

The king nodded his assent. A soldier was dispatched for the weapon, and shortly returned, bearing in both hands a maquahuitl so huge that a murmur of amazement arose from the spectators, who deemed it impossible that any man could wield it. But Tlahuicol received it with a smile of satisfaction, swung it lightly twice or thrice above his head, and then leaned upon it with an expectant air as though inviting his enemies to approach. No further invitation was needed, for no Aztec warrior worthy of the name was ever lacking in bravery. The young noble who wore the head of a fox sprang forward, and, with guarded movements, approached the chained but still terrible champion.

Cautiously the fox circled about his adversary seeking an unguarded point at which to strike. On account of his fettered leg Tlahuicol could only turn half-way round, but he would then whirl about so quickly that, in spite of his disadvantage, he presented no opening for attack for some minutes. At length, wearying of such fruitless play, he purposely made his movements slower, until the Fox, thinking his opportunity had come, sprang forward to deliver a deadly blow. In an instant his sword was struck from his hand. Broken and useless it was sent spinning to the further side of the arena, and the Fox reeled backward with the force of the blow. Recovering himself he sprang to a soldier who stood near, snatched a javelin from his hand, and hurled it with deadly aim at Tlahuicol's head. Without moving his body, the Toltec bent his head to one side, caught the hurtling weapon in his left hand, and, almost with the same motion, flung it back with such terrible force that it passed completely through the body of the Aztec and fell to the ground behind him. He staggered, fell, and was borne, dying, from the scene.

Instantly two of his companions took his vacant place. Filled with rage they advanced impetuously and somewhat incautiously. As their weapons were raised to strike, the terrible maquahuitl of Tlahuicol crushed the skull of one like an egg-shell, and then, with a fierce backward blow, sent the other reeling a dozen paces away, so severely wounded that it was doubtful if he might ever recover. Marvelous as this feat was, it did not wholly save the Toltec from the descending sword of his third enemy. The keen obsidian blade cut a frightful gash in his side, and he was instantly bathed in his own blood.

But the wounded warrior had no time to consider his own condition, for, almost before he realized that he had been struck, two fresh assailants were upon him. One of these was cleft from casque to shoulders by Tlahuicol's awful weapon, which seemed to the breathless spectators like a thunderbolt in the hands of a god. Ere the Toltec could recover himself, the other rushed in and bore him to the ground, where, falling uppermost, the Aztec hoped to deal a fatal blow with his dagger. Before he could accomplish his purpose the champion's arms had enfolded him in an embrace so deadly that the breath was driven from his body with a sound that might be heard in all parts of the amphitheatre, and his ribs were crushed like pipe-stems. Leaping to his feet, amid thunders of applause from the frenzied spectators, the Toltec flung the lifeless body from him, and regained his ponderous sword just in time to meet the onset of his sixth, and most powerful, assailant, he whose casque was fashioned in the likeness of an ocelot.

Now the breath of the champion came in sobbing gasps, and he was so weakened by loss of blood that it seemed impossible for him to withstand the furious onslaught of this fresh adversary. For the space of two minutes the exchange of blows was so rapid that there was but one continuous crash of sound. Then the ocelot leaped back beyond reach of his tethered opponent. The Toltec staggered and seemed about to fall. Suddenly, rallying his failing strength, he hurled his heavy weapon so truly, and with such mighty force, that the last of his assailants was swept over the edge of the platform on which they had fought, and rolled, to all appearance lifeless, to the base of the royal pavilion.

For an instant there was a silence as of death in the vast amphitheatre. Then it was broken by a thrilling cry in the Mayan tongue of "Father! Oh, Father! You have conquered! You are free!"

Tlahuicol, who had fallen to his knees with the force of his last effort, lifted his drooping head and looked to where Huetzin struggled in the grasp of two brawny priests. Then, very feebly, with his right hand, he made a sign such as but two persons in that vast concourse recognized. He touched his forehead, his breast, and both shoulders. It was the sign of the God of the Four Winds, the almost forgotten symbol of the Toltec faith. Huetzin knew it, and so did one of the priests who held him.

With the making of this sacred symbol of his race, the mighty warrior fell forward and lay prone on the bloody stone, unmindful of the wild storm of plaudits by which his unprecedented victory was hailed.

Suddenly, while all was confusion, the fierce figure of Topil, the chief priest, sprang to the platform, and, snatching the dread knife of sacrifice from his girdle, bent over the prostrate man. The next moment he rose, and with a savage cry of triumph held aloft the heart of the bravest son of Anahuac. The cheering of the multitude sank into a shuddering cry of horror at this dastardly act. Had another committed it he would have been rent in pieces, but the person of the chief priest was sacred.

Even the elements seemed aghast at the dreadful deed; for, though the sun had not yet set, the sky was darkened by a veil of inky blackness, and an ominous moaning filled the air.

Paying no heed to these portents, nor to the black looks of those about him, Topil screamed to his fellows that the son should share the fate of the father, and that the god was weary of waiting for the offering of their hearts. Then, bidding them follow him with the prisoner, he sprang up the steps of the great temple. With shrill cries the obedient priests forced a passage through the surging multitude, and hurried Huetzin in the same direction. Even the king had no power to stop them, for in Tenochtitlan the chief priest was mightier than he.

So the compact body of white-robed priests mounted flight after flight of steps, and swept around the four sides of the teocal along terrace above terrace. Finally they gained the summit of the lofty pyramid, and disappeared from the view of the silent throngs who gazed, as though fascinated, after them.

Inevitable and awful as was the fate before him, Huetzin had but one thought as he was dragged up those weary flights, and along those interminable terraces. It was not for himself, but for his sister Tiata, the dear one who, with his last words, the dead father had entrusted to his care. Without father, mother, or brother, what would be her fate? What would become of her? As they stripped him and stretched his naked body on the dread stone of sacrifice, he cried aloud in his agony:

"Tiata! Sister! To the god of the Toltecs, our father's god and our god, I commend thee!"

5

HUETZIN'S MIRACULOUS ESCAPE

AT THIS SUPREME moment in the life of Huetzin, the young Toltec, the scene, of which he formed the central figure, was of such a character as to inspire a nameless fear in the hearts of all beholders. To the silent multitude who, with upturned faces, were gathered about the temple of their most dreaded god, awaiting the wild chant of priests that should proclaim the sacrifice accomplished, the summit of the lofty pyramid was lost in the pall-like blackness of the heavens. Only a fitful gleam of altar-fire formed a point of light on which the eye could rest. The broad space surmounting the temple was the dramatic focus of the weird scene. About it moaned the spirits of upper air, as though with the voices of the innumerable dead who had breathed their last on that accursed spot. There was an absolute calm, and no breath of wind disturbed the straight column of altar-flame that cast a lurid light across the blood-stained platform. In front of the altar, and clustered in a dark mass about the stone of sacrifice, were the priests of Huitzil. Their white robes had been thrown aside, and all the hideous features of their blood-smeared bodies and streaming locks of matted hair were revealed. In their midst, cruelly outstretched on the mass of polished jasper, lay the naked body of the beautiful youth whose death was to close the pagan rites with which the great calendar stone was dedicated.

Suddenly the dread silence was broken by a single stroke upon the huge drum of serpent skins. Out through the blackness rolled its booming echoes, proclaiming to the utmost limits of the city, and far beyond, that the final act of the drama was about to be consummated. As the significant sound smote upon the ears of those gathered at the base of the teocal, a shuddering cry broke from the vast concourse. It was heard by Topil, the chief priest, who had just sounded the signal, and now strode, knife in hand, toward his waiting victim; but it only caused him to smile scornfully. It was but another tribute to his power, and he exulted in the natural accessories that rendered this final scene so impressive.

As Topil stood beside his victim, Huetzin gave utterance to the prayer recorded in the preceding chapter. Then the dread knife, that had drunk the blood of thousands, was uplifted. Ere it could descend there came, from out the enveloping blackness, a flash of light so vivid, and a crash of thunder so awful, that the very earth trembled with the shock and the mighty pyramid rocked on its foundations. A huge globe of fire, a veritable thunderbolt of the gods launched with unerring aim and irresistible force, had fallen on Huitzil›s temple. It burst as it struck the rock-paved summit of the teocal, and for a moment the whole space was bathed in leaping flames of such dazzling intensity that no mortal eye might gaze upon them. Many of the stone blocks were shattered into fragments, the altar on which burned the eternal fire was overthrown and its sacred flame extinguished. The priests, gathered about the stone of sacrifice, were flung, stunned and breathless, in every direction. Some of them, in the madness of their terror, even leaped from the edge of the trembling platform, and were dashed to the pavement of the courtyard far below.

An instant of darkness followed this first exhibition of the storm god's power. While it lasted, cries of terror and lamentation arose from all parts of the wide-spread city. From every quarter it was seen that the sacred fire no longer burned, and into every mind flashed the foreboding of calamity thus portended. Only for a moment was the wrath of the storm god stayed, and then bolt upon bolt crashed above the devoted city, their awful din mingled with the wild shriekings of unfettered winces, and a downpour of rain that seemed like to deluge the world.

With the first outbreak of the tempest, Huetzin, released by the terrified priests who had held him, rolled unconscious to the pavement beside the stone of sacrifice. When he recovered his senses and staggered to his feet, a furious storm of wind and rain was buffeting his naked body, while lightning glared and thunder crashed incessantly about him. But he still lived, and of those who so recently condemned him to death, not one was to be seen. A sudden hope sprang into his breast, and he glanced about for a way of escape. There was none. If he descended the long flights of steps he would certainly be apprehended in the walled court below. He might seek a temporary refuge in the shrine at one end of the platform; but at the best, that would only prolong his existence for a few wretched hours. Last of all, he might end his misery at once by a leap from the giddy verge of the platform on which he stood. Yes, that was best. There was no other way. As he was about to carry out this intention, a human figure rose from beyond the sacrificial stone, and stepped to where he stood. It was that of a priest, and, as a flash of lightning betrayed his presence, Huetzin's impulse to seize him and force him also to take the death-leap was checked by a sight that filled him with amazement.

A second gleam of lightning revealed the startling fact that this priest of Huitzil was making the sacred symbol of the Toltec faith, the sign made by his own father as his dying act, and which he deemed unknown to any in all Tenochtitlan save himself. As he stood motionless with amazement, the strange priest cried, in a voice to be heard above the tumult of the storm:

"Follow me and I will save you, for I, too, know the holy sign of the Four Winds! I, too, am a Toltec!"

With this he seized the youth's hand, and the latter allowed himself to be led away. Instead of turning toward the outer stairway, as Huetzin fancied they would, they entered the foul and evil-smelling shrine of the Aztec war-god. The monstrous image, with its hideous features, was dimly revealed by the intermittent flashes of lightning, and Huetzin shuddered as he stood before it. To him it was the embodiment of that cruel and cowardly religion with which the fair land of his ancestors was cursed, and could he have destroyed it at the expense of his own life, he would gladly have done so.

Passing swiftly to the back of the image, the priest, who had just proclaimed himself to be of the Toltec race, caused a panel of stone to slide noiselessly back in polished grooves, and disclosed a place of utter blackness. Entering this he drew Huetzin after him. Then he closed the opening, and, bidding the other stand motionless, passed his hands carefully over the stone floor at their feet. There was a slight grating sound, and Huetzin knew, by a sudden upflow of damp air, that some concealed passage-way had been opened.

"Now," whispered his guide, "we are about to descend a secret stairway known only to the chief priest and myself. Moreover, should he even suspect that I was possessed of its knowledge, my heart would smoke on Huitzil's altar. For this reason I claim thy oath, by the immortal God of the Four Winds, never to reveal this secret, so long as Huitzil sits upon his throne."

"By the sacred name of the Four Winds I swear never to reveal it," answered the youth.

Then they began to descend, carefully closing the opening above them, and feeling their way with the utmost caution. The air was damp and chill, the narrow stone steps were slippery with moisture. They formed a stairway of zigzags, and to Huetzin it seemed as though they must penetrate below the foundations of the temple, so long was it before the bottom of the last flight was reached.

At the terminus of the stairway was a closed door, which only those initiated into its secret might open. It admitted them to a long narrow passage, from which branched other passages, as Huetzin learned by coming upon them with his groping hands. His guide took careful note of the number of these passages, and finally turned into one that led at right angles to that they had been following. After a while it sloped upward, and at its end they found themselves in a small room, which at the same time seemed large and airy as compared with the suffocating narrowness of the various passages they had just traversed.

Bidding Huetzin remain here for a moment, the priest left him standing in darkness and silence that were absolute. So long a time elapsed before his com-

panion returned, that the young Toltec wondered if he
had escaped the altar of sacrifice only to be buried alive
in this mysterious place. While he dwelt with a sinking
heart on the awful possibilities thus presented, a door
was noiselessly opened, and a flood of light poured into
the apartment. The priest, bearing a torch in one hand
and a packet in the other, entered. He was followed by
a slave, carrying a basket, at sight of whom Huetzin
shrank back in alarm.

"Be not afraid," whispered the priest, noting the
movement; "he is blind and knows naught of thy presence."

As the slave set down his burden, he was dismissed
and retired, closing the door behind him. From the
packet that he bore the priest produced a robe of the
coarse cotton (nequen) worn by the lower classes, with
which Huetzin gladly covered his naked body, a pair of
grass sandals, and a dagger of itztli. The basket yielded materials for a bountiful meal, to which the young
man, who had tasted no food since the night before,
sat down with the appetite of one who is famished. His
companion also ate heartily, and as he did so conversed
with Huetzin, principally of his own affairs. Of himself
he only said:

"My name is Halco, and like thyself I am of the
Toltec race. Why I am here in this accursed guise, and
how I came to know the secrets of Topil, I cannot now
explain. Suffice it that I am one of the bitterest enemies
of Aztec priesthood and Aztec gods. Until the moment

of his death I knew not that thy father, the brave Tla-huicol, was a Toltec, or I might have saved him; when he made the sign it was too late. Now I can provide thee with means of escape. Make thy way to the camp of the white conquerors, of whom thou must have heard, and lead them to this city. In them lies our only hope for the overthrow of Huitzil and his bloody priesthood; when thou comest again thou shalt hear from me."

"But Tiata, my sister! I cannot leave her unprotected," interrupted Huetzin.

"Fear not for her. For the present she is safe, and if she were not thou couldst do nothing to help her. I will keep watch, and if dangers beset her while thou art with the white conquerors, thou shalt be informed. Now that thou hast eaten and regained thy strength, thy flight must be continued. Already Topil is aware of thy escape, and he has sworn by all the gods that thy heart shall yet smoke on Huitzil's altar."

6

TWO SLAVES OF IZTAPALAPAN

Following the mysterious priest, who bore the torch that illuminated their way, Huetzin was conducted through bewildering ranges of galleries, passages, and halls, until finally Halco paused, saying:

"Farther than this I may not go. It is high time that I showed myself among the priests, that my absence may not cause suspicion. Follow this passage to its end, where thy way of escape will be made plain. Now fare thee well, son of Tlahuicol, and may the god of the Four Winds guide and protect thee."

With these words, and without waiting for a reply, the priest turned abruptly away, and in another moment both he and the light of his torch had disappeared. For a minute or so Huetzin stood motionless where he had been left, but as his eyes grew accustomed to the darkness, he imagined that a faint light came from the direction he had been told to take. Walking cautiously toward it his ear caught the sound of lapping waters, and in a moment later he stood in the opening of a low water-gate that looked out on the broad lake of Tezcuco. The storm had passed and the stars shone brightly. The cool night air was delightfully refreshing, and Huetzin inhaled it with long breaths. As he looked out beyond the wall of the gateway, he saw a shadowy form of a canoe containing a single occupant, who appeared to be waiting. Believing this to be the means of escape indicated by the priest, he uttered a slight cough.

Instantly there came a whisper of: "Art thou he who would be set across?"

To which Huetzin replied, without hesitation: "I am he."

As the canoe moved to where he stood, he stepped in, and it instantly shot away toward the farther side of the star-flecked waters. Many boats, with twinkling lights, were seen, but all of them were skilfully avoided, until the canoe was among a cluster of little floating islands of artificial construction. Some of these were used as resorts by pleasure-loving Aztecs, and others as small gardens on which were raised vegetables and flowers for the near-by city market. As the canoe which bore Huetzin and his silent companion passed swiftly by one of these, a stern voice hailed them, demanding to know their business and whither they were bound.

Receiving no reply, the voice commanded them to halt, in the king's name.

"What shall I do?" asked Huetzin's companion, irresolutely.

"Do as he commands, and when his curiosity is satisfied so that thou art allowed to depart, come for me to yonder chinampa," replied Huetzin, in a whisper. As he spoke he pointed to one of the floating islands dimly outlined not far from them, and at the same time quietly slipped into the water. He swam noiselessly, but with such powerful strokes that a dozen of them placed him beside the tiny islet he had indicated to his companion. He made as though he would land on it, and then, with a sudden change of plan, the motive of which he could not have explained even to himself, he slipped back into the water and swam toward another chinampa that he could barely discern in the distance. It was well for him that he obeyed the instinct forbidding him to land on the first island; for, as he drew himself out on the second, and lay hidden in the tall grasses that fringed its edge, he heard the quick dip of paddles, and the sound of suppressed, but excited, voices coming from the direction of the other. He was startled by hearing his own name coupled with that of his father. It was borne distinctly to him over the still waters, and gave him a certain intimation that the bloodhounds of the chief priest were already on his trail.

Without waiting a further confirmation of his fears, Huetzin hastily crossed to the other side of the island on which he had taken refuge, almost stumbling against the tiny, grass-thatched hut of its proprietor as he did so. The man heard him, and shouted to know who was there. As Huetzin quietly entered the water and swam away, the man emerged from his hut, keeping up the angry shouting that the young Toltec would so gladly have silenced. He soon gained another island, fastened to which he discovered a canoe. Even as he clambered into it and shoved off, its owner, aroused by the distant shouts, came hurriedly to the place where it had been. In another moment his outcries were added to the others, as he discovered his loss. Fortunately the canoe had drifted so far under the impetus of Huetzin›s vigorous shove, that it was hidden by the darkness from the eyes of its owner, so that he could form no notion of who had taken it, nor why it had been stolen.

Huetzin lay motionless in the bottom of the frail craft so long as it continued to move. Then he raised himself cautiously and began to feel for a paddle. To his dismay there was none. The careful owner had carried it to his hut, and now the fugitive, though possessed of a boat, had no means of propelling it. Yes, he had his hands! And, kneeling in the bottom of the canoe, he began to urge it forward by paddling with them. It was slow and tedious work. Moreover, it was accompanied by a certain unavoidable amount of splashing. This sounded so loud to the strained senses of the poor lad, that he felt convinced it must reach the ears of his pursuers.

He had made considerable progress and was well-nigh exhausted by the unaccustomed nature of his efforts, but still hopeful of escape. Suddenly he heard voices behind him, evidently approaching rapidly, and his heart failed him as he realized the utter helplessness of his position. He listened fearfully to the approaching sounds, which were coming so directly toward him that discovery was inevitable if he remained in the canoe. All at once his ear detected something which caused such a sudden revulsion of feeling that he could have shouted for joy. The voices were those of a man and a woman, who were talking in the familiar Tlascalan dialect.

"Ho, slaves!" he called in an imperious tone, as the other canoe approached close to his own.

The paddling ceased and the man's voice, couched in submissive accents, answered, "Yes, my lord."

"Have you an extra paddle? Mine is broken and I am a King's messenger on a service that admits of no delay."

"We have but two, both of which are in use. But if your lordship desires one of them, and will make good its loss to our master——"

"Hand it to me at once," interrupted Huetzin, in as stern a tone as he could command. "Or better still," he continued as the other craft drew alongside, "I will come into your canoe, and you shall carry me to the further side of the lake. In that way I shall get on more quickly, and you will run no risk of losing your precious paddle."

Thus saying, Huetzin stepped lightly into the other boat, and peremptorily ordered its occupants to hasten forward with all speed, as his mission could not longer be delayed.

With an obedience born of long servitude, they resumed their paddles and labored to fulfill his wishes, without question. For some time they proceeded in silence. Then Huetzin's curiosity got the better of his prudence, and he asked the slaves what they were doing on the lake at so late an hour of the night.

"We carried a load of flowers from our master's garden, near Iztapalapan, to the market of Tenochtitlan," answered the man, "and delayed to witness the festivities until overtaken by the storm. When it abated so that we might put forth, it was near the middle watch. Since then we have been stopped and examined three different times by boats of the lake patrol."

"What sought they?" demanded Huetzin.

"An escaped prisoner."

"Heard you his name?"

"They said——," began the woman, timidly.

"No," interrupted her husband, sharply, "we heard it not. Where will my lord that we should land him?"

"Anywhere," answered Huetzin, carelessly. Then, correcting himself, he added: "That is, you may land me at the place to which you are going. I would not that you should incur your master's displeasure by further delay. You have a hut of your own, I suppose?"

"Yes, my lord."

"Then take me to it, for my garments are wet, and I would dry them before proceeding on my journey."

Although such a proposition from one who had recently claimed to be in the greatest haste, struck both the Tlascalans as peculiar, they were too wise to pass remarks on the actions of a king's messenger, and so received it in silence.

Guiding their course by the stars, they soon brought the canoe to land, and led the way to their humble hut of rushes, plastered with lake mud, that stood not far from the water's edge.

As the three entered it, the woman knelt to blow life into some coals that smouldered in a bed of ashes, on a rude hearth, while the man brought a bundle of twigs to throw on them. As a bright blaze sprung up, both turned to look at the stranger who had so unceremoniously thrust himself upon their hospitality. The firelight fell full on his face, and as the man caught sight of it, a startled cry burst from his lips. It was echoed by the woman.

"It is Huetzin the Tlascalan!" gasped the former.

"The son of Tlahuicol, our war chief!" cried the woman, with a great sob, and, seizing the young man's hand, she kissed it passionately.

7

LOYALTY OUTWEIGHS GOLD AND FREEDOM

THE DELIGHT of these humble Tlascalan slaves at discovering, and being permitted to serve, the son of their country's hero, knew no bounds. They wept with joy, and would have kissed his feet had he allowed it. The man provided him with dry clothing from his own scanty stock, while the woman hastened to make some tortillas, the thin cakes of meal and water, baked on the surface of a flat stone set at an angle before the fire, that to this day form the staple bread of all Mexico. They marveled at the story of his escape from beneath the very knife of sacrifice, and listened to it with ejaculations of thankfulness and amazement at every detail. They spoke with bated breath of Tlahuicol's brave fight, while the man declared proudly that the like had never been seen even in that land of battles, and that none but a Tlascalan could have performed such marvels. More than all were they proud that Huetzin had entrusted them with his life, and they wondered that he should have dared place himself at the mercy of strangers.

"No Tlascalan is a stranger to the son of Tlahuicol," answered the young man, simply.

"But how knew you that we were Tlascalans?"

"By the tongues with which you spoke. The voice of the mountaineer no more resembles that of a dweller in the valleys than the cry of the eagle is like that of a raven," replied Huetzin, with a smile.

Then they rejoiced that in all their years of slavery they had not lost their native accent, and recalled with simple pride how they had striven and helped each other to preserve this token of their birth, and sole reminder of their happy youth among the distant mountains. They told him of their captivity, and how they had been surprised, not far from their own home, by a party of Aztec slave-hunters, against whom the man's desperate resistance proved of no avail. "Though there were but few abler warriors than he in all the land," added the old woman, proudly, with a fond look at her old husband. They also told him of their only child, the little girl, Cocotin, who had been left behind and of whose fate they had gained no tidings in all these years. They told of their present life with all its toil and hardship, and, when the tale was ended they rejoiced that the gods had led them over the thorny paths of slavery to the end that they might be of service to the son of Tlahuicol, their country's hero.

With all this there was no intimation of the fact, that should they be suspected of aiding the escape of a victim doomed to sacrifice, or of having sheltered him for an hour, they would be condemned to death by torture. Huetzin, however, was well aware of this, and so, when he had eaten of their frugal fare and dried his wet garments, he would have taken his departure; but to this his entertainers would not listen.

"It is near morning, and with daylight your capture in this place would be certain," argued the man. "Tarry with us until the coming of another night, when I will guide you to a place from which you may reach the road to Tlascala."

"Would my lord snatch from us the great joy of our lives?" asked the woman, reproachfully, "and needlessly shorten the only hours of happiness we have known since last we looked on the face of Cocotin, our little one?"

"But if I am found here your lives will be forfeit," urged Huetzin.

"That is as the gods will," answered the man. "Our poor lives are as nothing, while the gods have shown that they are reserving yours for their own good purpose. Nay, my lord, depart not, but honor us with your presence yet a while longer, and all shall be well."

Thus urged Huetzin yielded, and, more weary than

he was aware of, flung himself down on a mat of sweet grasses in one corner of the room, where he almost instantly fell asleep. The old people watched him, sitting hand in hand and conversing in whispers of the wonderful event by which the hard monotony of their lives had been brightened. Every now and then the man went outside and listened. At daylight he was obliged to report for duty in the fields.

When he had gone the woman took a quantity of the maguey fibre, which it was her daily task to prepare for the cloth-weavers, and, with it, completely concealed the sleeping youth. So well was he hidden that even the prying eyes of a female neighbor, who ran in for a few moments' gossip while her breakfast was cooking, failed to detect his presence.

"Have you heard," asked the woman, "of the escape of a victim dedicated to Huitzil yesterday? In some manner—I have not yet learned the details—he succeeded in killing several of the holy priests, and escaping from under the very knife of sacrifice. The gods were so incensed that they extinguished the sacred fire with a breath. Nor will they be appeased until he is again brought before them, and his heart lies on the altar; for so say the priests."

"What is he like?" demanded the other, calmly.

"They say," replied the visitor, "that he is young, and as comely to look upon as Quetzal himself; but that at heart he is a very monster, and that his only meat is babes or very young children. I should be frightened to death were I to catch sight of him, though for the sake of the reward I should be willing to venture it."

"Is there a reward offered for his capture?"

"Yes. Have you not heard? It is proclaimed everywhere, that, to any free man who shall produce him dead or alive, or tell where he may be found, shall be given a hundred quills of gold and a royal grant of land. If any slave shall be the fortunate one, he and his shall be given their freedom, and twenty quills of gold. Oh! I would my man might set eyes on him. He is already searching, as are many of the neighbors, for it is said that the escaped one crossed the lake in this direction last night, after overturning several boats that were in pursuit of him, and leaving their occupants to perish in the water. Besides that, he killed or wounded near a score of chinampa owners, and set their canoes adrift. I know this to be so, for my man picked up one of the canoes on the lake shore, not an hour ago, and has informed the officers."

"Never did I hear of anything so terrible!" cried the Tlascalan woman, professing an eager sympathy with her neighbor's gossip. "We are all in danger of our lives."

"Yes," continued the other, "but he must be taken soon, for soldiers are scouring the country in all directions, and every house is to be searched. They will not find him in a dwelling, though, for the penalty is too terrible. The proclamation says that whoever shall give him a crust of bread, or a sup of water, or a moment's shelter, shall be burned to death, he and every member of his family. So the monster will get no aid, I warrant you. Well, I must go. I am glad you know nothing of him," she added, casting a searching glance around the interior of the hut, «for I should hate to be compelled to inform against a neighbor. What a fine lot of fibre you have prepared!"

"Yes," answered the Tlascalan woman, calmly, "and I am just about to take it out in the sun to bleach."

As the steps of the departing gossip died away, Huetzin, who had been aroused by her shrill tones, and had overheard all that she said, shook off his covering of fibre and rose to his feet, looking very pale and determined.

"I can no longer remain here," he said; "my presence would be discovered by the first who searched this dwelling, and I should only have devoted you and your husband to an awful fate. It is better that you should give me up and claim the reward."

At these words the woman gave him a look so reproachful and full of entreaty, that he hastened to recall them. "No," he exclaimed, "you could not! To a Tlascalan such baseness would be impossible! But you can at least let me depart."

"Yes," said the woman, "you must go, for you can no longer remain here in safety; but I am minded of another hiding-place in which, for a time at least, you can remain undiscovered. Come with me, and I will show it you."

So they left the hut together, Huetzin almost creeping on his hands and knees through the tall grasses which formed the only shelter from observation, and the woman bearing a great bundle of maguey fibre. This answered a fourfold purpose. The pretense of bleaching it gave her an excuse for going abroad. Its weight would account for the slowness with which she walked. She carried it so as partly to shield her companion from sight, and, had anyone approached, she would have dropped it over him while pretending to rest.

Thus the two proceeded slowly and fearfully until they reached the ruins of an ancient aqueduct, that had once brought water for the garden fountains of some long-forgotten Toltec noble. The aqueduct, which was a sodded dike enclosing a great earthen pipe, had been gullied by some short-lived but furious torrent, and its pipe was broken at the place where Huetzin and the Tlascalan woman now halted. There was an opening just large enough for a man to squeeze through; but, once inside the pipe, he could neither turn himself about nor assume any position save that of lying at full length. The bottom of the pipe was covered thickly with a slimy sediment suggestive of all manner of creeping and venomous things. It was indeed a dismal place, but it offered a chance for life which Huetzin accepted. As he disappeared within its dark recess, the woman resumed her burden of fibre and retraced her steps to her own dwelling.

Not long after her return to it, she was startled by

the approach of a squad of Aztec soldiers, guided by her husband, with anguish-stricken face. Entering the hut they searched it carefully, thrusting their spears into every suspected place, including the heap of maguey fibre on the floor, which they thoroughly prodded. The Tlascalan was amazed at his wife's calmness during these proceedings, as well as at the absence of the fugitive. He had been certain that the latter would be discovered there, even while he stoutly denied any knowledge of him or his whereabouts to the soldiers, who had forced him to accompany them to the search of his own dwelling. When they left to hunt elsewhere he was compelled to go with them. Thus it was not until nightfall, when he returned from his day's labor, that he learned of the safety of their beloved guest, and of the hiding-place found for him by the quick-witted Tlascalan woman. She had not dared go near him during the day, and it was not until after their usual hour for retiring, when all men were supposed to be asleep, that the brave old couple ventured forth to release the prisoner from his painful position in the ancient water-pipe.

8

TRAPPING A KING'S COURIER

BUT FOR A PROMISE he had given, to remain in his uncomfortable hiding-place until summoned by his friends, and but for the awful penalty they must have paid had their connection with him been discovered, Huetzin would long since have left the old water-pipe. His position in it was so painfully cramped that, as the long hours dragged slowly away, it became well-nigh insupportable. When he finally heard the welcome summons, and issued from the narrow opening, he was so stiff he could hardly stand. A brisk rubbing of his limbs soon restored their circulation; and, after partaking of a hearty meal in the cabin of his humble protectors, he was once more ready to venture forth. A wallet well filled with tortillas, provided by the woman to whom he already owed his life, was given him, and, bidding her a loving and grateful farewell, he followed the lead of the old mountaineer out into the darkness.

Making many detours to avoid dwellings, and after a narrow escape from a patrol of soldiers, suddenly encountered, who passed so close to where they crouched in a thicket by the wayside that they could have touched them, the fugitives finally reached the fresh-water lake of Chalco. Here Huetzin alone would have wasted much precious time, but his guide knew where to find a canoe. This he speedily drew forth from its hiding-place, and a half-hour of silent paddling set them across the lake. Although they approached the shore with the utmost caution, they were hailed from out its shadows, as they were about to land, by a hoarse challenge that sounded like a voice of doom. As they hesitated, irresolute, an arrow flew by their heads with a venomous hiss, and the old man cried out, in a tremulous voice:

"Hold thy hand, my lord, it is only I, a poor slave of Iztapalapan, seeking to catch a few fish for the morrow's food."

"Come hither, slave, at once, that I may examine thee, ere I drive an arrow through thy miserable carcass," cried the voice.

Making an awkward splashing with his paddle, under cover of which Huetzin slid into the water, the old man obeyed. He found but a single soldier awaiting him, though others, who came running up from either side, demanding to know the cause for shouting, showed that he formed but one of a cordon guarding the whole lake shore. These carefully examined the old man and his canoe. At length, satisfied that he was alone and bore no resemblance to the one whom they sought, they let him go, bidding him not to venture near the shore again as he valued his life. As he humbly thanked them for their forbearance, and slowly paddled away, they moved up the beach in search of other suspicious characters.

Huetzin, who had been standing in water up to his neck, where he would hear every word that passed, now attracted the Tlascalan's attention by a low hissing sound, grasped his hand in token of farewell, and made his way to the spot just vacated by the soldiers, correctly assuming that, for a short time at least, it would be safer than any other. Cautiously and noiselessly he crept up the bank, nor did he dare to move at more than a snail's pace until a good quarter of a mile had been put between him and his enemies. Then he set forth at such speed that, before morning, he had left the valley of Mexico behind, and was climbing the rugged slope of the mountains bounding it on the east.

At the coming of daylight the fugitive sought a cave, near which issued a spring of clear water; and here he passed the day, having no food save the water-soaked tortillas, already sour and mouldering in his wallet. When night came he again ventured forth, and found a field, from which he procured a few ears of half-ripened maize.

Thus for a week he hid by day and traveled by night, rarely daring to set foot on the highway by which the mountains were traversed, but scrambling through the dense forests that bordered it, and having narrow escapes from wild beasts and wilder men. His clothing and skin were torn by thorns, his feet were cut and bleeding from rude contact with jagged rocks, his blood was chilled by the biting winds of the lofty heights to which he climbed, and his body was weakened and emaciated by starvation. Only an indomitable will, the remembrance of his father›s death, and the thought of Tiata with no one in the world to care for her save him, urged the young Toltec forward.

Often during the day, from some hiding-place overlooking the public road, he watched with envy the king's couriers, hurrying east or west with the swiftness of the wind. Each of these, as he knew, ran at full speed for two leagues, at the end of which he delivered his dispatches to another who was in waiting at a post-station, and was then allowed to refresh himself with food, drink, and a bath, before being again summoned to duty. Such was the swiftness of these trained runners, and the perfection of the system controlling them, that dispatches were transmitted with incredible rapidity, and on the king's table in Tenochtitlan fresh fish were daily served, that were taken from the eastern ocean, two hundred miles away, less than twenty hours before.

Not only did Huetzin, barely existing on the few

tunas or acrid wild figs that he occasionally found, envy the king's couriers the comforts of the post-stations, to which he dared not venture, and which seemed so desirable as compared with his own surroundings, but he longed to know the purport of the dispatches that so constantly passed and repassed. That most of them contained information concerning the white conquerors, whose movements and intentions he was so anxious to discover, he felt certain. He knew that the penalty for molesting or delaying a king's courier was death; but that meant nothing to him, for the same fate would be his in any case if he should be captured. Thus, being already outlawed, he would not have hesitated to attack a courier and strive to capture his dispatches, but for the fact that they were strong, well-fed men, while he was weak from starvation. Moreover, they were armed, while he was not, even his dagger having been broken off at the hilt in an attempt to cut for himself a club early in his flight. At length, however, he contrived a plan that promised success, and which he at once proceeded to put into execution.

He had saved the broken blade of his dagger, and transformed it into a rude knife by binding one end with bark. With this he cut a tough, trailing vine, nearly one hundred feet in length, and, coiling it as he would a rope, made his way, cautiously, just at dusk, to the edge of the highway. He had chosen a place from which he could see for some distance in either direction; and, after making certain that no person was in sight, he fastened one end of his rope-like vine to the roots of a small tree. Then, carrying the other across the road, he stretched it as tightly as possible, and made it fast. The rope, so arranged, was lifted some six inches above the surface of the road. Having thus set his trap, Huetzin concealed himself at one side and impatiently awaited the approach of a victim.

Ere he had waited a half-hour there came a sound of quick foot-falls, and the heart of the young Toltec beat high with excitement. Now he could see the dim form of a man speeding forward through the darkness, and hear the panting breath. Now the flying messenger is abreast of the place where he crouches. Now he trips over the unseen obstacle, and plunges headlong with a startled cry and outstretched arms. Huetzin leaped forward and flung himself bodily upon the prostrate form. He had anticipated a struggle, and nerved himself for it, but none was made. The man's forehead had struck on the rocky roadbed, and he lay as one dead. Huetzin wasted no time in attempting to revive him; but, unfastening the green girdle that held the precious packet of dispatches, and at the same time distinguished its wearer as being in the royal service, and securing the bow and arrows with which the courier was armed, he plunged again into the forest and disappeared.

That night he was so fortunate as to discover a corn-field, for he had now passed the range of the great volcan, and descended to the fertile table-land on its eastern side. At daylight he had the further good fortune to shoot a wild turkey, and though, having no fire nor means of procuring one, he was forced to eat the meat raw, it greatly refreshed and strengthened him. By the time he had finished this welcome meal, and selected a hiding-place for the day, the sun had risen, and he eagerly opened the packet of dispatches.

For an hour he poured over them, and when it was ended the young Toltec was wiser, concerning some matters of vital importance, than the king himself. He had not only learned, as well as pictured likenesses could teach him, what manner of beings the white conquerors were, but a secret concerning them that might have altered the fate of the kingdom had Montezuma been aware of it at that moment. It was that the terrible beings who accompanied the conquerors, and were described as combining the forms of men and fire-breathing monsters, were in reality two distinct individuals, a man and an animal, also that they were mortal and not godlike. These facts were shown by pictures of a dead horse, and two of the white strangers, also lying on the ground, dead and transfixed by arrows. Near them stood a number of men, and several horses without riders, but all pierced by arrows, showing them to be wounded. It was evidently a representation of a battle-scene between the white conquerors, and— Could it be? Yes! There was the white heron, the emblem of the Tlascalan house of Titcala, the token of his mother's family! The white conquerors were at war with Tlascala!

This was a startling revelation to the son of Tlahuicol. He knew that his warrior father had deemed a union of the forces of Tlascala with those of the powerful strangers the only means by which the Aztec nation and its terrible priesthood could be overthrown. What could he do to stop the war now so evidently in progress, and bring about the desirable alliance? He could at least bear his father's last message, with all speed, to Tlascala, and he would. It should be heard by the council of chiefs ere the set of another sun. Thus deciding, and fastening the green girdle of the courier, the badge of royal authority, about his waist, Huetzin hastened to the highway, and set out boldly upon it, with all speed, in the direction of Tlascala.

9

WHO ARE THE WHITE CONQUERORS

Yes, the white strangers were at war with Tlasca-la; there could be no doubt of it. The meaning of the pictured dispatches was too clear on that point to be misunderstood. Which side would win in such a struggle? The pictures seemed to indicate that the strangers had suffered a defeat. Certainly some of them had been killed, as had at least three of the mysterious beings who had, until then, been believed to be gods. With such evidences of the superiority of his countrymen to reassure him, could the son of a Tlascalan warrior doubt which banner would be crowned with victory? And yet, if these white strangers should be destroyed, or driven back whence they came, what would become of his father's cherished plan for the overthrow of Montezuma and his bloody priesthood by their aid? Why

65

had Tlahuicol placed such confidence in their powers? Who, and what, were these white conquerors? Whence had they come? And what was their object in braving the dangers that must beset every step of their advance into the land of Anahuac?

With thoughts and queries such as these was the mind of Huetzin filled as he sped forward on his self-appointed mission. The question of food, that had absorbed so large a share of his attention on the preceding days of his flight, no longer gave him any anxiety. The sight of his green girdle and packet of dispatches caused his wants of this nature to be rapidly supplied from the several post stations, at which he halted for a moment without entering. To be sure his appearance created animated discussions after he had departed, but only when it was too late to make investigation. Thus Huetzin's mind was free to dwell upon the subject of the white conquerors and their war with his own people.

These "white conquerors," as Tlahuicol had termed them, formed the little army with which Hernando Cortes set forth from Cuba, in the spring of 1519, for the exploration and possible subjugation of the great western kingdom, concerning which fabulous accounts had already reached Spain. During the twenty-seven years that had elapsed since Columbus first set foot on an island of the New World, exploration had been active, and the extent of its eastern coast had been nearly determined. Sebastian Cabot had skirted it from Labrador to the peninsula of Florida. Columbus himself had reached the mainland, without realizing that it was such, and had sailed from Honduras to the mouth of the mighty Orinoco. Amerigo Vespucci and others had coasted southward as far as the Rio de la Plata. Balboa, with dauntless courage, had forced his way through the trackless forests of Darien, and from the summit of its lofty cordilleras sighted the mighty Pacific. The West Indian Islands were all known, and only the lands bordering the Mexican Gulf still remained unexplored.

In 1517 a Spanish slave-hunter, bound from Cuba to the Bahamas, was driven so far out of his course by a succession of easterly gales that, at the end of three weeks, he found himself on an unknown coast far to the westward. It was the land of the Mayas, who, having learned by rumor of the cruelties practiced by the Spaniards in the Caribbean Islands, greeted these new-comers with an invincible hostility that resulted in a series of bloody encounters. In most of these the Spaniards were worsted; some of them were taken prisoners by the Indians, and so many were killed that all notions of their godlike nature were destroyed. When the whites questioned those natives with whom they gained intercourse as to the name of their land, the answer always given was, "Tec-ta-tan" (I do not understand you), and this, corrupted into "Yucatan," is the name borne by that portion of the country to this day.

In spite of their reverses and failure to gain a foothold in this new country, the Spanish slave-hunters saw enough of its stone buildings, populous towns, cultivated fields, rich fabrics, and golden ornaments to convince them that they were on the borders of a powerful and wealthy empire. Thus, when they returned to Cuba, leaving half their number behind, either dead or as prisoners, they brought such glowing accounts of their discoveries that another expedition to extend them, as well as to procure slaves and gold, was immediately fitted out. Under the command of Juan de Grijalva, and embarked in four small vessels, it sailed from Santiago in May, 1518, and was gone six months, during which time it explored the coast from Yucatan to a point some distance beyond where the city of Vera Cruz now stands.

On the Mayan coast Grijalva met with the same fierce hostility that had greeted his predecessor, but among the Aztecs he was received with a more friendly spirit by a chieftain who had been ordered to make a careful study of the strangers for the information of the king of that land. This monarch, who was soon to become the world-famed Montezuma, also sent costly gifts to the Spaniards, hoping that, satisfied with them, they would depart and leave his country in peace. They did so, but only to carry to Cuba such wonderful tales of the wealth of the countries they had visited that a third expedition was at once undertaken. It was placed under command of Hernando Cortes, a trained soldier, about thirty-three years of age. His fleet consisted of eleven vessels, the largest of which was but of one hundred tons burden. Three others were from seventy to eighty tons, and the rest were open caravels. In these were embarked eight hundred and fifty souls, of whom one hundred and ten were sailors. Five hundred and fifty were soldiers, but of these only thirteen were armed with muskets, and thirty-two with crossbows, the rest being provided with swords and pikes. The remainder of the force consisted of Indian servants.

If this small force of men had been his sole reliance, Cortes would have accomplished little more than his predecessors; but it was not. He was well provided with artillery, in the shape of ten heavy guns and four small brass pieces called falconets, besides a bountiful supply of ammunition. Better than all, however, he had sixteen horses, animals up to that time unknown on the American continent, and well fitted to inspire the simple-minded natives with terror. Cortes was also fortunate in his selection of officers. Among them were the fierce Alvarado, who had already been on the coast with Grijalva, and who was afterward named by the Aztecs "Tonatiah," or the Sunlit, on account of his golden hair and beard, and Gonzalo de Sandoval, barely twenty-two years of age and slow of speech, but of such a sturdy frame, good judgment, and absolute fearlessness that he became the most famous and trustworthy of all the conqueror's captains. He was also the owner of the glorious mare Motilla, the pride and pet of the army.

With this force Cortes sailed for the Mexican coast filled with hopes of conquest and of abolishing forever

the cruel religion of the Aztecs, with its human sacrifices and bloody rites, concerning which the reports of his
predecessors had said so much.

The policy of Cortes was to gain his ends by peaceful means, if possible, and only to fight when forced to
do so. In pursuance of this plan of action he touched
at several places on the Mayan coast, before proceeding
to Mexico, and so won the good-will of those fierce
fighters by his courtesy and a liberal bestowal of presents, that they not only desisted from hostilities, but
delivered to him a Spaniard whom they had held as
prisoner for several years. This man, whose name was
Aguilar, could converse fluently in the Mayan tongue,
and was thus invaluable as an interpreter.

At the mouth of the Tabasco River, on the borders
of Aztec territory, where Grijalva had been so courteously received two years before, Cortes was greeted in
a very different manner. As the Tabascans had been ordered by the Aztec monarch to treat Grijalva's expedition kindly and gain from it all possible information
concerning the white strangers, they now received instructions from the same source to destroy this one. Accordingly a great army had been collected, and in spite
of Cortes's efforts to maintain peaceful relations, his
little force was attacked with the utmost fury as soon
as it landed. The artillery created terrible havoc in the
dense ranks of the natives; but so desperate was their
onset that the Spaniards would doubtless have been
defeated had it not been for the opportune arrival of

their cavalry, which was thus used for the first time in a New-World battle. Before these death-dealing monsters, whose weight bore down all opposition, and beneath whose iron hoofs they were trampled like blades of grass, the panic-stricken Indians fled in dismay.

The loss of the Tabascans in this first battle of the conquest of Mexico was enormous, reaching well into the thousands, while of the Spaniards a number were killed and some two hundred were wounded. Among the prisoners taken were several caciques, whom Cortes set at liberty and sent back to their own people with presents, and the message that for the sake of peace he was willing to overlook the past provided they would now acknowledge the authority of his king and abolish human sacrifices from their religious observances. If they refused these terms he would put every man, woman, and child to the sword.

This threat, together with the punishment already received, was effective. On the following day a delegation of head men came in, to tender their submission to the White Conqueror. They brought many valuable gifts, among which were twenty female slaves, whom Cortes caused to be baptized and given Christian names. The most beautiful of these, and the one who quickly proved herself the most intelligent, had already passed through a long experience of slavery, though still but seventeen years of age. Sold, when a child, by a step-mother, in a distant northern province, she had been carried to the land of the Mayas, educated there in the household of a noble, and finally captured by the fierce Tabascans. She was thus able to speak both the Aztec and the Mayan tongues, and so could interpret the Aztec, through the Mayan, to Aguilar, who in turn translated her words into Spanish. Thus, through this young Indian girl, the Spaniards were, for the first time, placed in direct communication with the dominant race of the country. The Christian name given her was «Marina," a name destined to become almost as well known as that of the White Conqueror himself.

From Tabasco Cortes followed the coast to the island of San Juan de Ulloa, inside which he anchored his fleet. Here, for the first time, he received an embassy direct from Montezuma, and saw the Aztec artists busily making sketches of his men and their belongings for the king's information. Here, too, he landed, and founded the city of Vera Cruz, to be used as a base of operations while in that country.

The Spaniards spent some months on the coast, and in the Tierra Caliente, or hot lands, immediately adjoining it. They formed an alliance with the Totonacs, a disaffected people recently conquered by the Aztecs, regained for them their principal city of Cempoalla, where they destroyed the Aztec idols, and devoted themselves to a study of the resources of the country they proposed to conquer and the character of its people.

In the meantime they received many messages from Montezuma forbidding their proposed visit to his capital, and commanding them to depart whence they came. As these messages were always accompanied by magnificent presents of gold, jewels, and rich fabrics, the Spaniards were even more tempted to stay and search for the source of this unbounded wealth, than to leave it undiscovered. So, in spite of Montezuma's prohibition, Cortes, after first destroying his ships that they might offer no excuse for a retreat, took up his line of march for Tenochtitlan, two hundred miles in the interior.

10

THE SIGN OF THE GOD
OF THE FOUR WINDS

IT WAS IN AUGUST, the height of the rainy season, that the little Spanish army of four hundred men, only fifteen of whom were mounted, took up their line of march from Vera Cruz for the Aztec capital. They carried with them but three heavy guns and the four falconets. The remainder of the troops, one horse, and seven pieces of heavy artillery, were left for the defense of their infant city. To drag their guns and transport their baggage over the mountains they obtained from Cempoalla the services of a thousand tamanes, or porters. An army of thirteen hundred Totonac warriors also accompanied them.

Their first day's journey was through the perfumed forest filled with gorgeous blossoms and brightly plumaged tropic birds of the Tierra Caliente. Then they began to ascend the eastern slope of the Mexican Cordilleras, above which towers the mighty snow-robed peak of Orizaba. At the close of the second day they reached the beautifully located city of Jalapa, standing midway up the long ascent. Two days later they came to Naulinco, whose inhabitants, being allied to the Totonacs, received them in the most friendly manner. From here they passed into the rugged defile now known as the "Bishop's Pass," where, instead of the tropic heats and sunshine to which they had become accustomed, they began to experience cold winds, with driving storms of rain, sleet, and hail, which chilled them to the marrow, and caused the death of many of the Indian porters. The aspect of the surrounding country was as dreary as that of its leaden skies. On all sides were granite boulders rent into a thousand fantastic shapes, huge masses of lava, beds of volcanic cinders and scoriæ, bearing no traces of vegetation, while, above all, towered snow-clad pinnacles and volcanic peaks. After three days of suffering and the most fatiguing labor amid these desolate scenes they descended, and emerged through a second pass into a region of exceeding fertility and a genial climate. They were now on the great table-land of Puebla, and seven thousand feet above the level of the sea. Here they rested for several days in the Aztec city of Cocotlan, the governor of which dared not resist them, as he had received no orders from his royal master to do so.

From Cocotlan they traveled down a noble, forest-clad valley, watered by a bold mountain-torrent, and teeming with inhabitants, who collected in throngs to witness the passing of the mysterious strangers, but made no offer to molest them. At the fortress of Xalacingo they came to two roads, one leading to the sacred city of Cholula, famed for its great pyramid, its temples, and its pottery, and the other leading to Tlascala. By the advice of their native allies the conquerors decided to take the latter way, and visit the sturdy little mountain republic which had maintained a successful warfare against the arrogant Aztec for more than two centuries, and with which they hoped to form an alliance. So an embassy of Totonac caciques, bearing an exquisite Spanish sword as a present, was dispatched to explain to the Tlascalan chiefs the peaceful intentions of the Spaniards, and ask for permission to pass through their territory.

The Christian army waited several days in vain for the return of these messengers, and at length, impatient of the delay, determined to push on at all hazards. Leaving the beautiful plain in which they had halted, they struck into a more rugged country, and at length paused before a structure so strange that they gazed at it in wonder. It was a battlemented stone wall nine feet high, twenty in thickness, six miles long, and terminating at either end in the precipitous sides of tall mountains too steep to be scaled. Only in the centre of this well-nigh impregnable fortress was there a narrow opening, running for forty paces between overlapping sections of the wall. This remarkable structure stood on the boundary of Tlascalan territory and, had the mountain warriors to whom it belonged chosen to defend it upon this occasion, the white men might have dashed themselves against it as fruitlessly as the waves of the sea against an iron-bound coast, until their strength was spent, without effecting a passage to the country beyond.

For days the great council of Tlascala had been the scene of stormy debate as to how the strangers applying for admission to their territory should be received. Some of its members were for making an immediate alliance with them against the Aztecs. Others claimed that these unknown adventurers had not yet declared themselves as enemies of Montezuma, nor had their vaunted powers been tested in battle against true warriors. "Therefore," said these counselors, "let us first fight them, and if they prove able to withstand us, then will it be time to accept their alliance." This advice finally prevailed, war was decided upon, and a force was dispatched to guard the great fortress. But it was too late. Cortes and his little army had already passed through its unguarded opening and gained the soil of the free republic.

After proceeding a few miles the leader, riding at the head of his horsemen perceived a small body of warriors armed with maquahuitls and shields, and clad in armor of quilted cotton, advancing rapidly. These formed the van of those who should have guarded the fortress. On seeing that the Spaniards had already passed it, they halted; and, as the latter continued to approach, they turned and fled. Cortes called upon them to halt, but as they only fled the faster he and his companions clapped spurs to their steeds and speedily overtook them. Finding escape impossible the Tlascalans faced about, but instead of surrendering or showing themselves terror-stricken at the appearance of their pursuers, they began a furious attack upon them. Handful as they were, they fought so bravely that they held their ground until the appearance, a few minutes later, of the main body to which they belonged. These numbering several thousand, and advancing on the run, at once gave battle to the little body of Spanish cavaliers. First discharging a blinding flight of arrows, they rushed, with wild cries, upon the horsemen, striving to tear their lances from their grasp and to drag the riders from their saddles. They seemed fully aware that rider and horse were distinct individuals, in which respect they differed from any of the natives yet encountered. Fortunately for the cavaliers the press about them was so great that their assailants found it almost impossible to wield their weapons, while from their superior elevation they were enabled to use their swords with telling effect. Still the Tlascalans succeeded in dragging one rider to the ground and in wounding him so severely that he soon afterward died. Two horses were also killed, and this formed by far the most serious loss yet sustained by the Spaniards.

Scores of the Tlascalans received mortal wounds, but the sight of their stricken comrades only served to animate the survivors with fresh courage and an increased fury. From their childhood the Tlascalans were taught that there was no glory so great as that to be gained by death on the field of battle, and that the warrior thus dying was at once transported to the blissful mansions of the sun. Nowhere in the New World had the Spaniards encountered such warriors as these, and it was with inexpressible thankfulness that the hard-pressed cavaliers beheld the rapid advance of their own infantry, and were able to retreat for a breathing spell behind their sheltering lines. A simultaneous fire of artillery, muskets, and crossbows so bewildered the Tlascalans, who now for the first time heard the terrifying sound, and witnessed the deadly effect, of fire-arms, that they made no further attempt to continue the battle. They did not fly but withdrew in good order, carrying their dead with them.

The Spaniards were too exhausted to follow up their victory, and were anxious only to find a safe camping-place for the night. During the hours of darkness they carefully buried the two horses killed in that day's fight, hoping that when the Tlascalans found no trace of them they might still believe them to be supernatural beings. A strong guard was maintained all night, and those who slept did so in their armor with their weapons in their hands.

On the following day the Spaniards resumed

their march, presenting, with their Indian allies, quite an imposing array. As on the previous day the pursuit of a small body of the enemy, who fell back as they advanced, led them into the presence of another Tlascalan army, headed by Tlahuicol›s nephew and successor, a fiery young warrior named Xicoten. This army met them in a narrow valley of such broken ground that the artillery could not be operated within its limits. Here thirty thousand warriors not only filled the valley with their numbers, but spread out on the plain beyond, presenting a confused assemblage of gay banners, glittering weapons, and many-colored plumes tossing above the white of cotton-quilted armor. Over all floated proudly the heron device of the great house of Titcala, to which Xicoten, the general, belonged.

The battle now fought was more stubborn and prolonged than that of the day before. Another horse was killed, and his mangled remains were borne off in triumph to be distributed as trophies through every Tlascalan village. A terrible hand-to-hand struggle took place over the prostrate form of his rider, who was finally recovered by the Spaniards, only to die shortly after of his wounds.

While the Christians, protected by their armor, received the showers of Tlascalan arrows and darts with impunity, their Totonac allies suffered heavily. All were nearly exhausted before the artillery was dragged clear of the broken ground and brought into play. Then, as on the previous day, the Tlascalans sullenly retreated before a deadly fire which they had no means of returning.

Again the Spaniards, weary with a day of fighting, sought only a safe place of encampment. This they found on the hill of Zompach, a rocky eminence crowned by a small temple, which they converted into a fortress. Here they rested and cared for their wounded during the succeeding day; but on the next, as provisions were running low, Cortes, taking with him only his cavalry, made a foray through the surrounding villages and farms. During this wild ride Sandoval, with the recklessness of youth, trusting to his good sword and the fleet Motilla for safety, allowed himself to become separated from the rest.

He was at some distance behind, and galloping furiously through a narrow street of a deserted village, when Motilla swerved so suddenly to one side as to almost unseat her rider, and then stood snorting and quivering with excitement. The object of her terror was the body of a young man who lay prone on the ground, bleeding profusely from a sword-cut on the head, evidently just given him by one of those who had passed on before. As Sandoval gazed at him with an expression of pity, for the youth was well favored and of about his own age, the latter lifted his right hand and made a few motions that, feeble as they were, almost caused the young Spaniard to fall off his horse with amazement.

He gazed for a moment longer, and then, moved by a sudden impulse, he sprang from Motilla's back, lifted the limp and unconscious form of the wounded youth to the saddle, remounted behind him, and, with only this strange prize to show as his share of booty, galloped back to camp. When the Spanish commander laughingly asked him what he was going to do with his captive, Sandoval answered:

"I am going to care for him until he recovers sufficiently to tell me how it came about that, when he thought himself dying, he made the sign of the cross."

11

HOW THE TLASCALANS FOUGHT

BESIDES THE MYSTERY of the sign, which was at that time supposed to be used only by those of the Christian faith, Sandoval found himself taking a deep interest in his unconscious prisoner for other reasons. To begin with, he had saved the life of the unknown youth, which would be sufficient to arouse a feeling of interest in the breast of any one who had done a similar deed. With the young cavalier this feeling was intensified by the fact that, while he had taken so many lives that he had come to regard the killing of an Indian much as he would that of a wild beast, this was his first attempt at rescuing one from death.

Then, too, being plain of feature himself, he had an appreciation of comeliness in others, and never had he seen a more perfect specimen of youthful manhood than that which lay motionless, but faintly breathing, on a straw pallet, in the Tlascalan temple, to which he had brought him. The olive-tinted features, but little darker than his own, were as delicate as those of a maiden, but clearly cut and noble; the forehead was broad, the mouth and chin bore the imprint of a firm will, and the face formed a perfect oval. The youth was taller and of more slender build than Sandoval, but his well-rounded limbs were of a symmetry only to be gained by an athletic training and constant exercise. Although he was thus an embodiment of manly beauty, this fact aroused no envy in the breast of honest Sandoval, but only increased the interest that he felt in his captive.

In addition to all this, the youth had worn the green girdle of a king's courier, and in his wallet was found a pictorial dispatch, evidently relating to the recent battles between Spaniards and Tlascalans that could only have been intended for Montezuma himself. This was even now in the hands of the White Conqueror, who with the aid of Indian interpreters was endeavoring to decipher it. And yet the youth did not have the appearance of a king's courier, who, as every one knew, were as well cared for as any of his servants. He was clad in a single garment of coarse nequen, soiled and ragged. His whole body was bruised, and his bare feet were cut and swollen. Besides, what could an undisguised Aztec courier be doing in Tlascala? Neither was it certain that he was an Aztec. Several of the Tlascalan prisoners, who were brought in to pronounce upon his nationality started at sight of him, and exhibited symptoms of deep distress. In explanation of this they would only say that he bore a striking resemblance to the son of one of their greatest warriors who, with his family, had been taken prisoner, and doubtless sacrificed to the Aztec gods, nearly a year before.

The trooper who had wounded him was found, and said that, as he was riding close behind the general, this youth had suddenly appeared and rushed at Cortes, apparently with evil intent, whereupon he— the trooper—had promptly cut him down and left him for dead. "And why not?" growled the trooper, who was disgusted at so much fuss over what he considered so paltry an object. "What matters the life of one, or even a thousand, of these idolaters?"

"It matters this," thundered Sandoval, angered by the man's insolent bearing, "that our mission to these Tlascalans is one of peace, and not of war, and that one of them alive is worth more than the whole nation dead. Besides, with the sign of the holy cross has this one, at least, proved himself no idolater, but as good a Christian as thyself. So then, sirrah! be more careful of thy blows in the future, lest they strike the steel of a Christian sword instead of the unprotected head of a weaponless youth."

While Huetzin's identity and the mystery surrounding him were being thus discussed, the gentle hands of Marina were tenderly bathing and dressing his wound, which, upon inspection, did not prove so severe as it had at first appeared. The blow had been a glancing one, rather than a downright stroke, and the gash, though ugly to look at, was not deep, nor did it penetrate the bone.

Marina's ministrations at length produced their desired effect, and Huetzin, opening his eyes, gazed in a bewildered manner about him. Finally his wandering gaze settled upon the fair face bending over him. He smiled faintly, whispered the one word, "Tiata," and almost immediately sank into the deep but healthful sleep of one who is utterly weary.

For the next twenty hours he remained in a slumber so profound that not even the tumult of a third great battle, fought within a short distance of where he lay, served to arouse him. In this battle were engaged, on the Tlascalan side, no less than fifty thousand warriors, selected from their own armies, and from those of their fierce allies the Otomies. The Spaniards were disheartened by the gaining of victories that only seemed to endue their enemies with fresh determination to destroy them, and to cause a succession of armies, each larger than its predecessor, to be brought against them. In the present instance they had ample cause to fear that they, the conquerors, were at last to become the conquered; for never had they beheld such an array as witnessed their defiant march down the hill of Zompach on that beautiful 5th day of September.

There was the same bewildering gorgeousness of the brilliant feather mantles, tossing plumes, and snow-white armor of the nobles and higher classes, the vividly painted bodies of the common soldiers, the flashing of itztli blades, and the waving banners that had greeted their eyes on former occasions, only on an infinitely greater scale. Six square miles of plain were covered by this New-World army, from which arose a deafening clamor of barbaric music and shrill war-cries. The weapons with which these hardy warriors were armed were slings, bows and arrows, darts, maquahuitls or war-clubs bladed with itztli, and javelins attached by long thongs to the wrists of those who bore them, so that they might be drawn back and their deadly thrusts repeated many times. They also bore shields, made of wood or leather, or more often a light wicker frame covered thick with quilted cotton, impenetrable to the darts and arrows of their own warfare, but offering a sorry protection against the musket-balls, steel-headed cross-bolts, Toledo blades, and lances of the foe whom they were now to encounter. High above all the glittering array gleamed, in the bright sunlight, a great golden eagle with outspread wings, the standard of the Tlascalan republic.

Had there been any chance of honorably avoiding a battle with this overwhelming force the little band of Spaniards would gladly have availed themselves of it; but there was not. They could but fight or die; and with a courage born of despair they awaited the attack.

On their side they had discipline, long experience in civilized warfare, armor, and weapons of steel, artillery, muskets, and horses, in all of which their opponents were lacking.

As the opposing forces neared each other the Tlascalans filled the air with such a hurtling tempest of missiles that the sun was momentarily darkened as by a passing cloud. In return the Christians delivered, at close range, a musketry and cross-bow fire, so deadly in its effects that the front ranks of the Indians were mowed down like grass before a scythe. For a moment the Tlascalans stood as though paralyzed. Then, goaded to desperation by their losses, and uttering blood-curdling cries, they leaped forward and rushed upon the Spaniards with the impetuosity of some mighty ocean billow whose fury none may withstand. For a few seconds the iron front of the white conquerors remained unbroken, and their compact ranks held together, though they were forced backward for more than a hundred yards. Then came a break in the front rank. An iron-clad soldier was felled to the ground, and ere the breach could be closed it was filled with maddened Indians. Instantly the close order of the Spaniards gave way, and every man found himself engaged in a hand-to-hand struggle with more assailants than he could count. Gasping, blinded, and overpowered, the white men fought doggedly, but without hope.

Suddenly, above the din of shrieks, oaths, and clashing weapons there rose a wild scream, and Motilla, goaded into fury by her wounds, reared high in the air and leaped over the heads of the combatants crowding about her. With the ferocity of a wounded tiger she plunged into the thickest of the dense Tlas-calan ranks, tearing at her tormentors with her teeth, and dealing death-blows on every side with her iron-shod hoofs. Above her the keen blade of sturdy Sando-val gleamed like a flame, darting to right and left, and shearing through armor, flesh, and bone, wherever it touched. The white charger of Cortes had echoed Mo-tilla›s scream, and was quickly battling at her side with a fury equal to her own. Nor was sorrel Bradamante, bearing her master, the golden-bearded Alvarado, far behind. Thus, fighting like demons rather than mor-tals, these six—three horses and three men—beat back the mighty Tlascalan wave until those behind them could reform and charge in turn.

All this while the artillery was thundering on the Tlascalan flanks, and creating a fearful havoc with its far-reaching missiles. Again and again did the warriors of the mountain republic charge, but never with such success as at first. Finally a quarrel among their leaders caused half their army to be withdrawn from the field, and, after four hours of desperate, incessant fighting, Xicoten ordered a retreat, and again left the white con-querors masters of the bloody field.

Nearly fifty of these had been slain, while most of the surviving men and all of the horses were wound-ed. Thus, as Sandoval grimly remarked on his return to camp, one more such victory would seal the fate of the Christians and consign their hearts to heathen altars.

12

A SON OF THE HOUSE
OF TITCALA

DURING THE PROGRESS of this fierce and sanguinary battle Huetzin slept peacefully as a child, and not until after the return of the weary, but victorious, Spaniards to their camp did he wake. In the earlier hours of the day Marina, from the roof of the temple in which he lay, watched the progress of the fight with a fearful interest that was yet divided in its loyalty. She had cast her lot with these strangers, who had rescued her from slavery, and treated her with courtesy. But for the shelter of their camps she was homeless, and but for their strong arms she was without a protector in the world. And yet, those with whom they now fought were of her own race. The defeat of either side would fill her with sadness. Would that they might be friends rather than enemies! Then, indeed, would she rejoice! How might such a happy result be brought about? What could she do to further it?

In spite of these crowding thoughts, and in spite of the thrilling interest of the battle raging with varying fortunes below her, the girl was not so unmindful of her duty but that she descended several times to look after the welfare of her patients. On one of these occasions, though the young courier still slept, she found him muttering incoherently, and, to her amazement his words were spoken in the Mayan tongue.

When Huetzin awoke, greatly refreshed and possessed of all his faculties, he lay motionless for a while, bewildered by his surroundings and striving to account for the strange sights and sounds about him. Many other wounded men lay on the floor of the room in which he now found himself, and, ministering to their wants were a number of women. He could see that while the former were of a strange race, the women were of Anahuac. Strange weapons, such as he had never seen, were scattered on all sides, and he heard rough voices speaking in an unknown tongue. He had thought, or dreamed, that his sister Tiata was with him, but now he looked for her in vain, and heaved a deep sigh that it must have been a dream.

Suddenly he realized that the wounded men about him were white and bearded. It flashed into his mind that they must be of those whom his father had termed the "White Conquerors." Gradually the past came back to him. He remembered his own flight from Tenoch-

titlan, the courier, and his dispatches telling of war between these strangers and the Tlascalans. He recalled
his own determination, and his efforts to reach Tlascala in time to put an end to fighting before either side
should be conquered. Then came a vision of terrible beings, armed with gleaming weapons, pursuing a crowd
of fleeing natives through the streets of a Tlascalan village he had just entered. He recalled his dismay at sight
of them, and his resolution in spite of it to intercede
with their leader and beg him to stay the hands of his
followers. After that all was blank.

Huetzin's head throbbed, and he raised his hand to
it. He felt that he had been wounded; but how, or by
whom, he knew not. Had he, too, been fighting? He
tried to rise, but fell back, amazed and indignant at his
own weakness. As though the movement had attracted
attention, one of the women hastened to where he lay
and knelt beside him. She was young and beautiful,
even more so than Tiata he thought, as he gazed into
her face. She spoke soothingly to him, and, to his surprise, her words were in the Mayan tongue, which was
also that of the Toltecs, and had been taught him by his
father. Then she left him, but soon returned bringing
broth and wine, of which he drank eagerly.

He asked her, in the Mayan language, who she was,
and where they were, receiving for answer that she was
Marina, and that they were in the camp of the Christians, from whom he had naught to fear. Then, saying
that he must talk no more but must again sleep, she left

him, and when he slept he dreamed of one called Marina, who was beautiful, more beautiful even than Tiata.

When the young Toltec next awoke, another day had come, and his strength was so far recovered that he sat up, and felt that he might walk if he were allowed to try. As he sat gazing with eager curiosity upon those about him, Marina came again, bringing him food, of which he ate heartily, but still forbidding him to rise. Then they talked together, and he told her, unreservedly, who he was, of his father's brave death in Tenochtitlan, of his own escape from a like fate, and why he had come to Tlascala.

Marina was amazed, and yet rejoiced, at what she heard. It seemed to her that through the influence of this stranger her own cherished hope of an alliance between Tlascala and the Spaniards might be brought about. Filled with this thought the girl spoke little of herself, but told him of what had taken place since the arrival of the conquerors in the republic, of the terrible battles already fought and her fears that more were to follow. Then she begged him to think of some way by which the fighting might be ended and peace declared.

While they talked a young man entered the place, and came directly to where they were. At sight of him Marina told Huetzin that it was he who had saved him from death and brought him to this place. Thereupon the young Toltec seized the other's hand and kissed it, and said many grateful things that were not understood. Then Marina, speaking in Spanish, of which by this time she had acquired a fair command, told Sandoval the story of Huetzin›s escape from the altars of Tenochtitlan in so vivid a manner that, when she finished, the listener crossed himself and uttered a pious ejaculation of amazement.

Nor was he less amazed when Huetzin excitedly sprang to his feet and asked if he too were a Toltec? If not, how came he to know and use the holy sign of the God of the Four Winds?

When the purport of this question was explained to Sandoval, he answered that he most certainly was not a Toltec, but was a Spaniard, and that the sign, just made by him was that of the cross, the sacred symbol of the Christian religion. Then, in turn, he bade Marina ask Huetzin whether he were a Christian, and, if not, how it came that he had made use of that same sign upon the occasion of their first meeting?

Without hesitation the other answered that while he knew not the meaning of the term Christian, he had made the sign of the cross, which was also the symbol of the god of his fathers, when he thought himself dying. He added that his warrior father had made the same sign as his last conscious act, and that, since it represented the religion of the white conquerors, both they and he must worship the same gods.

The translation of these words aroused the deepest interest in the mind of Sandoval, who recalled the ancient stone crosses that the Spaniards had seen and marveled at in the land of the Mayas. After some reflection he bade Marina ask if the gods worshipped by Huetzin were not also those of the Aztecs? The young man replied, indignantly, that they were not, adding that the gods of his Toltec fathers abhorred the bloody rites and human sacrifices of the Aztec priesthood, and demanded only offerings of fruits, flowers, and on great occasions the blood of beasts. He also explained that as his father's life had been devoted to the overthrow of the cruel Aztec gods, so should his own be devoted.

When this was understood by Sandoval, his eyes sparkled with gladness, and, grasping Huetzin's hand, he exclaimed: "Now I know for what great purpose I was moved to save thy life! Henceforth shall we be as brothers! Thy quarrel shall be mine, and mine thine! When thou art recovered thy full strength I will arm thee as becomes a Christian, and teach thee to fight as a Christian. In token of this thou shalt hereafter be called 'Juan,' which was the name of my own brother, now dwelling with the saints in glory."

Although Huetzin failed at the time to comprehend these words, he read the sentiment expressed in the other's face, understood the meaning of the sturdy hand-grasp, and was filled with a great joy. This was the end of conversation for the present; and, at Marina's suggestion, Huetzin was again left to rest.

That night the Tlascalans made an attack on the Spanish camp; and when the defenders returned from repelling it Sandoval was greatly concerned to learn, from Marina, that his newly adopted brother had disappeared, leaving no trace of where he had gone. To her news the Indian maiden added, mysteriously, that she did not believe they had seen the last of him; but she could not be persuaded to name her reason for so thinking.

By these repeated attacks not only was the Spanish force constantly weakened, but many of its members were so disheartened that they became clamorous for Cortes to give over his hopeless attempt to reach the Aztec capital, and lead them back to the coast. If this petty mountain republic could offer such determined opposition to their progress, what might they not expect from the powerful nation whom they had yet to meet? was the question that even the undaunted leader found it difficult to answer. At the same time the camp was filled with rumors of the gathering, for their destruction, of another Tlascalan army, greater and more formidable than any they had yet encountered. Food was becoming scarce with them, for they had wasted the neighborhood with fire and sword, there was much sickness in camp, and even the White Conqueror himself was ill of a fever, aggravated by anxiety.

The affairs of the Spaniards stood thus for several days: but one morning, when gloom and despair had well-nigh reached their climax, the camp was gladdened by the approach of a small but imposing body of Tlascalan chiefs, wearing white badges, indicative of a peaceful errand. At their head walked a young man whose noble appearance and martial bearing attracted admiration even from the Spaniards. Over a cuirass of golden scales he wore a magnificent feather cloak, in which were harmoniously blended the most brilliant colors. Boots of tanned leather, ornamented with gold and jewels, reached to his thighs. On his head he wore a golden casque, decorated with the graceful plumes of a white heron. This, and the colors of his cloak, designated him as belonging to the house of Titcala. His only weapon was a Spanish sword of the finest Toledo steel, which was recognized to be the one sent as a present by Cortes to the Tlascalans with his first embassy.

Proudly advancing between the curious but orderly ranks of Spanish soldiers, to where Cortes stood, surrounded by his captains, and with Marina near at hand to act as interpreter, the young man made respectful obeisance by touching the ground with his hand and raising it to his head. Then he said:

"My Lord Malinche (the native name for Cortes) I am commissioned by the Great Council of Tlascala to invite you, with your army, to become the honored guests of their city, and there discuss with them the terms of a solemn treaty of peace and alliance. Even now Xicoten, the war chief of all Tlascalan armies, follows me to pledge his friendship, and urge your acceptance of this invitation."

Then for a moment, forgetful of the dignity of his position, the young man turned to Sandoval, and lifting that sturdy soldier's hand to his lips, exclaimed: "My brother, to whom I owe my life, now will we indeed fight side by side!" to which the astonished captain replied, though in nowise comprehending the other's words:

"By the holy St. Jago! It is no other than Huetzin, my young Toltec, the captive of my bow and spear!"

13

HOW PEACE WAS BROUGHT ABOUT

WHEN HUETZIN was left alone on the night of the Tlascalan attack, and knew, by the sounds from outside,
that the entire Spanish garrison had gone to repel it,
he conceived the idea of leaving the unguarded camp,
making his way to that of Xicoten, and of endeavoring
to persuade that impetuous war-chief to put an end to
fighting. Although still weak, he felt that his will would
carry him through the undertaking. Making his cautious way to the outer door of the temple, he was there
confronted by Marina, who was just entering. Alarmed
at the sight of a patient thus disobeying her command
to rest quietly until he had recovered his strength, she
at once ordered him back to his bed.

Smiling, but resolutely disregarding the stern command of this gentle mistress, Huetzin led her outside

and there unfolded his plan. Marina replied that while it was a noble one, and met with her full approbation, he had not yet the strength to carry it out. Whereupon Huetzin suddenly threw his arms about her, lifted her lightly from the ground, kissed her full on the lips, and set her gently down again.

Springing to a safe distance, the girl, with burning cheeks and a well-assumed anger, abused him soundly for so shameful an act, and indignantly bade him begone, with the hope that she might never set eyes on him again. As he turned to obey her, she added that, if he ever dared to return, except as an ambassador of peace from Tlascala, she should certainly refuse to recognize him in any way. Then hurrying to the top of the temple, where, by the bright moonlight, she could discern something of what was taking place below, she prayed to the gods for the safety of the youth whom she had but now so bitterly denounced.

In the meantime Huetzin, filled with other thoughts than those of wounds or weakness, hurried down the hillside, on the opposite side from that on which the fighting was taking place, and, making a great circuit, gained the camp of the Tlascalans, who had just returned, filled with sullen rage, from the scene of their fourth defeat. Here he found it impossible to pass the guards, who, to his plea that he bore a most important communication for their general, replied that the latter would see no one that night.

Thus it was not until late on the following day that

Huetzin gained audience of his haughty cousin, who, smarting under his reverses, was in much the temper of a caged lion recently deprived of its liberty. Although he recognized the son of Tlahuicol he refused to admit that he did so. When the latter ventured to speak of the mission on which he had come, the irate war-chief broke forth in a tirade of abuse, not only against the Spaniards, who, he declared, he would yet sweep from the face of the earth, but against all Tlascalan traitors, who, if they had escaped the sacrifice they so well deserved, should no longer escape from the just wrath of their patriot countrymen. Then, calling in the officer of his guard, Xicoten commanded that the young rebel, as he designated Huetzin, be seized, conveyed to the city, and thrown into the deepest dungeon of the temple.

As resistance to this cruel mandate would have been worse than useless, Huetzin suffered himself to be led quietly away by a file of soldiers, and, on the following morning, was taken to the city of Tlascala. Here, as he was hurried through the narrow streets, seeking in vain for a friendly face among the multitudes who thronged them, his heart was filled with such bitterness that he almost regretted not having turned traitor to his country and remained to share the fortune or fate of the white conquerors.

While he was thus sorrowfully reflecting, and walking mechanically between his stolid guards, there came an obstruction in the street that compelled them to halt. Looking up Huetzin caught sight of that which caused his heart to beat with a new hope. A silver-haired old man, evidently blind, was being borne past in a splendidly appointed litter. Above it waved a panache of heron›s plumes, and its bearers wore the yellow and white livery of the house of Titcala. It was his own grandfather, the aged chieftain of Titcala, on his way to a meeting of the Great Council of the republic.

Freeing himself from his guards with a sudden movement, the young man sprang to the side of the litter, crying:

"My lord! Oh, my lord! I am Huetzin, son of Tlahuicol, and of thy daughter! I am, moreover, in sore distress! Extend to me thy protection, I pray thee!"

Thus suddenly aroused from a deep reverie, the old man at first failed to comprehend what was said or who was speaking; but, on a repetition of the words, he commanded Huetzin to approach that he might identify him. This he did by slowly passing his sensitive fingers over the young man's face, as he had been used to do in former years. Finally he exclaimed, in trembling tones:

"It is indeed Huetzin, son of my son, and blood of my blood! But how camest thou here? Did I not hear that thou wert dead? They told me that thou, and thy noble father, mine own sweet child, and the little Tiata, had all been sacrificed on the bloody altars of Huitzil. How is it? Do Tlahuicol and his still live?"

"No, my lord," answered Huetzin. "Both my brave father and my beautiful mother have departed to the realms of the sun. As for Tiata I know not if she still lives. I myself have thrice escaped; once from the altars of Tenochtitlan, once from the camp of the white conquerors, and even now from the soldiers of Xicoten, who would lead me to a Tlascalan dungeon. But my story will keep for a later telling. First, I must deliver the last message of Tlahuicol, which is of vital importance to the republic for which he gave his life. Is there no place other than this street where I may entrust it to thy ears?"

"If it concerns the republic," answered the aged chieftain, "then it is for the senate, who even now await my presence. Come thou with me, and deliver it directly to those who must judge of its importance."

In that city the will of its most honored councilor was supreme, and not even the soldiers of Xicoten dared dispute it. Therefore Huetzin's guard allowed him to accompany his aged grandfather to the senate chamber, making respectful way for them to pass, but following closely behind in readiness to prevent any further escape of their prisoner.

The councilors of the republic, assembled to discuss the momentous question of war or peace with the terrible white conquerors, whose coming had shaken the nation to its foundations, rose and stood with bowed heads as their aged president appeared and was led to the seat of honor. As he passed them, they gazed with surprise at the meanly clad youth who walked beside him with a bearing as proud as that of any prince, and marveled as to who he might be.

When the lord of Titcala faced them with his sight-less eyes, and announced that this same youth was his grandson, the son of Tlahuicol, and that he had but now escaped from Tenochtitlan, bringing them a message from his dead father, a murmur of recognition and amazement swept over the assembly.

Then Huetzin, standing before them in his robe of tattered and blood-stained nequen, told, in the simple language with which oratory is made most effective, his story of the past year. He told of Tlahuicol's unswerving loyalty to his adopted country, despite the splendid offers of Montezuma to desert her and enter his service. He repeated his father's last words in a voice that trembled with emotion, and described with thrilling effect the final battle of the great Tlascalan war-chief. He told of his own escape, through the direct interposition of the gods, from the very knife of sacrifice, and of his experience in the camp of the white conquerors. He described his leaving it and his reception by Xicoten. Finally, he concluded with so strong an argument in favor of a Tlascalan alliance with the powerful strangers, against the hated Aztec, that none who heard him could resist his eloquence; and, when he finished, he was greeted with such a storm of applause as had never before swept over that solemn chamber.

As Huetzin stepped back to his grandfather's side the aged chieftain embraced and blessed him, while tears streamed from his sightless eyes. Then, declaring that his vote should, now and always, be for an alliance with the Spaniards, and begging to be excused from the deliberations of that day, the lord of Titcala retired, taking Huetzin with him, to his own palace. Here the young man was bathed in perfumed waters and clad as became his rank, and here he rested, recovering his strength, during all of that day. In the meantime the news of his return had spread through the city, and was received with such joy that, the next morning, when he appeared in the streets, on his way to the senate chamber, to which he had been summoned, he was greeted with universal enthusiasm.

By the councilors of the republic the dignity of the command of a division of the Tlascalan army was conferred upon the young warrior; also, in consideration of the life services of his father, he was presented with the most valuable weapon in all Tlascala, the sword of Toledo steel that Cortes had sent as a gift to the republic. Last and best of all, the newly made chieftain was commissioned to proceed at once to the camp of the white conquerors, and invite them, in the name of the republic, to visit the capital city, there to settle upon the terms of an everlasting peace and alliance.

Thus was Huetzin's cup of happiness filled to overflowing. There was but one drop of bitterness mingled with it. He was instructed to visit his cousin, Xicoten, on his way to the Christian camp, convey to that arrogant general the command of the senate that there must be no more fighting, and invite him, as the war-chief, to head, in person, the embassy to Cortes.

So the son of Tlahuicol, who had entered his native city a despised prisoner, clad in rags, left it, the next day, an honored chieftain, robed with the gorgeousness of his rank, and heading the most important embassy the New World had ever seen.

When he reached Xicoten's camp that hot-headed warrior, while not daring to openly oppose the messenger of the senate, yet managed to delay him for a whole day, while he secretly dispatched spies to discover the condition of the Spaniards. If their report should prove favorable he was resolved on another attack, with the splendid army he had gathered, in spite of all the senators in Tlascala. Had this attack been made, the Spaniards, weakened by their previous losses, would undoubtedly have been destroyed, and all history would have been changed.

As it was, Cortes detected the spies, cut off their thumbs, and sent them back to their master with the message, that while the Christians never slept, and were ready for him at all times, they were also weary of waiting. Therefore, if he had not tendered his submission inside of twenty-four hours, they would desolate the land of Tlascala with fire and sword, until no living thing remained within its borders.

Thus was Xicoten's proud spirit humbled, and though he preferred to follow, rather than to accompany, Huetzin on his mission, the latter was no longer hindered from carrying it into effect.

14

A CHALLENGE, AND ITS RESULT

WHILE THE EMBASSY of Tlascalans, headed by Huetzin, was being received with all honor in the camp of the rejoicing Spaniards, another, consisting of five Aztec nobles, with a retinue of two hundred servants, bearing presents of great value, arrived from the court of Montezuma. They were sent by the trembling monarch to congratulate Cortes on his recent victories over the most redoubtable warriors of the Plateau, and to warn him against entering into an alliance with them. In reality the Aztec king, who had watched the movements of the white conquerors with deepest anxiety, and who had rejoiced when they took the road to Tlascala, still hoped that they might be destroyed by the armies of the mountain republic, and would have used any means to prolong the war just ended. Under pretence of needing time to prepare a suitable answer to his majesty, Cortes detained these ambassadors for several days, that they might witness his reception at the Tlascalan capital.

Preparations were now made for leaving the hill of Zompach, on which the conquerors had passed three memorable weeks, and its fortress-temple, the ruins of which are shown to this day as those of the «Tower of Victory." On the 23d of September, the anniversary of which is still celebrated by Tlascalans as a day of jubilee, the Christian army entered the capital of the brave little republic. The van of the procession consisted of a body of white-robed priests, chanting and scattering clouds of sweet incense from swaying censers. Next came Huetzin, proudly leading an escort of a thousand Tlascalan warriors. These were followed by Cortes and the Aztec envoys. After them marched the battle-worn Spanish troops, with their rumbling artillery and prancing cavalry bringing up the rear.

The eager multitude of spectators who thronged the streets and terraced roofs, and who were kept in check by an efficient body of native police, greeted the conquerors with acclamations, showering upon them garlands and wreaths of the choicest flowers. They even hung these over the necks of the horses, and on the black-muzzled guns. Arches of green branches, entwined with roses, spanned the streets, and the house fronts were gay with fragrant festoons.

A great feast was provided in the palace of Titcala for the entire Spanish army, and at the entrance the aged chieftain waited to welcome them. When Huetzin escorted Cortes to where the veteran stood, the latter passed his hands over the conqueror's face, and, tracing its lines of rugged determination, exclaimed:

"Now, oh, Malinche, do I understand the secret of thy success! Thou hast the will of a god; and when thy face is set, no mortal power may turn it to the right or to the left."

After the banquet the Spaniards were conducted to quarters prepared for them in the court of the temple. The festivities were continued for a week, during which time feasting was alternated with games and exhibitions of every description. The Tlascalans never wearied of witnessing the manœuvres of the Spanish horsemen, nor their displays of skill with the lance. In these, none so astonished the spectators as did Sandoval, with a feat that he performed, not only once, but many times in succession. It was to ride at full speed toward a paper target, and pierce, with the glittering point of his lance, a painted circle, no larger than a man's eye. Only one possessed of the steadiest nerves and keenest eyesight, trained by long practice, could have accomplished this feat. Even with these qualifications, the rider was so dependent on the steadiness of his horse, that on the back of any but his own Motilla, even Sandoval often failed to strike the tiny circle. With Motilla's aid failure seemed impossible, and of the plaudits that the feat drew from admiring throngs, it is doubtful if horse or rider received the most.

Nor was Huetzin at all behind his newly adopted brother in deeds of warlike skill. Standing at thirty paces from the same target used by Sandoval, he would hurl javelin after javelin through the tiny mark, each passing through the opening made by its predecessor without enlarging it. He could also shoot one, two, or even three arrows at a time from his bow, with equal precision, and could split the shaft of one, quivering in a mark, with the keen blade of another. Such feats, though rare, were not unknown to the Tlascalans; but to the Spaniards they seemed little short of supernatural, and, on account of them, Huetzin was treated with a greater respect by the white soldiers than any other native of the land.

During this time the young Toltec was eagerly acquiring two other accomplishments. From Marina he took daily lessons in the Spanish tongue, which she had learned to speak fluently during her six months of intercourse with the conquerors. From Sandoval he received an equal amount of instruction in the use of his highly prized sword. So carefully had he been trained by his warrior father in the handling of all native weapons, that, after a week of practice, he was nearly as dexterous with the Spanish blade as with his accustomed maquahuitl, a weapon that he was now inclined to despise. Something of this kind being intimated one day, within the hearing of Xicoten, that warrior, anxious to humiliate his cousin, whom at the same time he regarded as a rival, and jealous for the reputation of his national weapon, challenged Huetzin to a trial of skill.

Although the latter had not regained his full strength, and had but a few days of sword practice to match against the other's years of familiarity with the maquahuitl, his bold spirit did not permit him to hesitate a moment in accepting the challenge.

Sandoval was greatly troubled when he learned of the rash engagement entered into by his pupil. He expressed himself on the subject in vigorous language, ending with: "That rascally kinsman of thine is jealous of thee, Don Juan, and, if I mistake not, would gladly seize this flimsy pretext for putting thee out of the way. Canst thou not avoid him for the present, or until thou art better fitted to lower his pride?"

This being translated by Marina, who seconded Sandoval's appeal with a look from her own beautiful eyes that would have moved Huetzin from any purpose where his word was not pledged, he answered: "It may not be, my brother. I have promised to try a turn with him, and that promise I would redeem with my life, if necessary. But it will not be, I am convinced. Xicoten meditates no more harm to me than I to him, and the trial will be but a friendly one."

"Let him look to it that it is!" growled Sandoval, "and remember that I am to act as thy second."

The following day was set apart for certain games of wrestling, foot-racing, and other tests of strength or skill, and it was decided that these should end with the trial of weapons between Huetzin and Xicoten. There was an immense concourse of spectators to witness the games, and when at length the two Tlascalan champions stood forth, they were greeted with tumultuous applause. Each was accompanied by a second, pledged to see fair play. That of the war chief was a brother noble of gigantic size, and by Huetzin's side walked Sandoval, with a face as melancholy as though he were attending an execution.

There were no preliminary formalities. The contestants were placed two paces apart, Xicoten, armed with his maquahuitl, a tough oaken staff, some three and a half feet long, set with blades of itztli, and Huetzin with his sword of Toledo steel. Each bore on his left arm a tough leathern shield. Behind Xicoten stood his second, also armed with a maquahuitl, and a little to one side of Huetzin, Sandoval leaned gloomily on his great two-handed sword.

The contest began with a cautious play of fence, in which the adversaries displayed an equal skill, and which the spectators greeted with hearty approval. Soon, however, Xicoten's blows began to fall with a downright earnestness that boded ill for his slighter antagonist, and but for Huetzin's superior agility in springing back, and so evading them, it was evident that he would have come to grief. Several times was his guard beaten down by sheer force. The face of the young Toltec grew pale, his breath came in gasps, and it was apparent to all that his powers of endurance were nearly spent.

Finally blood began to ooze from the recent wound in his head, at sight of which murmurs arose from the spectators, and cries for the contest to end. Sandoval, who stood with half-closed eyes and an air of bored indifference, began to arouse. Huetzin deftly caught a cruel blow from Xicoten's maquahuitl on his shield; but beneath its force his left arm dropped as though numbed.

With blazing eyes Sandoval stepped forward and lifted his sword as a signal for the combat to cease. Disobeying the signal, Xicoten, blinded by a jealous rage, raised his weapon for yet another blow. Ere it could be delivered Sandoval's great sword was whirled about his head like a leaping flame, and in another instant it had shorn through the tough oak of Xicoten's weapon, as though it had been a reed. So complete was the severance that one-half fell to the ground behind the Tlascalan, leaving him to gaze at the other, still remaining in his hand, with such a bewildered air, that the vast audience broke into shouts of merriment. For a moment Sandoval glared about him as though seeking an excuse to repeat his mighty blow. Then, with a glance of contempt at Xicoten, he turned and stalked from the field.

On the next day, in spite of the protests from Montezuma's ambassadors, and the warnings of the Tlascalan counselors, the white conquerors prepared to resume their march to Tenochtitlan, which they proposed to reach by way of the sacred city of Cholula.

15

MARCHING ON
CHOLULA

WHILE THE SPANISH commander had never swerved
from his announced determination of penetrating to
the very heart of Anahuac, and establishing himself, either by peaceful or warlike means, in its capital city, he
was at all times confused by the contradictory advice of
the natives as to the route by which he should advance.
He had been advised to visit Tlascala, and urged not
to do so by those who feared that, after encountering
the unconquered armies of the mountain republic, he
would be so weakened that the Aztecs would easily destroy him. In this case he had relied solely upon his
own judgment, with the results already known. Up to
the moment of his triumphal entry into the Tlascalan
capital, every embassy from Montezuma, while striving
to gain his good-will by lavish and costly gifts, had also

endeavored to dissuade him from his purpose of visiting the royal city. The Tlascalans, too, protested against their new allies placing themselves at the mercy of the treacherous Aztec monarch by entering the island city of Tenochtitlan, where they could easily be cut off from all communication with the main land by the simple removal of the bridges on its several causeways. They assured him that the armies of Montezuma covered the continent, so that, in the event of battle, the Aztec king could well afford to allow the Spaniards to exhaust themselves with slaughter, and could then overwhelm them by mere force of numbers.

To this Cortes made the flattering reply, that no one who had been able to withstand the forces of Tlascala, even for a time, need fear all the other armies of the New World.

Finding him thus determined to advance to Tenochtitlan, the Tlascalans still urged him to avoid the perfidious city of Cholula, which, they said, was filled with a crafty priesthood, who would hesitate at no act of treachery for his destruction.

At this juncture two new embassies appeared upon the scene. One came from the Aztec king, bringing an invitation to the white strangers to visit his capital. He urged them not to enter into an alliance with the base and barbarous Tlascalans, whom he proposed shortly to exterminate. He also advised Cortes to travel by the easy and pleasant road leading through the friendly city of Cholula, where he had ordered a fitting reception to be prepared for him. The other embassy was composed of the head men of Cholula itself, and these second-ed the king's invitation, at the same time assuring the Spaniards of a cordial welcome to their city.

These embassies had hardly delivered their mes-sages, ere some Tlascalan scouts, returning from the neighborhood of Cholula, reported that a strong Aztec force was marching toward it, and that the inhabitants were actively engaged in strengthening the defenses of their city.

Perplexed by the conflicting nature of this advice and these reports, the Spanish leader called a council of his captains; but even they could not agree upon a course of action. Then Sandoval suggested that Huetz-in, the young Toltec, be admitted to the council, and that its decision be determined according to his advice. "So far as may be judged," argued the speaker, "he is a Christian like ourselves, but with a better cause than any here to hate the Aztecs, and desire their humilia-tion. Having lived among them, he must be acquainted with their method of warfare. He has already shown himself a brave youth, possessed of a wisdom uncom-mon among these barbarians, and has proved his devo-tion to our interest."

Struck by the force of these words, Cortes agreed to Sandoval's proposition, and sent for the young war-rior as well as for Marina, to act as interpreter. Huetz-in, greatly wondering for what he might be wanted, promptly obeyed the summons, and listened attentively while the situation was explained to him.

When his turn came to speak, he said to Marina: "Answer my lord Malinche, I pray thee, that my warrior father ever considered an enemy in the rear far more dangerous than one that might be faced. So, in the present case, I would advise that he pass not by Cholula without a visit. To do so would not only place him between two enemies, but would argue a fear of the one left behind. Thus would their confidence in their own strength be increased, and they would be persuaded to a more vigorous enmity."

Which speech being translated by Marina, was received with approval by all the members of the council.

"If I may be permitted to speak further," continued Huetzin, "I would say that if my lord Malinche will permit the Tlascalan warriors, who, under my command, have been chosen to accompany him, to encamp outside the city of Cholula rather than within its walls, I will undertake that no attack nor attempt against his safety shall be made from any quarter, without his previous knowledge."

To this Cortes replied: "Not only do I willingly accede to thy proposal, but such is my confidence in thy prudence and in the fidelity of thy Tlascalan warriors, that I would readily entrust the safety of my army to thy watchfulness. Now, then, gentlemen, having listened to the advice of our well-considered ally of Tlascala, what say you? Shall we visit this city of Cholula on our way to the capital, or shall we pass it by?"

"Let us visit it," was the unanimous answer. And thus it was decided.

During the past week Huetzin's time had not been wholly occupied with the study of Spanish, nor in learning the use of a sword. Upon the earnest representation of Sandoval, Cortes had requested of the Tlascalan senate that the son of Tlahuicol might be appointed to the command of the force they intended to send with him.

They had assigned Xicoten to this expedition, but that general, who regarded the Spaniards with a bitter hatred, claimed that it would be beneath the dignity of the war-chief of the republic to be subject to the orders of a stranger, even the White Conqueror himself, and begged to be relieved of the duty. So the position was left unfilled until Cortes made application for it on behalf of Huetzin. In spite of his youth the young Toltec had been trained for a military life from his childhood by his father, the greatest warrior ever known in Tlascala, and was thus well fitted for the position. Of his bravery there was no question, and, as a son of the house of Titcala, his rank was second to none. Besides all this, the young man possessed an invaluable knowledge of the Aztec capital, gained while a prisoner within its walls. In view of these facts there seemed to be no reason, except his youth and lack of experience as a commander, against Huetzin›s appointment, and these were overruled by the request of the all-powerful Spaniard.

Thus, to his amazement and great joy, Huetzin found himself placed in a position, and entrusted with a responsibility, such as most men only gain by long years of diligent and successful service. Not only would it permit him to fight side by side with Sandoval, for whom he had conceived a warm affection, but it clothed him with a power that might be used for the rescue of Tiata, if, indeed, she were still alive. There was also a thought of Marina, but this he strove to banish as being out of keeping with his military duties.

The young chieftain entered his new office with the greatest enthusiasm, and at once set about the selection, from nearly one hundred thousand volunteers, of the six thousand warriors which Cortes desired might accompany the Christian army. He believed that a greater number than this would only embarrass his own movements, while a force of this size might be subjected to a certain amount of drilling that would render them more effective than many times their number of undisciplined troops. In selecting his men Huetzin always chose those who had fought under his father's command, and who, in consequence, embraced the service of Tlahuicol's son with gladness.

As fast as enlisted, these were sent to a camp outside the city, where they were formed into companies of hundreds, each under command of a proved warrior. These companies were assembled into four bodies, or regiments, each containing fifteen hundred warriors, and named after the four great houses or states of the republic. Thus each regiment was entitled to a separate banner, while all were united under that of their young leader. The device chosen by Huetzin as his own was a rock on which stood the white heron of Titcala and a cross typical both of his Toltec origin and his present service. Marina claimed, and was gladly accorded, the privilege of making the first standard of the new alliance. On a blood-red field she embroidered the device in silver thread, and worked at it with such unflagging industry that, greatly to Huetzin›s satisfaction, it was finished and ready for display on the morning of the day appointed for departure.

Before daylight on that eventful morning, the young man entered the city and sought his grandfather, that he might receive his blessing before setting forth on this first great undertaking of his life. As the blind chieftain placed his hands on the head of the youth and blessed him, he added:

"My son, wherever thou goest, bear thyself modestly and be not puffed up, though thy station appear exalted among men. Remember always that the greatest is he who commands himself, rather than he who commands others. In time of battle forget not the bravery of thy father, and in the hour of victory recall the tender mercy of thy mother. Now, my son, farewell. Go to thy duty, and may the gods guide thee."

The departure of the army was witnessed by the entire population of the city, and it was accompanied for several miles by thousands who had relatives or friends in its ranks. At length the shining walls of Tlascala disappeared from view, the last of its shouting inhabitants was left behind, and the eventful march, toward the goal from which so many of those now pressing eagerly forward would never return, was begun in earnest. Although the distance from Tlascala to Cholula was but six leagues, so much of the way was over rough ground that it was after noon before the army descended into the great plain of Puebla, and night had fallen ere they camped on the bank of a small stream, within sight of the lofty pyramid and hundreds of smoking temples of the ancient Toltec city.

The next morning the Spaniards, leaving Huetzin and his Tlascalans in camp where they were, marched on amid ever-increasing throngs of eager sightseers, who, filled with an intense curiosity concerning the wonderful strangers, poured from the city gates by thousands. As the conquerors entered the city they, in turn, were filled with admiration at its cleanliness, the width and regularity of its streets, the solidity of its buildings, the number of its temples, the intelligent and civilized aspect of its people, and the richly embroidered mantles of its higher classes. They were also astonished at the surprising number of what they supposed were beggars, but who, as they afterward learned, were, in reality, pilgrims, attracted to this point from every corner of Anahuac by the fame of Quetzal, a god who was enshrined on the great pyramid of Cholula.

16

A SACRIFICE OF CHILDREN, AND WHAT IT PORTENDED

As THE ANCIENT capital of his father's race, Huetzin regarded the city of Cholula with an intense interest. It was a source of real sorrow to him that it, rather than another, should be selected as the sacred city of the Aztec priests. His eyes blazed with indignation on seeing the flames of Aztec altars rising from the mighty pyramid erected by his Toltec ancestors, a thousand years before, in honor of their bloodless religion.

This most colossal monument of the New World rose to a height of two hundred feet, and its base covered forty-four acres, an area twice as great as that occupied by the Egyptian pyramid of Cheops. It was a venerable pile when the Aztecs took possession of the land and erected on its summit a magnificent temple, which they dedicated to Quetzal. With the advent of their cruel religion began those daily human sacrifices that drenched its altars with blood for two centuries, or until the coming of the white conquerors. Other temples sprang up about that of Quetzal, each demanding human victims, until the number of those annually sacrificed, in Cholula alone, was over six thousand.

No sooner was Huetzin left with his command than he began to put into practice some of the lessons he had learned from his new friends. His first care was to establish a chain of sentinels and advanced pickets about his camp. Then he sent out small scouting parties in various directions to glean all possible information regarding any other troops that might be discovered in that neighborhood. Finally, after darkness had fallen, disguising himself in the coarse and mud-stained garments of a maker of pottery, whom he had caused to be captured for this purpose, he made his own way into the city.

Once among the streets he avoided those places in which the Spaniards were being lavishly entertained by the caciques of Cholula, and threaded the more distant but populous quarters. He was struck with the number of people still at work, in spite of the lateness of the hour. Masons appeared to be repairing house-walls in all directions, and quantities of stone were being carried to the roofs for their use. Laborers were making excavations in the streets, apparently for foundations; woodchoppers were hewing numbers of posts into sharp-pointed stakes. Many old people, women, and children were also to be seen, and all of these appeared to be removing household goods.

At length, in the most remote part to which he penetrated, Huetzin came upon that which caused his blood to boil, and, at the same time, filled him with horror. Several hundred persons were grouped about the entrance to a small temple. They were silent, almost to breathlessness, and were evidently intent upon some scene being enacted within. Every now and then a stifled cry, apparently that of a child, came from the interior of the temple.

Determined to discover what was taking place, Huetzin, by patient and persistent effort, finally forced his way to the very front rank of the spectators, and in another moment was as anxious to make good his retreat from this position as he had been to gain it. For fully a minute he was so tightly wedged in by the eager throng about him that to move was impossible, and he gazed with a horrible fascination at the awful scene disclosed through the open doorway by the flickering light of its lurid altar flames. It was a scene of human sacrifice, though not one of such every-day occurrence that the spectators were wholly hardened to it. It was a sacrifice of children; and, as one pitiful little victim after another was roughly seized by the blood-stained priests and laid beneath the merciless knife, a suppressed shudder passed through the gaping throng. Still no manifestation of disapproval was made, and every eye eagerly followed the motions of an aged priest, whose scanty white locks were blood-reddened like his body, and to whom each little heart was handed still palpitating, as it was torn from a child›s breast. He was an augur, and was watched with a breathless interest as he sought for omens from the dread thing held in his hand. As each was tossed aside, evidently unpropitious, a murmur of disappointment arose from the spectators, and more than once Huetzin heard the remark: "The hour is not yet come."

Finally, sick with horror, and raging with a furious anger, the young Toltec could bear it no longer. With a stifled cry he burst through the encircling throng of human wolves, and in spite of angry words and even blows, forced his way into the open space beyond them. When once more free he fled, he knew not whither, filled with a tumult of thought the central idea of which was vengeance. At length he reached his own camp, heart-sick, and exhausted by the strength of his emotions. Here he received the reports of his scouting parties, and learned several things, which, added to his own information, kept him in a state of wakeful anxiety until morning.

At the earliest possible hour he sought an audience with the Spanish leader, to whom he imparted his fears that some deep-laid plot for the destruction of the invaders at this point was in preparation. He told Cortes of the Aztec army discovered by his scouts hidden in a valley but a short distance from the city; of the exodus of those too old or feeble to fight; of the piles of stones secretly accumulated on the house-tops adjoining certain streets; of the pits dug in those same streets and artfully concealed, after being lined with sharp-pointed stakes; of the various chance expressions that he had overheard; and of the awful, but unusual, sacrifice of children of which he had been an unwilling eye-witness. At the same time he expressed it as his belief that the hour had not yet come for springing the trap thus set. It was evident that the portents were not yet favorable, and everything seemed to be awaiting further orders, probably from Montezuma himself. From the nature of the preparations it seemed likely that nothing would be undertaken until the Spaniards were ready to leave the city and continue their march.

Marina, who interpreted this communication, added some suspicions of a similar character, that she had gleaned from certain unguarded utterances of the wife of a Cholulan cacique, with whom she had formed an acquaintance.

Although the conqueror was not one to be easily alarmed, yet he was prudent and ever on the watch for treachery among those surrounding him. So important did he deem the information just given him, that he at once doubled his precautions against a surprise. After thanking the young leader of Tlascalans for his vigilance, he requested him to return to his own camp, continue his work of acquiring a knowledge of what was taking place in and about the city, and to hold his warriors in readiness for instant action.

When Huetzin had departed, Cortes turned his attention to his immediate surroundings. He ordered that no Spaniard should pass beyond the walls of the temple enclosure in which they were quartered. Nor should one lay aside his arms, on any pretext, for a moment. The horses of the cavaliers were kept saddled and bridled, ready for instant service, and the artillery was posted beside the three gateways in the temple walls, in a position to sweep the streets leading to them.

While these preparations were being made, Marina's new acquaintance, the garrulous wife of the cacique, came to pay her a visit. In a short time the Indian girl, pretending to be anxious to escape from the Spaniards, had drawn from her a full account of the conspiracy, which, she said, originated with Montezuma. The Christians, on attempting to leave the city, were to be led into the streets prepared with pitfalls, into which it was expected the cavalry would be precipitated. In the resulting confusion they were to be attacked from the housetops and by the Aztec army that was in waiting, when their easy destruction was deemed a certainty. Even a division of the anticipated captives had already been made, and, while a certain number were to be retained for sacrifice on Cholulan altars, the remainder were to be led in triumph to Tenochtitlan, in the leathern collars, affixed to the ends of stout poles, that were even then prepared for them.

Having agreed to a plan for taking flight to the house of this talkative acquaintance that night, Marina dismissed the woman and hastened to lay the plot before Cortes. The latter, summoning his captains, disclosed it to them and asked their advice as to what course should be pursued. Some of them, in despair at the imminence of the threatened peril, advised an instant return to Tlascala, if not to the coast. Sandoval, Alvarado, and others of stouter hearts, declaring that such a retreat would certainly insure their destruction, advised that in boldly facing the danger, and continuing their onward march at all hazards, lay their only safety. Cortes agreed with this, and added that at no time since they entered the land of Anahuac had the thought of retreat been further from his mind than now.

He then sent for some of the Cholulan caciques and announced his intention of leaving their city early on the following morning. He desired that they should furnish him with a thousand porters for the transport of his artillery and baggage, and should themselves act as his guides to the limits of their domain. These requests they willingly promised to grant, and were dismissed.

That night there was little sleep in the Spanish army, and all held themselves in readiness for an attack. The period of darkness was, however, passed in peace, and through the night no sound broke the stillness of the city, save the hoarse voices of the priests proclaiming the hour from the summit of its lofty teocallis.

17

PUNISHMENT OF THE CONSPIRATORS

CORTES HAD DETERMINED to anticipate the treachery of the Cholulans and the meditated destruction of his army, by a punishment so terrible that its effect should be felt throughout all Anahuac. He intended that a wholesome dread of the white conquerors should be implanted in every Aztec breast. By earliest dawn he was on horseback, perfecting his arrangements for the coming tragedy. The musketeers and cross-bowmen were placed close under the walls of the temple court-yard, and the pikemen were stationed near the three entrances. Here, too, the gunners, under command of Mesa, chief of artillery, renewed their primings and blew their matches into a brighter glow. The cavalry, headed by Cortes in person, was held in reserve to act as emergencies should dictate.

At the same time, silent but active preparations were being made in all parts of the city, though, of course, unseen by the Spaniards, for their destruction. As every Cholulan to whom the secret was known fondly hoped, the hour was at hand in which the boasted prowess of these invaders should come to naught and they should be sacrificed to the wrath of the Aztec gods. Everywhere the exulting natives swarmed to the housetops along the designated line of march, and stationed themselves near the ample stores of missiles already gathered; or they collected in armed bodies, whispering, but jubilant over the perfection of their plans, in the side streets, from which they were to leap, like mountain lions, on their helpless prey. The Aztec army, secretly prepared for this emergency, entered the city, and so swelled the number of assailants that no Cholulan doubted for a moment as to which side should be granted the victory in the coming conflict. So, impatiently and joyously, they awaited the signal with which their triumph would begin.

Outside the city Huetzin's grim Tlascalans, each with a fillet of grass bound about his head to distinguish him from an Aztec or a Cholulan, awaited the signal that should send them into action with an equal impatience. They too were without a doubt as to the result of the battle. Had they not fought against the white conquerors? And did they not know, from bitter experience, the extent of their terrible powers? What would avail the puny efforts of the pottery-making

Cholulans against beings before whom even the mountain warriors of Tlascala could not stand? That they should dare, for a moment, to oppose the white conquerors, to say nothing of themselves, was a subject for scornful mirth in the Tlascalan camp. As for Huetzin, he was filled with the nervous anxiety of a young commander about to engage in his first battle. Of this, however, he effectually concealed all traces in the presence of his warriors, to whom he presented a calm and cheerful countenance. His friend and brother, Sandoval, had urged him to don a cap of steel, such as were worn by the conquerors themselves; but this, Huetzin had firmly declined, saying that he would wear no armor that could not be equally shared by his warriors. Now, therefore, he was clad as they were, in a doublet of quilted cotton, and wore on his head a simple fillet of grass. Above it waved the graceful plume of a white heron, which, with his Spanish sword, formed the distinguishing badges of his rank.

The sun had hardly risen before the Cholulan Caciques, who were to guide the Spanish army through the city streets, presented themselves at the temple and were admitted. They were followed by a thousand or more of tamanes, who, as the quick eye of Cortes instantly detected, were all armed with weapons, of one kind or another, thrust into their girdles. These were halted in the centre of the court, while the Caciques advanced, with smiling faces and complimentary words, to where the Spanish commander sat on his gray steed. Their smiles were quickly exchanged for expressions of consternation; for, with scornful words, Cortes began to charge them with their treachery, and showed himself to be acquainted with all the details of their conspiracy. He recalled the apparent friendliness with which they and their king had invited him to Cholula, and the mask of hospitality with which they had covered their base designs. Now he demanded to know what they had to say for themselves, and whether any form of punishment could be too severe for such perfidy.

The trembling Caciques were overwhelmed by these terrible words, and a memory of the supernatural powers credited to these mysterious strangers, who seemed able to read their most hidden thoughts, came back to them. They dared not deny the accusation just made, and so made a full confession of the conspiracy, only striving to lay the entire blame upon Montezuma, by whose orders they claimed to have acted, and whom they dared not disobey.

Merely regarding this as a further evidence of Cholulan cowardice, and declaring that he was now about to make such an example of them as should cause their false-hearted king to tremble on his throne, Cortes raised his hand. At the signal every Spanish musket and cross-bow was leveled, and so deadly a volley of bullets and bolts was poured into the dense body of natives, huddled together like sheep in the middle of the court, that they fell by scores. Then the soldiers leaped forward to complete their work with sword and pike.

In another moment the combined throngs of Cholulans and Aztecs, gathered outside the walls, hearing the sounds of strife, advanced, with exulting cries, to an attack upon the Spaniards. As they rushed forward there came a burst of flame full in their faces, and, with a thunderous roar, increased tenfold by reverberations from enclosing buildings, Mesa's guns hurled forth their deadly tempest. Ere the bewildered natives could comprehend the nature of what had happened, the cavalry was upon them with sword, lance, and trampling, iron-shod hoofs. By the onrush of succeeding hosts these were driven back; but again Mesa's reloaded guns swept the narrow streets. Again and again were these tactics repeated with frightful losses to the natives and almost none to their adversaries.

In the mean time, Huetzin's warriors, dashing forward like tigers at sound of the first volley, fell on the rear of the swarming Aztecs with such fury that none could withstand them. Dismayed and panic-stricken the townsmen gave way and took refuge in their houses. Even here the fierce Tlascalans pursued them, and setting fire to such structures as were of wood, soon caused whole blocks of buildings to be enveloped in flames.

Ever in the front, using his keen Toledo blade with deadly effect, Huetzin cheered on his followers. Suddenly he detected a body of skulking priests who had come from all the temples of the city to share in the anticipated victory of their benighted adherents. Now they were seeking safety in flight. Like a flash of light came a vision of innocent children torn to death by these human wolves, and, with an inarticulate cry of rage, the young Toltec darted after them. A number of his warriors sprang to his side, and, as the priests dashed up the long flight of steps leading to the summit of the great pyramid, the Tlascalans were close on their heels. Hardly had the panting fugitives gained the upper platform, ere others, who had already sought this place of refuge, rolled great stones down on the heads of their pursuers.

Many a mountain warrior was swept, lifeless, to the bottom of the vast pile before the survivors obtained a foothold on its summit; but, once there, these took ample revenge for the death of their comrades. The cowardly priests, who had heretofore urged others to fight, but who had themselves wielded no weapon save the bloody knife of sacrifice, now fought for their lives, but with no more effect against Huetzin and his fierce Tlascalans, than if they had been so many carrion crows. The face of the murdered Tlahuicol rose before his son's vision, and the despairing cries of thousands of priestly victims rang in the ears of the young Toltec as he closed with the mob of blood-stained wretches who sought in vain the protection of their gods. With no thought save of vengeance, he leaped among them, his sword drinking life blood with every stroke. Animated by his example, his followers dealt death-blows on all sides with a fury only excelled by his own.

From the top of the wooden temple in which the image of the god was enshrined, the Cholulans poured down javelins, stones, and burning arrows. Snatching a blazing brand from an altar, Huetzin set fire to the building, and, with the aid of some Spaniards, who now appeared on the scene, he dragged the great idol from its pedestal, and hurled it, crashing, down a side of the lofty pyramid, at the base of which it was shattered into a hundred fragments.

Priest after priest shared the fate of the god, by leaping from the blazing turrets of the temple, or flung over the parapet by the Tlascalans. Finally Huetzin, with the fury of battle in his face and the blazing eyes of a young war god, looked about him in vain for another victim. None was left, and, for the first time in two centuries the great temple of his Toltec ancestors was freed from its defilement of blood-thirsty Aztec gods and their vile priests.

As he realized this, a solemn joy took possession of the young warrior, and, though he was bleeding from many wounds he felt them not. He seemed to hear the myriad voices of his forefathers united in praise and blessing, and for a moment he stood in rapt unconsciousness of his surroundings. Then, lifting his eyes to the glowing noonday sky, he reverently and slowly traced the sacred symbol of the God of the Four Winds.

At this moment he was recalled to earthly things by a mighty hand-grasp, and the hearty tones of Sandoval's voice, saying, "Thou hast done nobly, my warrior brother! I came in time to witness the conclusion of thy fighting, and never saw I a more finished bit of work. Thou hast indeed smitten the idolater in his stronghold, and here, on the site of yonder smoking temple, shall thou and I erect a goodly cross, the holy symbol of thy religion and of mine."

18

FIRST GLIMPSE OF THE MEXICAN VALLEY

AFTER FOUR HOURS of fighting and slaughter, Cortes concluded that the lesson thus given the Cholulans was one that would not be speedily forgotten. So he withdrew his forces to their own quarters, at the same time ordering the Tlascalans back to their camp. The mountaineers bore with them quantities of plunder, mostly things of every-day use in Cholula, but so rare in the poorer city of Tlascala as to be deemed luxuries. They also carried off nearly a thousand prisoners whom they intended to devote to slavery. Through the influence of Huetzin, who vividly remembered his own sufferings as a prisoner of war, and recalled the charge given him by the chief of Titcala to be merciful in the hour of victory, these were ultimately released and allowed to return to their homes.

The young Toltec, with the permission of Cortes and accompanied by Sandoval, also visited every temple in the city, and, throwing open the doors of their cages or dungeons, gave freedom to hundreds of wretched prisoners who had been doomed to sacrifice. The only service required of these, in return for their liberty, was that they should bury the victims of the recent battle. As the dead numbered nearly three thousand, and as their bodies were exposed to the hot sun in all parts of the city, their speedy removal was a matter of prime necessity.

In spite of this sad record of fighting, burning, slaughter, and pillage, no woman or child in all Cholula had been harmed by either Spaniard or Tlascalan. This fact went so far toward restoring confidence in the honor and forbearance of the white conquerors that, when Cortes issued a proclamation inviting all citizens to return to their homes with an assurance of safety, the invitation was generally accepted. Thus, within a few days, the city had nearly recovered its former air of peaceful prosperity. Markets and workshops were re-opened, the streets were filled with a busy population, and only the blackened ruins lining certain streets remained to tell of the fiery ordeal through which Cholula had so recently passed.

During this period of peaceful occupation by the conquerors, not only was no human sacrifice offered to the humbled Aztec gods, but no priest dared show himself in the presence of Huetzin, the Toltec. From the hour of his terrible vengeance upon the priests of Quetzal's temple, he was known through the length and breadth of Anahuac as a bitter enemy of the Aztec gods and a relentless persecutor of their priests. He aided in erecting the cross of stone and lime on the summit of the great teocal, that Sandoval had promised should stand there; and, as he gazed at it in earliest morning light, or when bathed in the glory of a setting sun, he felt that the spirits of his ancestors must, indeed, be regarding his work with approval.

As the news of the punishment inflicted by the white conquerors upon the treacherous Cholulans spread through the land, numerous embassies began to pour into the Christian camp, with tenders of allegiance from provinces and cities, which gladly seized this opportunity for throwing off the galling Aztec yoke. All brought the same tales of cruelty and extortion; of oppressive taxation that left them impoverished; of their young men forced to serve in Montezuma's armies, and of the yearly tribute of slaves, which they were compelled to furnish from their own families.

Besides these petty, but always welcome, embassies, there came an imposing one, laden with presents, from the Aztec king. It brought assurances of that monarch's distinguished regard for the noble Spaniards, as well as his regrets for the unfortunate affair of Cholula. He disclaimed any share in the conspiracy, and rejoiced that so summary a punishment had been meted out to its authors. He explained the presence of one of his own armies in the vicinity of the city, on the ground that it had been sent to protect the Spaniards from any treachery on the part of their base Tlascalan allies.

Pretending to believe these fair, but false words, Cortes dismissed the embassy courteously, but without any message to their royal master. This, he said, he would shortly deliver in person, as he intended to proceed, without further delay, to Tenochtitlan.

After spending a fortnight in Cholula, and strengthening his position on all sides, the Spanish commander issued orders for leaving the sacred city and resuming the march toward the Aztec capital. On a glorious morning of early November, therefore, the allied forces again set forth, filled with the high hopes inspired by their recent victory, and impatient to enter new fields of conquest.

For several leagues their way lay through a smiling country of broad fields, luxuriant plantations, and thrifty villages, watered by numerous clear streams pouring down from the adjacent mountains. During their passage through this pleasant land Huetzin heard frequent rumors from friendly Indians of trouble that was in store for the invaders in the mountains that must be crossed before the Mexican valley could be reached. He faithfully reported these rumors to the commander, and, in consequence of them, the march was conducted with every precaution that prudence or military science could suggest. Advance and rear guards of cavalry were always maintained, while small bodies of Tlascalan scouts were thrown out on either side.

Although it was thought to be somewhat beneath the dignity of his rank to do so, Huetzin generally led one of these scouting parties in person, so anxious was he to prove his vigilance. At length he was rewarded by the capture of a courier, who was attempting to avoid the army by taking a wide circuit around it. From this prisoner he gained the information, that of the two roads crossing the mountains before them, one had been rendered impassable by orders from Montezuma. On the other, which was so rugged as to present almost insurmountable difficulties, an Aztec army was stationed in ambuscade for the destruction of the invaders.

Hastening to convey this important item of news to Cortes, Huetzin found the army halted at a place where two roads forked. One of them, as he had already learned, was filled, farther than the eye could reach, with great boulders and the trunks of trees. The other was open, and at the outset looked to be much the easier and better of the two. At the moment of the young Toltec's arrival, the Aztec ambassadors who still remained with Cortes, had nearly persuaded him to take the open road. They assured him that the other would be found impassable for his cavalry and artillery, even if it were cleared of its obstructions.

The Aztec nobles were greatly confused when they heard Huetzin›s report to the commander. They attempted a blunt contradiction of his statements; but

Cortes, paying no further attention to them, warmly thanked his young ally for his timely service, and ordered that the obstructed road be cleared. To this task Huetzin set a thousand of his hardy mountaineers. These worked with such willing industry that, within two hours their task was accomplished, and the highway was open to the passage of the army. Thus the ambushed Aztecs were allowed to wait indefinitely for the coming of their expected victims, who, in the mean time, were proceeding cheerfully on their unmolested way.

The invaders now left the pleasant plateau on which they had lingered so long, and began the ascent of the bold mountain ranges separating it from the valley of Mexico. On their left towered the grand peak of Popocatepetl, clouded with smoke and fire, and lifting his majestic head nearly eighteen thousand feet above the level of the sea, or more than two thousand feet higher than Mont Blanc. On their right rose the vast proportions of snow-robed Iztaccihuatl, the "white woman." Between the two extended a steep barrier of bare, wind-swept rock, up which the rough road zigzagged its tedious way. From the snow-peaks came icy winds, chilling man and beast to the bone, while they were continually buffeted by fierce snow-squalls or tempests of cutting sleet. Dark gorges yawned on either side, and from their profound depths came dismal moanings, as though the storm demons were already lamenting the anticipated fall of the Aztec gods. Amid these surroundings the little army toiled painfully on, until darkness shrouded the dreary landscape, when, utterly exhausted, they clamored for a halt, declaring that human endurance could hold out no longer.

Again Huetzin came to the rescue with a knowledge of the road gained from his recent bitter experience as a hunted fugitive, in those same mountains. He assured them that a cluster of commodious post-houses, erected for the shelter of Montezuma's own troops and couriers, stood but a short distance ahead. Thus cheered, the Spaniards struggled on to the welcome haven so unwittingly provided by their enemy, where, by the aid of rousing fires, the fuel for which they found already cut and stored, they passed a night of comparative comfort.

Early on the succeeding day they passed the crest of the divide, and, feeling that the worst of their trials were now left behind, they advanced with buoyant steps down the western slope of the sierra. Suddenly a glad shout from the front woke the mountain echoes, and startled those who came behind. The leaders had turned an angle, and, as though by magic, the promised land was outspread before them. The superb valley of Mexico, unrivaled in the world for the exquisite beauty of its scenery, lay smiling in unclouded sunshine at their feet.

In an emerald setting of verdant fields, orchards, groves, and stately forests, blended with areas of yellow maize and blooming gardens, five lakes of heavenly blue shone like brilliant jewels. Clustered thickly about them, and even resting on their dimpled bosoms, were scores of white-walled cities, towns, and hamlets, all distinctly visible through the rarefied atmosphere. Most conspicuous of all, fairest and most stately of all, sat the Queen City of the New World. Tenochtitlan, the royal city of their hopes and dreams, was no longer an elusive mystery, but a visible reality. Near it rose the dark mass of Chapultepec, home of Aztec kings, crowned with the same majestic cypresses that shadow it to this day. It was a sight to repay years of suffering toil, and it is no wonder that these first white men gazed on it in spellbound silence.

19

MONTEZUMA WELCOMES THE CONQUERORS TO TENOCHTITLAN

As THE WHITE conquerors descended by easy stages into this marvelous valley, making frequent pauses to admire the fertility of its fields, or the beauty of its white-walled villages nestled in green nooks, they were everywhere hailed by the people of the country as deliverers from the harsh tyranny of Montezuma. These received the all-powerful strangers with shouts and songs of rejoicing, at the same time showering upon them gifts of food and flowers. Thus, the march resembled the return of a victorious army rather than one of invasion and conquest. They were also met by another of Montezuma's numerous embassies bearing, as usual, gifts of gold, jewels, and rich mantles of fur or exquisite feather-work. Threats and persuasions having proved unavailing to check the progress of the conquerors, Montezuma was reduced to bribery as a last resort. This embassy brought the offer of two hundred pounds of gold to Cortes, fifty to each of his captains, and an annual tribute to the Spanish king if the strangers would return whence they came.

When this offer was refused, as all others had been, and it became clear that nothing would check the victorious advance of the Christians, the Aztec monarch shut himself up in his palace, refused food, and devoted himself to prayer and sacrifice. He saw his mighty kingdom slipping from him, and, with a fatal superstition that forbade him to oppose the will of the gods, he refused to make an effort for its defense. Cuitlahuac, his warlike brother, Guatamotzin, his impetuous nephew, and others of the bolder spirits among his nobles, urged him to summon his armies and make at least one heroic effort to save his tottering throne. Tlalco, the Toltec priest, who had so worked upon the king's weak nature as to become his chief adviser, said: "Leave to the gods the honor of annihilating these unbelievers in their own good time," and the king listened to the voice of the priest.

So Montezuma prepared to send forth his last embassy to the advancing conquerors, and ordered Cacama, Prince of Tezcuco, with a noble retinue, to meet and welcome them to Mexico. This meeting took place amid the beautiful gardens and stately residences of the royal city of Iztapalapan, situated between the fresh waters of Lake Chalco and the salt flood of the broad Tezcuco. Here the Spaniards were entertained with regal splendor, and here they passed the last night before entering the capital.

Never did nature assume a fairer aspect than when, on the following morning, the clear-voiced Spanish trumpets set the little army in motion for the final march of their eventful progress through the land of Anahuac. A mere handful of men, cut off from all communication with their own race, they had traversed the breadth of a wealthy and populous kingdom, overcome its hostile armies, captured one after another of its strongholds, and were now about to make a triumphant entry into its capital city. Their record was without a parallel in the history of the world. Thus it was with swelling hearts and a proud bearing that they stepped on the superb stone causeway spanning the waters of the salt lake, at the distant end of which lay the queenly city of Tenochtitlan.

This causeway was one of the noblest works of New World civilization. Constructed of huge blocks of stone, it was wide enough for ten horsemen to ride abreast, and stretched for more than a league, in a perfectly straight line, across the lake. At several points it was cut by canals for the passage of boats, and these were crossed by drawbridges, which, when lifted, barred all communication by land with the city. Midway of its length stood Xoloc, a stone fort of immense strength, flanked by towers, and giving passage through a battle-mented gateway.

At this point, as the Spaniards advanced with silk-en banners streaming bravely out in the fresh morning air, burnished mail, and glittering weapons, proudly prancing steeds and rumbling guns, they were met by immense throngs of spectators, who had poured from the city to witness the strangest sight ever beheld in Anahuac. Not only did the astonished natives line both sides of the causeway with dense walls of curious humanity, but the waters of the lake were alive with thousands of their canoes. With equal, but restrained, curiosity did the Spaniards gaze on them; on the won-derful floating islands that, covered with a luxuriant vegetation, and even with miniature forests, appeared on both sides, gently undulating with the swell of the waves, and upon the vast extent of the stately city they were nearing.

As they approached the end of the causeway, and crossed its last bridge, they perceived the brilliant reti-nue of the king advancing to meet them, and halted to receive it. The royal palanquin, plated with burnished gold, was surrounded by a glittering throng of nobles, four of whom, barefooted, with downcast eyes and walking with slowly measured pace, supported it on their shoulders. Four others bore aloft the royal cano-py of brilliant featherwork, powdered with jewels and fringed with gold. It was preceded by three princes bearing golden wands, and having robes of the most exquisite plumage thrown over their golden armor.

When the dazzling train had reached a convenient distance it halted, and Montezuma, descending from his litter, advanced on foot, leaning on the lords of Tezcuco and Iztapalapan. He was still shaded by the feathered canopy, and his golden sandals touched only the rich tapestry spread down before him by attendant nobles. His thronging subjects prostrated themselves to the ground as he passed, and no eye dared gaze on his countenance.

The king was simply clad in a broad embroidered maxtlatl, or waist sash, and the voluminous tilmatli, or Aztec cloak; but above his head, held in place by a golden fillet, nodded a panache of green plumes, such as he alone might wear.

Dismounting from his horse, and tossing his reins to a page, Cortes, attended by Sandoval and Alvarado, stepped forward to meet the monarch. As they came face to face these two gazed for a moment, in silence and with a curious interest, at each other. Then Montezuma welcomed his guests with a kingly courtesy, and announced that his brother, the Prince Cuitlahua, would conduct them to the quarters prepared for their reception.

His words being translated by Marina, Cortes responded with a few courtly expressions of profound respect, hung about the king's neck a glistening chain of colored crystals, and the momentous interview came to an end.

Montezuma, returning through the prostrate ranks of his people, re-entered his litter and was borne back into the city with the same state in which he had left it. The Spaniards followed with colors flying, drums and trumpets arousing the echoes with strains of martial music, and with the trampling of horses and the rumble of heavy guns sounding for the first time over the cemented pavements of Tenochtitlan.

As they marched, with heavy tread, up the principal avenue of the city, the troops gazed with undisguised amazement at the evidences of wealth and civilization surrounding them. For miles the way was lined with the residences of nobles. They were built of a handsome red sandstone, and though generally of but one story in height, each covered a large area. Although the flat, battlemented roofs of these buildings showed that they were capable of being converted into so many fortresses, this military character was softened by the beds of flowers and perfumed shrubbery with which most of them were covered. Often broad, terraced gardens appeared between the dwellings, and the straight lines of their monotonous architecture were broken, here and there, by the pyramidal bulk of some teocal, lifting its fire-crowned summit high above all other structures, the fountains and porticos of a square, or the crossing of a canal.

The profoundest impression was, however, created by the dense population, who swarmed on the house-tops, in the streets and squares, and on the canals, in

such numbers as the Spaniards had not believed exist-
ed in all Anahuac. These everywhere greeted the white
strangers with cheerful smiles and acclamations, mingled with expressions of wonder at their horses, weapons, costumes, and beards. But when the cavalry, infantry, and artillery had passed, the dark ranks of Tlascalan
warriors, who followed, were met with the scowls and
mutterings of an undying hatred. These were not lost
upon Huetzin, who, proudly marching at the head of
his mountaineers, returned them with interest. Whenever he passed a temple he sincerely hoped that some
day he might lead his fierce warriors to its destruction.
When he finally came in sight of the great teocal, where
his noble father had died, and where he had so nearly
lost his own life, his eyes glistened with a light that
boded ill to this dwelling of the gods if ever he should
be allowed to have his way with it.

Opposite the western side of the temple stood a
vast and commodious range of buildings surrounded
by a stone wall. These had formed the palace of Montezuma's father, and were now given over to the strangers,
to be their place of abode so long as they should remain
in the city. As they entered these quarters the king himself, surrounded by his nobles, stood in the courtyard
waiting to receive them.

After his departure, Cortes made a careful inspection of the buildings, which were found to be ample for
the accommodation of the entire army, and assigned
to whites and Tlascalans their respective quarters. He

then stationed the artillery so as to command the gateways, posted sentinels, ordered that no soldier should
leave the enclosure without permission, and in every
manner that his prudence dictated, guarded against
attack or surprise. When this had been accomplished,
the army was allowed to partake of the bountiful meal
provided for it. Later in the day Cortes, accompanied
by Marina and his captains, visited the palace of the
king, by whom they were granted a long audience, and
presented with costly gifts. At sunset the Spaniards
celebrated their entrance into Tenochtitlan with a simultaneous discharge of all their artillery. This awe-inspiring sound, and its thunderous reverberations, combined with the sulphurous fumes of powder, filled the
superstitious Aztecs with dismay, and convinced them
that they were indeed entertaining beings of more than
mortal powers.

After this two days were passed quietly, or in the in-
terchange of ceremonious visits; but on the night of the
third Huetzin, tired of inactivity, and disguising himself in a peasant's robe of nequen, sallied forth into the
city. He had a vague hope of thus learning something
of Tiata, which thus far he had been unable to do. Ever
since sighting the Mexican valley her image had been
constantly before him, and he was strongly impressed
with the belief that she was still alive.

The streets were as well filled with people as they
had been on the eve of the festival of the great calendar
stone. In the brilliantly lighted porticos of the squares,

in which pulque, chocolatl, or cooling sherbets were sold, at the corners, before the open doorways, on the bridges, and at the landing-places of the many canals, were gathered animated groups discussing the arrival of the white strangers, which still formed the all-absorbing topic of public interest. There was little laughter or singing, but much earnest conversation, of which Huetzin caught such scraps as he could while passing, for he dared not join himself to any group, for fear of disclosing his identity. For an hour he wandered aimlessly to and fro, shunning lighted places as much as possible, and seeking friendly shadows. At the end of this time he suddenly became filled with the uneasy sense of one who is secretly observed, and looking about him, he strove to discover if this were the case.

20

HUETZIN IN THE POWER OF THE CHIEF PRIEST

THUS FAR HUETZIN had felt almost certain that he had escaped recognition in Tenochtitlan. By the Spaniards he was invariably addressed as Don Juan, while his own followers spoke and thought of him only as their chieftain, giving him always the title of his office. Although, under the circumstances of his present appearance in the city, he did not fear any evil consequences to himself from being identified with the prisoner who had escaped from Huitzil's altar only three months before, he thought it best, for Tiata's sake, to remain unknown as long as possible. Nor did he esteem this a difficult matter. While the personality of the Spaniards was of great interest in the court of Montezuma, that of their despised Tlascalan allies was not deemed worthy of consideration. Who, then, would concern himself as to the name, title, or previous history, even of their chief? As Huetzin answered to himself "No one," he forgot that the anger of a baffled priest never slumbers, forgives, nor forgets. He forgot Topil.

Thus, when the young Toltec finally discovered a shadowy form, that seemed to move when he moved, and to halt when he halted, though always at a distance from him, he became interested rather than apprehensive, and wondered for whom he was mistaken. In his efforts to obtain a closer view of his shadow, he tried disappearing around corners and then quickly retracing his steps, hiding in dark angles, and various other plans, but always without success. At length he lost sight of the figure, and was beginning to think he must be mistaken in his suspicions, when he was startled by a whisper in his ear: "If you would know of Tiata, follow me!" Then a dark form moved swiftly ahead of him.

For a moment the young Toltec stood irresolute. The utterance of his sister's name showed that he was indeed recognized. He longed above all things for news concerning her, but should he, for that reason, throw prudence to the winds and follow the first stranger who bade him do so? Certainly not. At the same time his curiosity was so aroused that he determined to overtake the mysterious person, if possible, and force an explanation from him. The shadow was still in sight, though at some distance, and, under the impulse of the resolve just made, Huetzin started swiftly after it. As he ran, so it fled, always almost, but not quite, within reach.

A touch of its fluttering garments led him to believe that the chase was nearly ended, and in his exultation he failed to notice that he had passed through a wide gateway. Again, as he was about to grasp the figure, it darted through an open door; but here the pursuer paused. He would follow no further.

At that moment there came a shrill scream from within. It was a woman's voice, and it seemed to cry: "Huetzin! Oh, Huetzin!" Impulsively the young man sprang forward. He had hardly passed the dark portal, when he was seized by several pairs of strong hands and thrown to the ground. A minute later he was led away, helplessly bound, through the darkness. At length he was rudely thrust into a wooden cage, such as were used for captives destined for sacrifice, and there left to his own sorrowful reflections.

He could no longer doubt that he had been recognized, his every movement watched, and his capture devised by means of the simple trap to which he had fallen so easy a victim. Fortunately for him, Topil, the chief priest, had that day gone on a secret mission to Tezcuco. He did not return until near noon of the following day. As soon as he reached the temple he was informed that the young Tlascalan, upon whom he had so long desired to lay hands, once more awaited his pleasure.

Topil's eyes lighted with a fierce gleam as he muttered, "Ha! Son of Tlahuicol, and avowed enemy of the holy priesthood, thou shalt not escape me now!" Then,

aloud, he said: "Away with him to the altar of Huitzil, to which I will shortly follow. With this sacrifice
shall the anger of the gods be averted, and all shall once
more go well with Anahuac."

In obedience to this order, Huetzin was dragged
from his cage, to which no ray of light had penetrated
since he was thrust into it, was blindfolded, and bound
to the back of a sturdy tamane, or porter of the temple.
In this manner, and surrounded by a strong guard of
priests, he was borne for a long distance, and, as he
could distinguish from the motion, up many flights of
stairs. When he was at length set down, although the
bandage was not removed from his eyes, he felt certain that he once more stood on the horrible platform
crowning the great teocal of Huitzil.

As he stood there, feeling that now his last hour
had indeed come, he vaguely calculated the chances of a desperate plan for wrenching himself free, at
the last moment, seizing the chief priest, who he was
sure would conduct the sacrifice in person, and leaping
with him from the giddy height. All at once he became
conscious of a mighty hum of voices rising from far
below, and gradually swelling into acclamations. Then,
although he could not see him, a priest came running
breathlessly up the stairway that led to the platform.
Huetzin did, however, hear the words, "They are coming here! Away with him! Another time will do as well!
Even his dead body must not be discovered!" Then the
prisoner was seized and dragged into a building, which,

by the horrible odor pervading it, he recognized as the shrine of the god. Here he was thrust into some sort of a room or closet, and its door was closed behind him.

In the meantime, Huetzin's former preserver, Tlalco, the Toltec priest, had been well aware of his arrival in the city, but had not yet found an opportunity to communicate with him. With all his secret means of acquiring information, he had not known of the young chieftain's capture and imminent peril until Topil's return from Tezcuco. Then he overheard the communication made to the chief priest, and, without an instant's delay, hastened to the king's palace. Montezuma was not there, nor were his attendant nobles. They were escorting the Spaniards on a visit to the places of greatest interest within the city.

Sandoval had been greatly concerned to learn, upon inquiring for his friend Don Juan, just before setting forth on this excursion, that the young Tlascalan had not returned to his quarters since leaving them late on the previous evening. He would have instituted an immediate search for the missing youth, had not the arrival of the king at that moment demanded his service. Filled with an ever-increasing uneasiness, the young Spaniard was compelled to visit, with his commander and the other cavaliers, the great market-place of Tlateloco, where not even the thousand strange sights, that so interested the others, could distract his mind from its one all-absorbing thought. What had become of the friend whom he had learned to love as a brother?

Was he in danger? If so, what was its nature?

He rejoiced when the tedious inspection of the market-place was ended, and the Spaniards were conducted toward the great temple, which Cortes was especially desirous of visiting. They were still some distance from it, when a page from the palace, mingling unnoticed with the throng, managed to attract the attention of Marina, who accompanied the party as interpreter, and delivered to her a whispered message. She turned pale as she gathered its import, and beckoning Sandoval to the side of her litter, said, in a low but thrillingly earnest tone:

"I am just told to inform the lord Sandoval that, if he would save his brother's life, he must make all speed to the summit of the great temple."

For a moment Sandoval was bewildered. His brother? Then it flashed into his mind that Huetzin, the missing one, must be meant. He also recalled the dread fate already escaped once by the young Toltec on the summit of that same pyramid of horrors. Huetzin had never been very clear in his account of how he escaped on that occasion, but it was likely that a similar method was well guarded against this time, if, indeed, he were in a similar danger.

While thus thinking, the young captain, saluting his commander, and obtaining leave to take a handful of men and act as an advance guard in clearing the streets, clapped spurs to Motilla and dashed away with a haste that occasioned general surprise. It was his impetuous arrival at the foot of the teocal that had occasioned such consternation on its summit, and the chief priest was but one flight of stairs ahead of him as he made his way, with all speed, up the long ascent. He was reckless of the fact that he had far outstripped his followers and was alone. Even when he gained the summit and found himself in the presence of a large body of scowling priests, he had no thought of his own danger. Drawing his sword, he advanced toward them with such a threatening air that they instinctively fell back at his approach.

"Where is he? What have you done with him? Answer me, dogs, ere I loosen thy false tongues with a taste of Spanish steel!" he cried, in savage tones, forgetting that they could understand no word of what he said.

As the priests retreated, so that his eyes could take in the whole of the broad platform, he saw that the object of his search was not there, nor was there any appearance of blood having been spilled that morning. Still he was not satisfied, and as his followers joined him, he led them, careless of the protests of the chief priest, into the foul shrine, where, in spite of its sickening odor, he searched every nook and corner, feeling with his sword in all places that he could not otherwise reach.

When the rest of the visiting party gained the summit of the teocal, the priest made such bitter complaint, to Montezuma, of the insult thus offered to their god that, for the first time during his intercourse with the whites, the king expressed anger at their proceedings, and declared that he himself must do penance for their sacrilege.

21

A SUPERSTITIOUS KING

WHILE THE PRIESTS were making their complaints to
Montezuma, Cortes and his companions were gazing
with fascinated eyes over the incomparable scene outspread on all sides of their lofty observatory. At their
feet lay the city, its terraced roofs blooming with flowers, its streets and shining canals intersecting each other at right angles, and the four great avenues, three of
which connected with as many causeways leading to
the mainland, stretching away in unbroken lines from
the four gates of Huitzil's temple. The avenues, streets,
squares, and canals were filled with a cheerful activity, and thronged with natives in gay and picturesque
costumes. Beyond the clustered buildings of the wide-
spread city sparkled the waters of the lake in which it
stood, and on its distant shores could be seen other
cities, nestling villages, and the white walls of many a

tall teocal rising above dark groves. Far across the broad valley the glorious sweep of view was unbroken until it rested on the encircling range of mountains that bounded it on all sides. From these many a frosty peak pierced the blue heavens, and, high over all trailed the smoke banners of Popocatepetl.

Their enjoyment of this enchanting scene was cut short by the king advising Cortes of the sacrilege committed by Sandoval and his followers in ransacking the sacred shrine. He requested that, on account of it, the Spaniards should at once depart, leaving him and the priests to win forgiveness of the gods for the offence, if indeed that were possible. Although Cortes would gladly have seconded Sandoval's blunt proposal to tumble the stony-eyed god down a side of the pyramid, and fling the priests after it, he knew that the time for such heroic measures was not yet come, and so yielded to the request of the king.

The Spaniards, including Sandoval, who was more than ever perplexed and uneasy concerning the disappearance of his friend, had hardly taken their departure before the chief priest advanced toward Montezuma with a smiling face.

"Oh, mighty lord, and lord of lords!" he exclaimed, making a deep obeisance, "know that I have this day secured a victim for Huitzil's altar, the sacrifice of whom will not only banish from the mind of the gods the recent insults of the white zopilotes (vultures), but will restore their favor to thee and thy people. He is no other than that son of Tlahuicol, the Tlascalan, who is the avowed enemy of the gods, and defied their wrath by his sacrilege at Cholula. Ever since I learned of his coming I have had a score of trusty fellows pledged to his capture, and even now he is at hand, in a secret chamber of the shrine, where the prying eyes of the lime-faced strangers failed to discover him. I fear, however, that, by some mysterious power known only to themselves, they have gained a knowledge of his capture, and are secretly in search of him. If it is thy will that he be immediately sacrificed, and his body given to the sacred flame, then will their search be in vain, and the manner of his disappearance will never be known."

"Bring him forth and let him be sacrificed," replied the king. "The times are urgent, and no means for winning back the favor of the gods must be left untried. If it be not speedily restored, then shall king and priest fall together, and the glory of Anahuac pass forever. So hasten and produce thy victim, for I must shortly return to discover what new mischief these insolent invaders may be meditating."

Filled with a savage joy that his revenge was about to be gratified, and pleased to be able to celebrate the coming of the king with so worthy a sacrifice, Topil hastened to the secure hiding-place in which he had left Huetzin. So long was he gone that the king, impatient of waiting, dispatched one of the lesser priests to bid him produce his victim without further delay. This messenger returned with the startling information that no trace of either the chief priest or his prisoner was to be found.

With an exclamation of anger, Montezuma himself entered the shrine and made a personal search of every room, closet, nook, and corner of its three stories. Finally he was compelled to admit that, in some mysterious way, and for some unknown reason, Topil had disappeared, leaving no trace of his presence. As even the king knew of no mode of exit from the shrine, save its one visible doorway, he could in no way account for this disappearance. Its mystery filled him with such a superstitious dread of the place that he made haste to leave it, and was borne back to his palace a prey to the most gloomy forebodings.

As the king, refusing the attendance of his nobles, entered his private apartments, he was stupefied with amazement to see, standing before him, holding a bloody human heart in his hand, the figure of Topil, the chief priest. For a few seconds he gazed in motionless terror, then he managed to gasp: "Art thou a spirit or a reality? Speak! I command thee!"

To this Topil answered: "I know not, O king, whether I am truly the one or the other. Hear thou my tale and then judge. When I left thee, but now, on the summit of Huitzil's holy temple, I went to bring forth a prisoner whom I had in safe keeping. Upon entering the place where he had been I found naught save traces of unquenchable fire, such as is used by the gods, and this heart. I was not terror-stricken, nor even greatly surprised, for I have known of other cases in which the gods, impatient of delay, have slain impious victims by means of their own awful weapons. I was only amazed to see that the heart of this sacrifice was left as fresh and whole as though just torn from the living body.

"Lifting it, I instantly observed it to be covered with omens so favorable to thee as have never before been seen in all the years of thy glorious reign. I was about to hasten to thee with the joyful tidings, when I was suddenly enveloped in a whirling cloud of dazzling radiance and borne I know not whither. While in this state I was granted a vision. It was of the white strangers now within thy walls; but they were no longer proud, nor were they victorious. They seemed to be without a leader, and were being driven, like leaves before the wind, by the warriors of Tenochtitlan.

"This being interpreted, O king, means that if thou canst but deprive them of their leader, the accursed strangers shall fall beneath thy sword as falls the brittle chian before the reaper's sickle. Thus, O Montezuma, shall the immortal gods be vindicated and thy king-dom established forever.

"When I awoke from this glorious vision, behold, I was standing here, as thou seest me, with the heart of the son of Tlahuicol in my hand as a proof that I had not dreamed a dream."

Such was the story of Topil, the chief priest, and this was the flimsy argument by which he persuaded Montezuma to embrace the first opportunity for the destruction of the Spanish leader. It was a bold device, and it served to conceal the fact that the son of Tlahuicol had again escaped from the altar. For fear its falsity should be discovered, Topil urged immediate action according to his plan; but Montezuma would only promise that, if possible, it should be carried out on the following day.

When Huetzin found himself respited from immediate sacrifice and thrust into another cage, or cell, his first act was to tear the bandage from his eyes. Although the darkness in which he stood was absolute, and he could see no more than before, his brain seemed to act more clearly now that he was no longer blindfolded. With a new hope springing in his heart, he felt on all sides for traces of a door. If he could only get out he might hide in some recess of the temple, and ultimately effect an escape. Of course the chances were a thousand to one against him, but he would thankfully accept even that poor one. So he felt carefully round and round the rough stone walls, but nothing yielded, and there was no trace of an opening. All at once it flashed into his mind that he had been within the narrow limits of these impenetrable walls before. He was almost certain that he stood in the pedestal of Huitzil's image, and just above the narrow stairway down which Tlalco had conducted him on the occasion of his former escape from the altar of sacrifice.

If it should be! And if he could only discover the secret of the opening leading to the stairway, how gladly would he brave the underground terrors to which it would conduct him, for the sake of its one slender chance of escape! Kneeling on the floor he passed his fingers, again and again, over every inch of its cold surface. The result was the same as had attended his efforts against the walls. He could find no trace of an opening nor of a projection by means of which a trap-door might be raised.

Finally, abandoning himself to despair, the young Toltec flung himself at full length on the floor and beat with his clenched fists upon its stony surface. As he did so, it seemed to sink beneath him with a slight grating sound. There was an upward rush of cool, damp air, and, in an instant, Huetzin was standing at the head of a flight of steps, while above him the ponderous stone door, that had opened for his passage, swung noiselessly back into place.

With a wildly beating heart the fugitive began cautiously to descend the unseen stairway. When midway down the second flight, a sound struck upon his ears that froze the blood in his veins. It came from above, and was that of some person rapidly descending behind him. The chief priest, for it must be he, had discovered his escape and was in hot pursuit, probably accompanied by others, all well-armed, and thirsting for his blood.

Thus thinking, Huetzin listened for an instant to the advancing sounds, and then plunged forward, almost headlong, through the darkness. Down flight after flight of the interminable steps he dashed with reckless haste, often slipping, falling, and rolling, but ever keeping in advance of his pursuers. As he neared the bottom, the horror of the secret door, there to be encountered, fell on him, and he cried aloud in his agony. Like a mocking echo, his cry was repeated from above.

When he reached the bottom of the last flight of steps, and could go no farther, then he would turn and fight to the bitter end. They should never again lay his breathing body on the hideous stone of sacrifice.

Thus Huetzin determined; but when he came to the door, and the pursuing footsteps were close upon him, it stood open. Hardly crediting this wonder, the fugitive sprang through the opening thus miraculously provided, and slammed the heavy door behind him. Then he again ran forward through utter darkness. Feeling for the side passages that he remembered, he at length found and entered one. In this he ran, until suddenly he brought up against a solid wall, where he fell, panting, bruised, and almost unconscious, to the ground.

22

SANDOVAL PLIGHTS HIS TROTH

When sandoval returned with the others to the Spanish quarters, after leaving the temple, he urged Marina to find out who had sent the message that had dispatched him on so fruitless an errand to Huitzil's shrine, and, if possible, what it meant. This Marina was only too glad to undertake; for she, as well as the young Spaniard, was anxious and unhappy concerning the fate of him who had been her patient in Tlascala.

In the meantime Sandoval, visiting the Tlascalan quarters, found the fierce warriors very angry, and inclined to quarrel with some one, on account of the loss of their well-liked young chief. They could form no idea of what had become of him, but declared that if he were not restored to them soon, and in safety, the city that had swallowed him should be made to feel their vengeance. The matter was becoming so serious that it must be reported to Cortes. Upon hearing of it, the Spanish leader declared his intention of immediately visiting the king, and demanding any information he might possess upon the subject. To this end, he summoned Marina to accompany him as interpreter.

The Indian girl had but just discovered the page who had brought her the message, and gained from him the information that it had been sent by one of the court ladies, who was even now walking in the king's gardens, and to whom he would willingly conduct her. As Marina must attend the Conqueror in his audience with the king, she turned the page over to Sandoval, with instructions to lead the young cavalier to the gardens instead of herself, and point the lady out to him.

Then the same party, that had made a tour of the city that morning, set forth for Montezuma's palace. After they had entered its grounds, Sandoval, keeping a tight hold of his page, managed to slip away unnoticed. He was pleasantly conscious that at length he, like other young men whom he had known, was setting forth in search of a romantic adventure. The feeling was an entirely novel one; for the plain-faced young soldier, though expert in the art of war, was awkward of speech, and so diffident that, since his childhood, he had hardly exchanged a dozen words with any woman. Marina was, of course, excepted, but he regarded her more in the light of a fellow-soldier than as a member of the dreaded sex.

He wondered if the woman he was about to see would be old or young, attractive or otherwise. He finally decided that she would be middle-aged, as dark-skinned as were most of the Indian women he had seen, and that she was probably the wife of some court noble, who had let drop a chance expression concerning Don Juan, which she had misunderstood. While thus cogitating, Sandoval was led through a maze of shaded alleys and perfumed shrubberies until he was as bewildered as one without a compass in mid-ocean.

At length, after a long search, he and the page detected the sound of voices; and, as they emerged from behind a dense thicket of laurel, the latter pointed, with a triumphant air, to two female figures pacing slowly along the borders of a miniature lake, and engaged in earnest conversation. One was dark, middle-aged, and stately. She answered so well Sandoval's mental picture of the woman he wished to discover, that he accepted her as such without a question. The other woman appeared to be younger, but he could not see her face.

Unobserved, they walked toward the two women, and Sandoval had already lifted his steel bonnet, preparatory to addressing the elder, when the page, pulling at his arm, pointed to the other, thus intimating that it was she who had sent the morning's message. At that moment, startled by the sound of their footsteps, the younger woman turned upon the young soldier a face more gloriously beautiful than any he had ever seen or dreamed of. It was that of a girl just entering womanhood, and was fair almost to whiteness, but with a dash of carmine glowing on cheeks and lips. The little head bore a wealth of hair that was dark brown, instead of jetty black, as was the case with most Aztec maidens. It was poised like that of a princess, but the great brown eyes were fixed upon Sandoval with a startled, pleading expression that, as he afterward said, pierced him like the keenest of Toledo blades.

So taken aback was he by this sudden apparition of youthful beauty, that the steel bonnet, with which he was prepared to make an elaborate bow, slipped from his hand and fell, with a loud clatter to the marble pavement. It would have rolled into the water had not the page captured and returned it to its owner. At this mishap the girl laughed, just a little rippling laugh, the elder woman bit her lip, and poor Sandoval, the picture of despairing mortification, looked as though about to hide his confusion in flight.

At this juncture the girl put some question to the page. At his answer she became very grave, and again looked appealingly at Sandoval. He, realizing that the time had come when he must either speak or ignominiously retreat, and so become a fit subject for mirth throughout all Mexico, opened his mouth and, after several abortive attempts, blurted out:

"I——that is, señorita, you——! I believe my brother, Don Juan——! You have exhibited an interest—— May I ask——? I mean, did you——?"

Here he paused, recalled by the expression of bewilderment on the girl's face, to the fact that she could not understand a word of what he was saying. She answered him, for all that, speaking so earnestly and with such musical accents, that poor Sandoval was completely bewitched, and, in spite of his ignorance of her meaning, would willingly have undertaken to listen to that sweet voice forever.

As she ended the words whose melody would linger in the ears of the embarrassed and shame-faced young soldier to his dying hour, there came a sound of other and harsher voices. Hearing them, the elder woman caught her companion by the arm and led her hastily away. Ere they disappeared, the girl looked back with a ravishing smile that said, as plainly as words of purest Castillian:

"I do not think you plain or awkward, or ill-favored, for I know you to be as true and brave a knight as ever plighted his troth to a maiden," and, from that moment, in his heart of hearts, was Sandoval's troth pledged.

Now he looked for the page on whom he relied to lead him from this enchanted wilderness. The boy had disappeared, and in his place stood two grinning dwarfs, with huge heads, grotesquely misshapen bodies, and thin, little legs that seemed illy calculated to support them. As Sandoval stared at them they returned his stare with interest, at the same time making diabolical faces and winking maliciously.

When he sternly demanded that they should lead

him to the palace, they broke forth with a harsh cackle of laughter and danced about him like hobgoblins. Finally, tormented beyond endurance, he drew his sword as though about to attack them, whereupon they retreated beyond his reach with the lightness of thistle-downs, and a speed that showed how little chance he had of capturing them. For an hour or so they amused themselves with impish torments of this young giant. When they at length disappeared, Sandoval found himself, flushed and breathless, standing before a cage of solemn-looking apes, whose appearance was so like that of his recent tormentors, that he could not help laughing in spite of his disgust. Fortunately, he was here discovered by some of the king's animal-keepers, who conducted him to a place from which he could see the Spanish quarters.

While Sandoval was undergoing these various and unique experiences in the royal gardens, Cortes and his companions were admitted to the presence of the king. Not having any reason to expect a visit from them at this hour, he was engaged in giving audience to many distinguished personages; ambassadors from other countries of the Western World, princes of tributary provinces or cities, caciques of recently conquered tribes, generals of his army, and the like, who had petitions to prefer or business to transact that required his personal attention.

Each of these was conducted into the throne-room by young nobles, who acted as ushers, and each, no matter how exalted his rank, was obliged to cover his gorgeous raiment with a robe of coarse nequen, and enter the presence barefooted. Approaching the king with many obeisances, and finally making the sign of servitude by touching first the ground and then his head with his right hand, the petitioner stood with downcast eyes waiting to be addressed before daring to speak. Each, as he was dismissed, retreated backward, and continued to make humble obeisances until he had passed from the room.

After watching this scene for some time with great interest, Cortes stepped forward, and, through his fair interpreter, abruptly demanded what had become of his young chief of Tlascalans.

"He is dead," answered Montezuma, simply, at which Marina staggered as though struck a heavy blow, and was scarcely able to translate the reply to Cortes.

"By whose hand?" demanded the Spanish leader, hotly.

"By the hand of no man, but by that of the gods."

"Where is his body?"

"No trace of it remains. If it were to be found I would deliver it to thee. If he had been slain by mortals they should be given to thee for punishment," replied the king, solemnly.

Nothing more was to be elicited; and, filled with rage, Cortes and his companions hastily departed, to consult as to what mode of revenge they should take, and upon whom.

They were followed, a few minutes later, by Sandoval, who, as he neared the Spanish quarters, was startled by seeing a man running toward him, hotly pursued by a crowd of priests and citizens brandishing weapons, and evidently intent upon taking his life. As he gazed curiously on this scene the young soldier was horror-stricken to recognize, in the well-nigh exhausted fugitive, his adopted brother, Huetzin the Toltec. Drawing his sword and springing forward with a loud cry, he succeeded in checking the pursuit long enough to enable the pursued to dart through a gateway of the old palace. As the rescuer quickly followed it was violently closed in the faces of the angry throng, whose prey was thus snatched from their very grasp.

23

IN THE PASSAGES
BENEATH THE TEMPLE

ALTHOUGH HUETZIN felt certain that some secret door or panel must offer a passage through the wall, against which he had run with such rude force, he realized, from past experience, the folly of attempting to discover it. Therefore, when he had somewhat recovered from the shock just received, he slowly and carefully retraced his way along the passage, in search of some other opening leading from it.

In the meantime the chief priest, who had discovered no sign of the fugitive since the door at the foot of the stairway was flung to in his face, had hastened on out of the underground labyrinth. He posted guards at all its exits, with the information that an escaped prisoner, who must be seized the moment he showed himself, was wandering about in it, and ordered a victim, selected at random from the temple cages, to be killed and his heart torn out. With this in his hand Topil made his way, undiscovered, to the private apartments of the king, reaching them just in time to anticipate the return of the monarch from the temple.

Feeling well satisfied with this portion of his morning's work, and being also convinced that the prisoner, who had twice eluded him, was still within his reach, the chief priest, after leaving the palace, made several calls on powerful nobles well know as being opposed to the king's present method of treating the invaders of Anahuac. These he invited to attend a secret meeting, to be held that very day, in a place well known to all of them, and in every case the invitation was gladly accepted.

While the priest was thus engaged Huetzin was wandering hopelessly through the black mazes of the underground passages, stairways, rooms, and hidden doorways, that he had entered so easily, but from which he now found it so impossible to escape. Some of the passages that he followed ended, as the first had done, with blank walls, while others led into chambers of greater or less size, as he discovered by groping his way around them. He was faint, weary, and aching in every joint, tortured by the pangs of hunger and a burning thirst. Above all, it seemed to the young Toltec that he must be going mad, as the horrors of his situation crowded thick and fast upon him. In spite of his dread of being recaptured by the priests, he shouted at the top of his voice, and the underground echoes jeered at him with hollow mockery.

Finally he found himself in a hall or chamber that seemed much larger than any he had yet entered, and here he managed to lose touch of the rough wall, along which he had felt his way until the ends of his fingers were worn to the quick. As he moved forward with uncertain steps, seeking to regain it, he stumbled against some large object, fell, and rolled partly under it. So far as he could tell by the feeling, it was a stone altar or table, covered with a heavy tapestry that hung in folds to the floor on all sides.

It was pleasant to encounter something besides cold stone, and instead of rising at once Huetzin lay still, passing his hands mechanically over the soft cloth. His thoughts became hazy and he seemed to be drifting into space. How much better it was to lie there than to wander aimlessly through those interminable passages as he had been doing for days—or weeks—which was it? He tried to remember, but could not. At any rate it was a long time, long enough for one to be dead, buried, and forgotten in. Perhaps he was dead! Yes, there came the white-robed torch-bearing priests who were to bury him. How perplexed they would be if he should hide his body so that the ceremony could not proceed. Of course he would give himself up after a while. Smiling to himself at the thought of this trick, Huetzin rolled still farther under the stone table, until he was completely hidden by its drapery. He lay very still, and must have fallen into a doze. At least he was not conscious of what was taking place about him until he was suddenly aroused by the word "Malinche."

Malinche was the native name for Cortes, and some one was saying, "Malinche must then be slain as he visits the king on the morrow. It is so decided. After his death the destruction of his army will be an easy matter, and Huitzil's altars shall not want for victims. As for the vile Tlascalans, they will serve to feed the altars of the lesser gods for many days of rejoicing."

No longer was Huetzin dozing, nor were his thoughts vague and uncertain. He was, of a sudden, as wide awake as ever in his life, and as clear-headed. Hunger, thirst, terror, and pain were all forgotten. He was listening to the details of a plot for the destruction of his friends and followers, and for the establishment on a firmer basis than ever of the cruel Aztec religion and its blood-stained priesthood. He dared not move, nor even to peep from behind his sheltering curtain to discover who these conspirators were. He hardly dared to breathe, and wished he could silence the beatings of his heart that seemed to him distinct above all other sounds.

From a faint glow that came through the tapestry he knew that the chamber was lighted by torches, and from the sound of footsteps on the stone floor he judged that a number of persons were implicated in the conspiracy. At length the glow began to fade and the footsteps to retreat. The meeting had broken up and its members were departing. Venturing to peer out Huetzin saw the last torch on the point of vanishing in the distant blackness, and springing to his feet he ran noiselessly after it.

He was thus guided along a narrow passage similar to those in which he had wandered so miserably, and around several corners. All at once he saw a torch coming directly toward him. A priest had been sent back for some mislaid article. The young Toltec crouched close beside the wall. The priest did not discover him until he was within a few paces of the crouching figure. Then, as he peered uncertainly at it, Huetzin launched himself forward with a spring like that of an ocelot. In an instant the priest was borne to the ground, while the torch, flung far from him, flickered and expired. He attempted to cry out, but a fierce clutch at his throat changed his cry into a choked gurgle. His struggles were futile in the iron grasp of this monster of the darkness, and within a minute he was bound hand, foot, and mouth with strips torn from his own robes.

Leaving him thus, Huetzin sped noiselessly and swiftly away in the direction taken by the others. He was so fortunate as to again see their lights as the last one was passing through a doorway leading to a flight of steps. He heard a voice say, "Let it remain open for Amatli," and was content to wait until all had ascended the stairway and disappeared.

Then the young Toltec crept cautiously up the stone steps, which were disclosed by a subdued but blessed daylight. From their top he could see a door opening on to a street. Between him and it were two armed guards engaged in earnest conversation. Their backs were turned to him, and stealing breathlessly to where they stood, he bounded past them to the doorway. They were after him in an instant, with loud cries, but he had already gained the street. He knew not where he was, and ran blindly, though with the fleetness of a deer, while an ever-increasing mob of soldiers, priests, and citizens followed in hot pursuit. Had he not caught sight of the great temple he must have fallen an easy prey to this army of pursuers. Even with the hope inspired by this familiar landmark his strength would have failed to take him to the shelter of the Spanish wall, had it not been for the opportune appearance of Sandoval with his flashing sword and gallant war-cry.

Once inside the gate, and realizing that he was again safe from his fierce pursuers, the unnatural strength that had sustained him so long gave way, and Huetzin staggered as though about to fall. Numbers of Spaniards and Tlascalans sprang to his assistance, but Sandoval was the first to reach him, and lifting the youth in his mighty arms as though he had been an infant, he bore him to his own quarters. Here, under the rough but skillful ministrations of the young soldier, Huetzin revived sufficiently to beg for water and food, neither of which he had tasted for many hours. These being brought, he ate and drank until, fearful that he would do himself harm, Sandoval took them from him.

Greatly refreshed and strengthened, Huetzin now asked for Marina, and when the girl appeared, full of wondering pity at the evidences he bore of his recent experiences, he requested her to obtain for him an instant interview with the commander concerning a matter of vital import. Cortes had just learned of the reappearance in the flesh of one whom the king had, but an hour before, declared dead, and was coming to investigate the miraculous resurrection when Marina met him with Huetzin's request.

The young chieftain had expected to go to the General, and was covered with confusion when the latter came to where he was, as though he had sent for him. He would have risen, but the commander insisted that, by his sufferings, he had won the right to lie still. So, seating himself beside the pile of mats that formed Sandoval's couch, and on which Huetzin now lay, Cortes listened with the gravest attention to an account of all that had happened to the young warrior since the preceding evening. When the latter came to a description of the underground meeting of conspirators, the leader's face grew very stern, and at the conclusion of the recital he exclaimed:

"Thou hast done well, my young lord of Titcala, and even thy recent sufferings are amply rewarded by the news obtained through them. Thus forewarned I am of the opinion that we shall find some means for checkmating these burrowing water-rats. How say you, Don Gonzalo?"

"If not, then shall we well deserve the fate they plot for us," answered Sandoval, to whom this question was addressed.

"Art sure that thou hast a heart still beating in thy breast?" suddenly demanded the General of Huetzin. "I was told, not long since, that a god had torn it from thy bosom, also that a fair lady of the king's court was expressing anxiety concerning thee."

"My heart is still in my own keeping, in spite of gods and fair ladies," replied Huetzin, though with Marina's blush reflected on his own face; "neither do I know any lady of Montezuma's court, unless indeed it be my sister Tiata, who is but a child, and is, I fear, no longer to be found in any earthly court or city."

24

MONTEZUMA
IS MADE PRISONER

THAT NIGHT Cortes convened a council of his captains, whom he told of the plot to kill him. He proposed to defeat this by being first in the field and making a prisoner of Montezuma himself. As an excuse for so high-handed a proceeding, he would bring up an affair, of which he had learned while at Cholula, but had deemed best to keep to himself until now. It was nothing less than an attack on the Spanish garrison at Vera Cruz, by an Aztec cacique named Quapoca, who claimed to have acted by direct orders from the king. In this engagement, though the Indians were ultimately defeated, the Spaniards, including Juan Escalante, the commandant, had been killed.

Armed with this excuse, Cortes, having requested and been granted an audience with the king, set forth for the palace at an early hour on the following morning. He was accompanied by Sandoval, Alvarado, and three other cavaliers in full armor. One of these was Huetzin, clad in armor provided for the occasion, and differing in no point, that the eye could detect, from a Spaniard. It was arranged that after Cortes and his companions were admitted to the king, other Spaniards, to the number of a score or so, should stroll into the palace, a few at a time, and remain within supporting distance in case of need. The rest of the troops, with the exception of a strong patrol on the avenue leading to the palace, were drawn up, under arms, in the courtyard of their quarters.

Montezuma received his guests with the utmost composure, and, through Marina's interpretation, chatted pleasantly with them for half an hour. At the end of that time Cortes, perceiving that a sufficient number of his men had assembled just outside the audience chamber, demanded of the king why he had ordered an attack to be made on Vera Cruz.

Although startled by the suddenness of the accusation, the king denied that he had done so.

Cortes professed himself willing to believe this, but requested that the cacique who had led the attacking force be sent for, that he might be examined.

To this Montezuma consented, and handed his signet to an officer, with the brief command that Quapoca be brought to Tenochtitlan.

After the officer had departed the Spanish commander proposed that, in order to prove his sincerity and place himself beyond suspicion of such an act of treachery against his Spanish friends, the king should transfer his residence to the palace occupied by them and remain as their guest until all questions in connection with this unfortunate affair should be settled.

As he listened to this proposal Montezuma turned deadly pale, and then his face flushed with indignation. "Do you dare doubt my word? The word of a king!" he demanded.

"Did not your majesty inform me of the death of my chief of Tlascalans but yesterday?" asked Cortes.

"If I did, it is because he is dead! A king cannot lie!" was the passionate answer.

"But he may be mistaken, and if so in one case, possibly in another," replied Cortes. At the same time he beckoned to Huetzin to step forward and unbonnet.

The young man did so, and as the king gazed on his well-remembered features it seemed for a moment as though he would fall in a fit, so terrified and horror-stricken was his expression. For a minute he could not command his voice, then, in a low tone, he said:

"The victory is thine, Malinche! So long as this son of Tlahuicol lives, the anger of the gods will not be averted from me or my kingdom. I will go with you."

Cortes immediately issued orders for the royal litter to be brought, and as the nobles who bore it hesitated to obey the stranger, the king assured them that it was his pleasure to visit his white friends. As the royal train, under a strong Spanish escort, passed through the street, its nobles walking with bowed heads and sad faces, the news spread like wildfire that the king had been taken prisoner, and was being carried off by force. On every side armed men seemed to spring from the ground. Ere they were half-way to their own place, the Christians were confronted by such a furious mass of humanity that, but for the intervention of Montezuma himself, they would have been forced to fight against desperate odds. Actuated either by superstitious cowardice or policy, the king assured his tumultuous subjects that he was going, of his own free will, to visit his friends, and ordered them to retire peaceably to their homes.

Thus, without a drop of bloodshed, was the powerful but superstitious monarch of the great Aztec nation taken prisoner by a handful of determined white men, and kept under their guard for months in the very heart of his own capital. It seems incredible that such could have been the case, but all historians vouch for its truth.

Montezuma was allowed spacious quarters and every semblance of royal authority, but was never again given his liberty. Quapoca came, was tried, condemned, and executed by the Spaniards, but their greater prisoner was not released. His subjects were granted daily audience with him, but they were only admitted a few at a time, and must pass the scrutiny of a strong Spanish guard always maintained in the royal antechamber.

This new order of things was hardly established before Sandoval began making inquiries as to the name, rank, and nationality of the beautiful girl with whom he had held so delightful, and, at the same time, so unsatisfactory an interview in the royal gardens. To his dismay he could learn nothing. No one to whom he applied could tell him aught concerning her, and she seemed to have disappeared as absolutely as though translated to another sphere. Even the page who had conducted him to her was not to be found. Sandoval enlisted the services of both Marina and Huetzin in the search, but they were equally unsuccessful with himself.

The young Toltec had, by this time, acquired so fair a knowledge of Spanish that he was able, after a fashion, to converse with his friend without the aid of an interpreter. Taking advantage of this, Sandoval would talk with him for hours concerning the object of his incessant thoughts. He declared his willingness to resign all the treasure he had acquired since coming to Mexico, if, by so doing, he could gain another interview with the maiden. This was no mean sum, for, in one way and another, the Spaniards had collected some six and a half millions of dollars in gold alone, to say nothing of an immense quantity of silver, jewels, and costly fabrics.

With all his wealth and bravery, poor Sandoval could discover no means of accomplishing the desire of his heart, and so sank into such a state of melancholy as to attract the attention and arouse the anxiety of Cortes himself. This acute observer, believing hard work to be the best lightener of a heavy heart, and being in want of a trusty governor for the important post of Vera Cruz, forthwith appointed the unhappy young soldier to the position, and dispatched him to his new sphere of action.

By this time the entire Aztec kingdom seemed truly to have passed under the dominion of the white conquerors, and that almost without a struggle. Not only did Cortes levy tribute and dispense justice in the name of the king, but he compelled Montezuma to publicly announce himself a vassal of Spain. Although the Aztec priesthood and religion were not yet overthrown, the Spaniards had erected a cross on the summit of the great temple, and here their worship was conducted by the side of that of the Aztec gods. Two brigantines, or small sailing vessels, were built and armed, for the command of the Tezcucan lake, and in no direction was the power of the Spaniards disputed. Several incipient rebellions had been so promptly reported to the Conqueror, though in so mysterious a manner that he could not trace his information to its source, that he was enabled to crush them before they came to a head. In the name of the king, who was but a passive tool in his hands, he arrested and held captive several reputed leaders of these rebellions, and among them Cacama, Prince of Tezcuco.

Some months were passed thus peacefully, and

Huetzin, tired of inactivity, as well as hopeless of discovering the fate of Tiata, whom he mourned as dead, was about to apply for permission to return to Tlascala, when one day there came a letter from Sandoval that changed the whole current of events. It contained the intelligence that a Spanish hidalgo, named Narvaez, in command of a fleet of eighteen vessels, and an army of a thousand men, well supplied with horses, artillery, muskets, and ammunition, had landed on the coast. This new-comer claimed to have authority from the Governor-General of the New World to supersede Cortes, and assume supreme control of the great kingdom he had conquered. By virtue of this authority he had summoned Sandoval to surrender Vera Cruz, and announced his intention of immediately marching on Cortes in Tenochtitlan. Upon this Sandoval had placed his little garrison in the best possible state of defense, answered Narvaez that he would surrender when he had orders from his commander to do so, but not before, and now awaited instructions.

In this grave emergency the white conqueror did not hesitate a moment to consider his course of action. Taking with him two hundred troops, he set out at once for the coast, where he proposed to at least test the strength of the new-comer before submitting to his authority. He left Alvarado, the «Tonatiah" of the Aztecs, behind in command of the city; with him were also left one hundred and forty Spaniards, Huetzin with his Tlascalans, and all the artillery.

As Cortes and his little army marched out of the city, Montezuma, in the royal litter, accompanied him as far as the great causeway. There, on the spot where they had first met, these two parted, with every mark of mutual esteem.

25

CORTES CAPTURES AND ENLISTS THE ARMY OF HIS RIVAL

HASTENING WITH ALL speed back over the road he had learned so well a few months before, Cortes led his little band across the valley, over the lofty pass of its mountain wall, to the wide-spread table-land of Puebla. Traversing this, by way of Cholula and Tlascala, the Conqueror finally crossed the eastern Cordilleras, and plunged into the sea of tropic vegetation that revels in the damp heats of the Tierra Caliente.

Narvaez had established himself at Cempoalla, with the intention of using the Totonac city as a base of operations against Vera Cruz. But Sandoval realizing that with a force of sixty men, as opposed to a thousand, discretion was by far the better part of valor, did not wait to be attacked. He slipped away during a night of stormy darkness, and when, on the following morning, his empty and echoing barracks were summoned to surrender, their late occupants were effectually hidden behind a league or more of the well-nigh impenetrable forest in which they had disappeared. Making a great circuit, so as to elude pursuit, carefully avoiding all highways, and suffering incredible hardships in trackless forests and wild mountain defiles, Sandoval and his handful of men at length effected a joyful junction with the slender force under Cortes.

They brought such news of the carelessness with which the camp of Narvaez was guarded, and concerning the dissatisfaction of his troops with their leader, that Cortes determined to attack him without delay. Through the alternate downpours and steaming sunbursts that mark the rainy season of the tropics, the little army advanced to the bank of a small river in the vicinity of Cempoalla, without being discovered. Here, while they lay concealed, they had the satisfaction of seeing Narvaez sally forth at the head of his troops, march as far as the opposite bank of the swollen stream, receive a thorough soaking from a heavy shower, and then, apparently convinced that his rival was nowhere in that part of the country, march back again to his comfortable quarters.

That night, in a pelting storm, the veterans of Cortes forded the stream, bracing themselves against its rushing current with the long copper-headed chinantla pikes obtained from the Aztecs. Two only were carried away by the flood, and the rest, advancing swiftly and stealthily, soon found themselves in the deserted and storm-swept streets of Cempoalla. Here, ere an alarm was given, they were so completely masters of the situation that, although Narvaez and his guard made a brave show of resistance, the moment the former fell, dangerously wounded, his entire army surrendered.

On the following morning their submission, which was accompanied by the laying down of their arms, was formally accepted by Cortes. Then the troops so recently opposed to him were re-enlisted, but this time under his victorious banner. Not only were their arms and other property restored to them, but they received liberal presents of the gold he had won from Aztec treasure-houses. Narvaez and his principal adherents were sent in chains to Vera Cruz, and his fleet was dismantled of its sails, rigging, and portable iron-work. Thus Cortes became again, without question, the supreme ruler of Mexico.

Just as these matters were so happily adjusted, and he was considering an extensive plan of new exploration and conquest, his attention was abruptly recalled to Tenochtitlan. Late one night a weary and way-worn native warrior reached the Christian camp, and, being halted by a sentry, who was one of Narvaez's men, demanded, in broken Spanish, to be conducted to the General, for whom he claimed to have an important communication. The sentry, being extremely suspicious of all Indians, including those who spoke

Spanish, stood stoutly on the defensive, with leveled pike, and called loudly for the captain of the guard. This officer, who happened to be Sandoval, came hurrying to the post, attended by the watch, one of whom bore a lantern. The sentry had only begun to tell of the treacherous Indian who was seeking admission to the commander, undoubtedly with designs against his life, when the lantern light flashed full in the warrior's face. As it did so a cry of delighted recognition came from the captain of the guard. Springing forward, he embraced the newly arrived stranger, calling him Don Juan and his brother, to the intense mystification of the gaping soldiers, who were witnesses of this unprecedented performance.

Bidding the watch retire, and the sentry resume his beat, Sandoval led Huetzin to his own quarters, where, after he had partaken of the food he showed every evidence of needing, the latter inquired:

"Hast thou not heard of the uprising in Tenochtitlan, and the perilous situation of thy friends?"

"Not a word," replied Sandoval.

"Then were the messengers captured as we feared. Full a dozen were sent out, but in each case the altar of the great temple was shortly after drenched with human blood. Two were Spaniards, and the rest warriors of my own band. We were hemmed in on all sides, nearly all were wounded, and all were exhausted with fighting and constant alarms. Without succor we could hold out but a few days longer.

KIRK MUNROE

"At length, satisfied that no one of our messengers had escaped from the city, I sought, and obtained permission from the lord Tonatiah to make the attempt. It was granted and I ventured forth. I could not escape by water, as the city is surrounded by an unbroken chain of canoes, and so was forced to seek the causeway of Iztapalapan. It was night, and being disguised, even as I now am, to resemble a tamane, I set forth with strong hopes of escaping unnoticed. They were unfounded; for before I had gone a hundred paces from the gate I was conscious of being observed and followed. As far as the end of the causeway was I allowed to go, but there I was waylaid and overcome by so strong a force that even had I been armed, resistance would have been in vain.

"As I was being led toward the temple by my captors, who shouted for joy that Huitzil would not lack for a victim that night, we were met by a priest, who called on them to halt until he could examine their prisoner. A light was brought, that exhibited my features without revealing his. He evidently recognized me, for he said, in a low tone and in the Mayan tongue: 'If thou canst escape the altar of Huitzil for this, the third time, O son of Tlahuicol, then will the power of the blood-loving gods be broken forever. Go, and may the gods of thy Toltec ancestors go with thee.' Then, with an angry voice he roundly abused my captors, saying to them that they had made a mistake, and arrested one who was a patriot like themselves. While he thus held

205

their attention I slipped away, and now, the causeway being unguarded, I escaped across it, and have in three days› time made my way to this place."

"But why should an Aztec priest exert himself in thy behalf?" demanded Sandoval.

"Because," answered Huetzin, "he was Tlalco the Toltec, of whom I have told thee as aiding my first escape."

"Tlalco," mused the other; "was not that the name of a priest who was ever about Montezuma, and apparently exercised so great an influence over him?"

"He is the same."

"Then he is the priest of all priests whom I am most anxious to meet. I have cause to believe that he can give me information concerning the lady of my heart, over whose loss I do so grieve that until I find her again I am unfitted for a soldier."

"From what source gained you this idea?" queried Huetzin.

"I heard, not long since, from him who was a king's page. He is some kin to the Totonac cacique, and in return for a favor I rendered the latter, he sent me word that my life's happiness was in the hands of Tlalco the priest. At first I could make nothing of so ambiguous a message, but after much consideration I think I have solved its meaning. Now, therefore, the dearest hope of my life, next to one, is to meet with this same Tlalco."

"Then!" exclaimed Huetzin, "as he is not to be

met short of Tenochtitlan, let us hasten the meeting as much as we may, by reporting the present state of affairs at once to my lord Malinche. It grieves me to think of the hunger and suffering, the weariness and despair of thy countrymen and my brave Tlascalans, whom I left penned in yonder city like trapped eagles. Speaking of pages, I heard that in spite of the strict watch maintained about our quarters a new one gained admittance in some way, and was taken into the king's service the very day I left. They said he was one of those handsome youths for whom the king expresses such a preference."

As Sandoval's impatience to make a start for the Aztec capital was equal to Huetzin's own, they proceeded to the quarters occupied by Cortes, and in spite of the lateness of the hour, obtained an audience. To the commander the young Toltec gave a full and detailed account of what had taken place in Tenochtitlan since his departure from that city. According to this Alvarado had been secretly informed that the Aztec priests, taking advantage of his weakness, had planned his destruction, and the rescue of Montezuma, by a general uprising, which was to take place during the feast of the Incensing of Huitzil. As the day of the feast approached they asked that the king might be permitted to assist them in their ceremonies. This request was refused, and Alvarado, recalling the summary vengeance taken by his commander on the Cholulans for planning his destruction, determined to adopt similar measures in the present case. He therefore caused the greater part of the force at his command to gather about the scene of festivities as though out of curiosity. At a given signal these fell upon the priests, nobles, and others, engaged in the ceremonial dance, and slew them to the number of six hundred.

At this the whole city rose in arms, drove the Spaniards to their quarters, and, in spite of a devastating fire of artillery, made assault after assault against the walls. Only at command of their king, whom Alvarado persuaded to appeal to them, did the assailants withdraw. Then they began a regular siege, burning the Spanish brigantines, throwing up works about their quarters, cutting off their supplies of water and provisions, and arresting all who attempted to pass either in to or out from them. "So desperate is their condition," concluded Huetzin, "that, unless my lord furnishes speedy relief, there is naught before them save starvation or the altars of the Great Temple."

For answer, Cortes simply said, "The army marches at daylight, and do thou, Gonzalo, give instant orders, in my name, to that effect."

26

TIATA'S BRAVE DEATH
AND SANDOVAL'S GRIEF

So UNTIRING WERE the efforts of Sandoval and his asso-
ciates during the remainder of that night, that by sunrise the army of rescue had left Cempoalla. It consisted
of about one thousand infantry, of whom nearly one
hundred were armed with muskets, and as many more
with cross-bows, a hundred cavalry, and a well-pro-
visioned train of artillery. In three days they reached
Tlascala; and Huetzin, who had obtained permission
to hasten to this point in advance of the army, rejoined
it with a welcome reinforcement of two thousand Tlascalan warriors, all eager to be led against their heredi-
tary foe.

While the army halted at Tlascala, the aged chieftain of Titcala offered to one of the newly arrived cavaliers so great a sum in gold dust for his horse, a dainty

sorrel mare, that the offer was promptly accepted. This purchase was immediately transferred to Huetzin, of whom his grandfather was so proud, that he was determined to give the young warrior an opportunity for making as brave an appearance as any of his white comrades. Thus Huetzin, raised to a pinnacle of proud happiness by his new possession, became the first native of the new world to own and bestride one of those marvelous animals which, but a year before, had been spoken of throughout all Anahuac as either gods or devils. He named his mare «Cocotin" (little girl), and, under the skillful teachings of Sandoval, who was almost as delighted to see him mounted as he was to be so, he soon became an expert horseman.

From Tlascala the conquerors made all speed over the rugged Cordilleras, though this time, as a measure of precaution, taking a more northerly route than that traversed before. On the western brow of the mountains it presented the broad Mexican valley from an entirely different point of view. It gave, however, the same exquisite picture of shimmering lakes with white-walled cities and villas resting on their bosoms, fire-tipped teocallis, dark groves, blooming fields, and encircling walls of distant blue, that some of them had gazed on before. At their feet lay the city of Tezcuco, shaded by cypresses, while, far across the shining waters, rose the inscrutable walls of Tenochtitlan, either the prison or the grave of their friends.

Their fears that it was the latter were aroused, as

they descended into the valley, by the coolness and even rudeness of their treatment by its inhabitants. As they entered the city of Tezcuco, where they proposed to rest for the night, their reception was even more chilling than any yet experienced. No one came forth to give them welcome, and, as they marched through the silent streets, only a furtive face, peering now and then from a doorway, proved that any living soul still remained in the city. These things raised uneasy forebodings, not only in the mind of Cortes, but throughout all his army, as to the fate of Alvarado and those with him, and they would have given much for news from the distant city. Not only would it put an end to their suspense, but by it their future movements could be determined. At a time and in a manner that they least expected it, the news came.

The night had passed quietly, and Huetzin, who had charge of the morning watch, stood on the shore of the lake, noting the rosy flush of morning redden the snow-fields of towering Popocatepetl. A mist hung over the waters that hid their farther shore and the city in which he had dared and suffered so much. As he gazed in the direction of Tenochtitlan, he became aware of moving forms out on the lake, dimly disclosed through the lifting fog. They were advancing toward him, and soon resolved themselves into two canoes, one behind the other. In a moment Huetzin saw that in the first a slight youth was paddling with a desperate energy, and evidently endeavoring to escape from the other. In the second a man, clad in the white robe of a priest, was laboring with an equal effort, and, by his superior strength, was surely gaining on the other. After them more canoes shot out of the mist, all coming from the same direction, and all advancing at their utmost speed.

A light craft lay drawn up on the shore, not far from where the young Toltec stood, and, as a wild cry for aid came quavering across the waters from the foremost canoe, Huetzin, first giving an alarm to his own men, sprang into it, and put forth to the assistance of the hard-pressed fugitive. As he did so, the man robed like a priest, who led the pursuit, dropped his paddle, seized a bow lying in the bottom of his boat, and stood up, with a copper-tipped arrow drawn back to its head. Huetzin uttered a cry of horror as the cruel shaft sped on its deadly errand, and sank deep in the back of the flying youth, striking him squarely between the shoulders. As the stricken lad fell forward, there came an exultant cry across the still waters: "Thus deals Topil with the enemies of his gods!" Then his canoe was spun around, and joined those of the other pursuers in an unharmed flight across the lake, though a dozen bullets were sent whistling after them, by the few musketeers who had been attracted to the shore.

Although Huetzin heard the priest's words plainly enough, he did not, at the moment, realize their full meaning. Filled with sorrow for the young stranger whom he had just seen so cruelly shot down, and who he felt must be a friend, he drove his own craft rapidly to where the other lay drifting. Its occupant, who seemed a mere boy, clad in the picturesque costume of a king›s page, lay, face downward in a pool of his life›s blood that was forming in the bottom of the canoe. The arrow had been sped truly, and with a deadly force.

As Huetzin, stepping into the canoe, lifted the lad to an easier position, a filmy scarf wound about his head, fell off, and a wealth of auburn hair tumbled over his shoulders. Then a pair of glorious, brown eyes were opened, and fixed full on the face of the Tlascalan warrior. The latter grew rigid, as though from a numbing shock. The very blood in his veins turned chill. A voice that he had thought never again to hear, came to his ears. It was very faint, but the words were clear and distinct:

"Huetzin, my brother! My dear, dear, brother! I knew you would come, though they said you were dead. You are fighting for the true faith, for the old faith, are you not, dear? I, too, have done what I could. Now I am dying for it. Gladly. Help me to make the sign, Huetzin. The holy sign of the Toltecs. There. Now it— is well. Huetzin!—Father!—Mother!——" The brown eyes closed gently, like those of an infant dropping into peaceful slumber. The queenly head sunk back on the strong arm supporting it; there came a soft sigh, and, as the rising sun burst in full glory from behind snow-crowned Popocatepetl, the spirit of Tiata mingled with its flood of brightness.

Like one who dreams, Huetzin sat with the light

burden in his arms, gazing at the calmly beautiful face of his dead sister, but seeming to see far beyond it. There was that in his expression that caused those who came to his assistance to respect his silence, though they knew not that the form, which he held, was other than what it appeared. Very gently they led his canoe to land, and, when its prow grated on the beach, he rose and stepped out, still bearing his burden. They offered to relieve him of it, but he paid no heed. As he lifted it a letter addressed to the Spanish commander fell to the ground. It was from Alvarado, and it contained the news, so longed for, that the garrison still held out. It concluded: "Were it not that I realize the great importance of this word to you, and that your movements will be guided by it, I should not strive to send it. Almost certain death awaits any messenger who attempts to pass the lines that the priests, who are heading this insurrection, have drawn about us. No ordinary dispatch bearer could cross them. I am sending this by a king's page, a brave lad, who has volunteered for the service, and will get through the lines if it be in the power of mortal to do so. I heartily recommend him to your favor, and pray that no harm may befall him."

While this letter, borne hastily to Cortes, was being read by him, Huetzin, taking no notice of proffered assistance, and still appearing like one in a dream, bore his dead to his own quarters, and laid the slender form on his own bed. He had barely deposited his sorrowful burden, when Sandoval, who, hearing that something had gone amiss with his friend, had hastened with ready sympathy to find him, entered the room.

"What has happened thee, Don Juan, my brother?" he began. Then, catching sight of the dead girl, lying so peacefully, he stopped as though struck with an instant dumbness, clutched at his own throat, and staggered back so that, but for the wall, he must have fallen.

Surprised from his own grief for the moment, Huetzin sprang to his friend, crying: "What is it? What ails thee, my brother? Art thou stricken with death?"

With a mighty sob, that sounded like the breaking of a heart, Sandoval answered: "Thou hast said it, for I am indeed stricken with death. There lies she who held my life, and if she has taken it not with her, still it is gone from me, so that none other may ever hold it. I know not even the name by which she was called, yet did I know her soul as though it were mine own."

"She was Tiata, my sister," answered Huetzin, in a whisper.

"Then are we indeed brothers, and more than brothers," replied Sandoval. With these words he left the room, nor was he seen again by living soul that day.

27

THE CONQUERORS ARE BESIEGED IN THEIR QUARTERS

THE BRAVE GIRL who had risked and lost her life in bringing Alvarado's message to Cortes, was buried that same day, at sunset, amid the drooping cypresses and perfumed flowers of the royal garden of Tezcuco. During the day, Marina, and a few young Tezcucan girls whom she persuaded to venture timidly forth from their homes, lined the grave with a plait of sweet-scented grasses. When Tiata had been laid gently within it, there was erected above it a snow-white cross, the symbol of the Toltec faith, for love of which she died. It was a day of sadness in the deserted city, for the story of the great sorrow that had fallen on both Huetzin and Sandoval was known to every soldier and warrior. At the young Tlascalan leader they cast glances of respectful sympathy, but Sandoval was seen of no man that day. When, on the following morning, he reappeared among them, none dared speak to him of what had happened, for to his face had come that look of sternness that it held to the day of his death, and which caused even the boldest to shrink from incurring his displeasure.

From Tezcuco the army swept around the southern shore of the salt lake, to that same great causeway over which the first triumphal entry had been made into Tenochtitlan. Then, they had barely found room to advance amid the welcoming throngs of spectators with which it was crowded. Now, save for their own heavy tread, it was silent and deserted. Then, the sparkling waters on either side had swarmed with swift canoes filled with eager sight-seers. Now, only an occasional craft was to be seen stealthily regarding their movements from a distance and darting away like a frightened water-fowl when attention appeared to be attracted to it. Even from the far-reaching city, before them came no sound, nor was there sign of life. A death-like stillness brooded over the entire scene, and it filled the hearts of the advancing troops with an ominous dread. To dispel this, Cortes ordered the trumpets to sound a merry blast. Its echoes had hardly died away before they were answered by a glad roar of artillery from the distant fortress, in the heart of the city.

With this evidence that the little garrison still held

out, and that the cross was still uplifted in the very shadow of Huitzil's temple, the troops entered Tenochtitlan with lighter hearts and a brisker tread. As they marched through its silent streets, these appeared even more deserted than had those of Tezcuco. The active population of former days had vanished, and the tramp of iron-shod hoofs only awoke melancholy echoes from empty houses. The veterans, who had seen these same streets teeming with eager multitudes, gazed about them in bewilderment, while the levies of Narvaez jeered at them for having, with all their boasted prowess, only conquered a city of the dead.

Finally they came to the Spanish quarters. The great gates behind which their friends had been besieged so long, were flung joyously open, and the new-comers were received with greetings as hearty as they were sincere. To the veterans little seemed changed since their departure. Some traces of the siege, in the shape of fire-blackened buildings and shattered walls, were to be seen here and there, but Montezuma was still a prisoner; military order still prevailed, and, with the advent of this fresh army, there was every reason to believe that the former state of affairs would speedily be restored. Thus Cortes believed, and thus he wrote to the officer whom he had left in command at Vera Cruz.

Only two comparatively unimportant matters gave him any uneasiness. One of these was the escape of Cuitlahua, the king's brother, and thus heir to the Aztec throne, which had been made only a few days before.

The other was Montezuma's complaint that Tlalco, his favorite priestly adviser, was no longer permitted to visit him. When Cortes questioned Alvarado concerning this, the latter denied having refused admittance to any person whom the king desired to see. He added that he had noted the absence of this particular priest, but had accounted for it by supposing that he had joined his fellows in inciting the present insurrection. Both Huetzin and Sandoval deeply regretted that they were unable to question Tlalco concerning certain matters. Knowing what they did of his personality, they feared lest it should have been discovered by the chief priest, in which case they knew there was little hope of ever again meeting with the devoted Toltec.

A day or two after his arrival, Cortes, having completed his dispatches for Vera Cruz, entrusted them to a messenger who was ordered to proceed to that fort. He set forth; but in less than half an hour, came flying back, terror-stricken and covered with wounds. "The city is in arms!" he cried. "The drawbridges are raised, and no avenue of escape is left!"

Even as he spoke, his words were confirmed by a dark flood of Aztec warriors, sweeping down the great avenue, like some mighty tide that has burst its limits. At the same time the parapeted roofs of neighboring buildings were covered with a multitude of slingers and bowmen, who seemed to spring into existence as though by magic. As the astonished Spaniards gazed on this sudden repopulating of the deserted city with warriors instead of traders, the dread tones of the great serpent drum, thundering forth from Huitzil's temple, proclaimed that the Aztec gods had at length awakened and were about to wage a pitiless, unrelenting war against all followers of the cross.

The ominous booming of the war-drum was instantly answered by the ringing notes of Christian trumpets, summoning every man within the palace-fortress to his post. Their call was so promptly obeyed that ere the tawny Aztec wave reached the wall, every musketeer, cross-bowman, and gunner was in place, and waiting.

A blinding flight of arrows, darts, and stones, from the Aztec front, and a storm of missiles from the house-tops, together with a fierce yell from ten thousand Aztec throats, opened the battle. In reply came a rattling volley from Spanish guns, that mowed down hundreds of the advancing hosts. But they did not falter. Again and again they charged, dashing themselves with impotent fury against the low stone wall separating them from their enemies, and, time after time, the same murderous volley drove them back. Hundreds of them, upborne by hundreds more, scaled the walls, only to fall victims to the Tlascalan maquahuitls, that sprang to meet them from the opposite side. They tried to effect a breach with battering-rams, and to set the quarters on fire with blazing arrows. The woodwork of some of the buildings was soon burning briskly, and a few rods of wall were leveled; but the fire died out without injuring the more substantial portions of the buildings, and a grinning battery lay in wait behind the breach. Like crouched tigers the black guns seemed to leap at the swarming foe, and in a few minutes the breach was choked with lifeless human bodies. Still the battle raged with unabated fury until, with the coming of night, both sides were thankful for a respite.

With earliest sunrise the Spaniards were again under arms and at their posts, but only to see the streets and squares swarming with a more numerous and determined foe than had attacked them on the preceding day. In its approach to military order the hand of the warlike Cuitlahua was visible. Instead of being a disorderly mob, the Aztec force was drawn up in compact bodies, each under its own leader. Above them streamed banners emblazoned with the devices of many cities, while over all soared a golden eagle, bearing in his talons a writhing serpent, the proud cognizance of the Montezumas, and the standard of the Aztec nation. Among the crowded ranks, fierce priests were everywhere to be seen promising the protection of the gods, and inviting their followers to deeds of valor. The gorgeous feather mantles and golden bucklers of the nobles glistened in the morning sun, while above the cotton-armored, or naked ranks of the humbler warriors, a forest of tossing spears reflected his rays from their myriad gleaming points.

As Cortes had determined to take the offensive in this day›s fight, he ordered a general discharge of artillery and musketry to be poured into the thickset

Aztec ranks before they had made a movement of attack. Under cover of the resulting confusion, the gates were thrown open, and out of the smoke clouds the Spanish cavalry dashed forth in a resistless charge. They were supported by Huetzin with a thousand Tlascalan warriors, and such was the fury of their onslaught that, for several blocks, the Aztecs were swept helplessly before it. Their precipitate flight ended at a barricade of timber and stones, that had been thrown across the great avenue during the night. Here they made so determined a stand that the Spaniards, galled by their hurtling missiles, and an incessant rain of stones from the neighboring house-tops, were compelled to retire.

Two heavy guns, advanced on the run by scores of lusty Tlascalans, soon leveled the barricade. But it had served as a rallying-point for fresh battalions of the enemy, by whom an attempt of the Spaniards to repeat their brilliant charge was doggedly and successfully resisted. Regardless of wounds or death, numbers of them would, at a signal, dart under the horses' bellies and cling to their legs, while others strove to fell the riders from their saddles.

It was fortunate for the bulk of the Spanish army that the efforts of the Aztecs were invariably directed toward the taking of prisoners, rather than to the killing of their enemies; though to the unfortunates thus captured and dragged away for sacrifice, instant death would have been infinitely preferable. Everywhere the Spaniards found barricades erected, and at these points were massed fresh bodies of Aztec troops, impatiently awaiting their turn to plunge into the fray. No matter how often they were repulsed or how many of them were killed, they appeared to the disheartened whites to swarm in undiminished numbers, and with unabated courage.

So the day was spent in a steady succession of petty, but desperate engagements. At its close, although the Spaniards had been everywhere victorious, they were exhausted and filled with gloomy forebodings, while their adversaries seemed more confident and in a better humor for fighting than at the beginning of the struggle.

All night long they gathered outside the Spanish quarters, taunting the invaders with their helplessness, now that the gods were awake. "The altars of Huitzil thirst for your blood!" they cried. "But soon they will be drenched with it, and the wild beasts of the palace shall feast on your carcasses! The knives of sacrifice are sharpened!—and cages for fattening await the lean and hungry Tlascalans!"

28

A BATTLE IN MID-AIR

So FIERCE WAS THE Aztec temper, that, with earliest dawn of the third day of fighting, they were swarming at the walls. So determined was their assault, that, ere they could be driven back, nearly a thousand of them had leaped inside, and gained the courtyard. Although these fought with a desperation that resulted in serious injury to the garrison, most of them were quickly dispatched by the Tlascalans, among whom they had appeared. A number, however, escaped, and darted into the numerous buildings of the old palace. Here, though the Tlascalans pursued them like ferrets after rats, they managed to set numerous fires, kill or wound several persons, stab Cortes himself through the hand, and do an immense amount of mischief before being finally hunted down and destroyed. A few more assaults as desperate and successful as this would seal the fate of the besieged, and, even to the bravest, their situation began to appear alarming.

In this strait, Cortes appealed to his royal prisoner and urged him to use his influence with his subjects to bring about a cessation of hostilities. This, Montezuma at first refused to do; but, when assured that the invaders would willingly leave the city if a way were opened to him, he finally consented. Arrayed for the occasion in his most kingly robes, he was escorted to the roof of the central turret of the palace by a brilliant retinue of those Aztec nobles who still shared his fortunes, and a number of Spanish cavaliers.

In the streets below the battle was raging furiously; but, as his subjects recognized their monarch, the din of clashing weapons and fierce war-cries instantly ceased. The tumult of war was succeeded by a stillness as of death. Many of the Aztecs prostrated themselves to the ground; others bowed their heads; but some gazed, unabashed, and even defiantly, at the king, whose weak-minded superstition had lost him his kingdom. More than one of these daring spirits secretly fitted an arrow to his bowstring, and nervously fingered it. In more than one breast a sacrilege was meditated that, though certain to be avenged by the gods, might, after all, be for the best. But first they would hear what this dishonored king had to say.

He was bidding them disperse, and do no further harm to his friends the white men, who, if allowed, would willingly return whence they came.

This would never do! The priests of the war-god were greedy for the victims, who were on the point of surrendering themselves. Should they be balked of their prey by this king, who was already as good as dead? Never! Let him die, and be no longer an impediment to their vengeance! With him out of the way, the destruction of the Christians and their base allies would be an easy matter! Then would the gods rejoice! Then would their favor be restored! And again would Anahuac take her proper place as leader of the nations! Down with Montezuma! Long live Cuitlahua! To the altars with Spaniard and Tlascalan!

So whispered the busy priests, darting from one to another. The whisper grew into a murmur, and it quickly rose to a storm of fierce cries.

Now was the time! An arrow, aimed by a subject at his king, hissed through the air. A cloud of arrows followed it. Spanish bucklers were interposed too late, and, as Montezuma fell, a frenzied yell of triumph arose from the multitude.

Then a reaction set in. What would the gods do? "To the temple!" was the cry. "The priests must plead for us!" The priests themselves spread this shout, exulting, as they did so, in its evidence of their unimpaired power. So the throngs hastened away toward the temples, until, in a short time, not a person remained in the great square fronting the Spanish quarters.

In the meantime, Montezuma, borne tenderly below, and laid on his royal bed still dressed in his robes of state, was dying. The priests of his own race came not near him. They had no use for a dying king! Already were they busy with preparations for crowning another, who would heap their altars with victims, and add to their power, until they should become objects of fear and worship, even as were the gods themselves. Already was Topil, the chief priest, preparing a sacrifice such as had not been known at an Aztec coronation for nearly four centuries. He had a Toltec in reserve for the altar. Not only that, but a Toltec who had masqueraded as an Aztec priest, and had been detected in a vile conspiracy against the gods. Besides, he had a few Spaniards in his dungeons, and when had Christian blood been spilled at an Aztec coronation? Never before!

So Montezuma, the king who might have been all-powerful, died, because of his superstitious weakness, and the gods did not avenge his death, but allowed Cuitlahua, his brother, to reign in his stead.

The great temple of Huitzil stood so near the ancient palace in which the Spaniards and their allies were quartered, as to overlook it. A quantity of stones and heavy timbers had been conveyed to its summit under cover of darkness, and one morning the Christians were dismayed to find these thundering down on them from the lofty height. At the same time came such flights of arrows, as denoted the presence on this vantage ground of a large body of warriors. In connection with this attack, came another of those furious assaults on their works, of which the enemy seemed never to tire. It was at once realized that if they would escape speedy destruction, the temple must be carried, and Cortes detailed one hundred men, under Escobar, the chamberlain, for the purpose.

Three separate charges did this officer and his brave followers make in their effort to capture the huge teocal; but each time they were repulsed with serious loss. Finally, Escobar returned with but half his men, leaving the others where they had fallen. He, and all of the survivors, were wounded, some of them so severely that they died soon after, and the capture of the temple was reported to be an impossibility.

Cortes declaring that nothing was impossible, that the place must be captured, and that he would either accomplish it or die in the attempt, detailed another storming party of three hundred Spaniards, and two thousand Tlascalan warriors. These last were headed by their young chieftain, while the whole force was led by the General in person. Fifteen minutes of furious fighting forced a passage through the throng of Aztecs occupying the temple court, and placed the assailants at the foot of the first of the five flights of stone steps by which the top was to be reached.

Leaving the Tlascalans and a score of musketeers to repel the Aztecs, who were making constant efforts to regain possession of the court, the leader, closely followed by Sandoval, Huetzin, and the other gallant cavaliers of the storming party, sprang up the first stairway. On each of the terraces above them stood strong bodies of the enemy to dispute their passage. These showered down arrows and darts, together with great stones and massive timbers. Most of the latter bounded harmlessly over the heads of the scaling party, but every now and then one would crash into their ranks, and, sweeping some of the unfortunate Spaniards from their narrow foothold, hurl them lifeless to the bottom. In spite of the terrible odds thus presented, the dauntless conquerors fought their way foot by foot, from terrace to terrace, and from stairway to stairway, ever upward, until at length the lofty summit was attained.

Here, in sight of the whole city the opposing forces closed in furious combat, of such a phenomenal nature, that all other hostilities were suspended by mutual consent, in order that this death-struggle in mid-air might be watched without interruption. The priests of the temple, seeming more like demons than human beings, with their blood-clotted locks and savage aspect, fought like such. They rushed at the Spaniards with incredible fury, and, in many cases, forced them over the awful brink, willing to sacrifice their own lives in the leap to death, if they could only carry the hated Christians with them.

Once, in the midst of the fighting, Huetzin heard his own name called in accents of despair, and saw his brother Sandoval whose sword had snapped off at the hilt, struggling with half a dozen of these fiends, who had forced him to within a few feet of the edge. In a moment the young Toltec had hewed a way to his friend's side, and in another Sandoval was free to snatch the sword of a dying cavalier, and plunge once more into the thickest of the fight. For three dreadful hours did the combat rage. At the end of that time a remnant only of the gallant band of assailants remained masters of the bloody arena. Every Aztec, priest, noble, or warrior, had either been slain, or hurled from the giddy height.

Some of the survivors entered the sanctuary where sat the frightful image of Huitzil, the war-god. Bound to the altar in front of it they discovered a man. His eyes were torn from their sockets; his limbs were broken, and he bore other evidences of the most diabolical tortures. That he still lived, in spite of all, was attested by his feeble moanings. For a moment the victors paused aghast at the sight. Then one from among them sprang forward, and knelt beside this pitiful victim of the most hideous religion known to the New World. He was Huetzin, and in the cruelly mutilated form before him, he still recognized Tlalco the Toltec, the priest who, on three separate occasions, had saved him from a like awful fate.

29

THE GLORIOUS TRIUMPH OF TLALCO

TLALCO THE TOLTEC, one of the few survivors in Mexico of that mysterious race to which Huetzin traced his own ancestry, had, like Tlahuicol, been born in the land of the Mayans. Here he was educated as a priest of that gentle religion of love and peace, whose gods were the Four Winds, and other forces of nature, and the symbol of which was a cross. It had at one time been the faith of all Anahuac; but, with the coming of the conquering Aztecs, it was supplanted by the cruel worship of Huitzil, the war-god, whose blood-stained priests demanded the sacrifice of thousands of human victims every year.

The young Toltec first heard of these abominations with horror, but not until his only brother, to whom he was passionately attached, was captured by an Aztec war party and doomed to sacrifice in Tenochtitlan, did he conceive the idea of devoting his life to conflict with the gods who exacted them. His first act was to secretly enlist a number of young men whose enthusiasm in the sacred cause was equal to his own. Then, like a crusader of the old world, he entered Anahuac at the head of his little band. Its members were distributed by twos, in various places, from which they were to maintain a regular correspondence with him. By this means he gained early information of all important occurrences throughout the kingdom, and was able to lay his plans accordingly. He established himself in Tenochtitlan. Here he bearded the lion in its den, by entering the service of the temple, and becoming a candidate for the priesthood of Huitzil. While thus engaged he first heard of Tlahuicol.

Tlalco's nature was to plot and work by hidden means; but he could rejoice in the downright blows of the warrior, who fought openly against those of whom he was the secret enemy. Though he did not meet Tlahuicol, nor even learn that he, too, was a Toltec, until the very hour of the latter's death, he made himself familiar with every event of the great warrior's career. He augmented the prestige of the Tlascalan war-chief by originating, and spreading, the prophecy that through Tlahuicol should Huitzil fall. It was this prophecy, a knowledge of which had become general at the time the Tlascalan was captured by his enemies, that caused Topil, the chief priest, to regard him with such a bitter hatred, and demand his life of Montezuma.

After the death of Tlahuicol, and the startling discovery that he, too, was a Toltec, Tlalco determined to protect the children of the hero so far as lay in his power, and at the same time to use them in furthering his own life-work. All his hopes of ultimate success now centered in the mysterious white conquerors, who, bearing a cross as their symbol of faith, had recently arrived on the coast. Therefore, after rescuing Huetzin from the knife of sacrifice, he bade him seek and join himself to them, thus, unwittingly, reiterating the last instructions of Tlahuicol.

Tiata, he saved from Topil's vengeance, by causing the praises of her beauty to be so artfully sounded within hearing of Cacama, Prince of Tezcuco, that the latter demanded her in marriage of Montezuma. By Tlalco's instructions the girl claimed the privilege of a year's mourning for her parents, before becoming a bride. This was granted; but in accordance with established custom, she was compelled to reside at the Court of Tezcuco, in charge of a noble lady of the prince's household. From here Tiata, who was now enlisted heart and soul in the cause of the Toltec, for the overthrow of the hated religion to which her parents had been sacrificed, constantly furnished Tlalco with important information. Under the strict watch of her duenna, she was permitted to visit Tenochtitlan, to witness the first entry of the white conquerors, and her heart swelled with pride at the sight of her brother leading his army of

Tlascalans. No opportunity was allowed her for communicating with him, ere he was spirited away through the efforts of the chief priest.

When Tlalco learned that Huetzin was, for the second time, about to be led to the altar of sacrifice, he was for a moment at a loss how to act. Had the message sent to Sandoval been traced to him, his influence with Montezuma, as an Aztec priest, would have been destroyed. Then he remembered Tiata's presence in the palace, and sent the message through her. That very evening, after her strange interview with Sandoval, the Toltec maiden was compelled to return to Tezcuco, where, for many weeks, she was so closely watched, that she could gain no intelligence of her brother's fate.

At length, wearying of Cacama's unwelcome attentions, Tiata found means of sending an appeal to Tlalco for aid in escaping them. At the same time she informed him that the Tezcucan prince was secretly raising an army with which he proposed to destroy the Spaniards, and usurp the Aztec throne. Tlalco immediately caused this information to be conveyed to Cortes, who as promptly effected the arrest of Cacama, whom he afterward held as a captive in the Spanish quarters.

After the departure of Cortes to meet Narvaez, Tlalco found that, by his constant intercourse with the king, upon whose superstitious nature he had been able to exert a powerful influence, he was exciting the jealousy and suspicions of Topil. Therefore, as a measure of precaution, he suddenly ceased his visits to the captive monarch. At the same time, in order that he might still be kept informed of all that was taking place in the palace, he conceived and carried out the plan of having Tiata, disguised as a youth, installed as a king›s page. Before she found an opportunity of communicating with her brother, she heard that he was to take the dangerous task of conveying the news of Alvarado›s desperate situation to Cortes, and this was the first bit of information that she sent to Tlalco. He, knowing only too well what precautions were taken to prevent the escape of any such messenger, and the terrible fate already suffered by those previously sent out, for a moment believed the son of Tlahuicol to be lost. Then a high resolve filled his breast.

Although not a warrior, he determined on a course of action from which many a one entitled to the name might well have shrunk. He knew himself to be an object of such suspicion to Topil, that the spies of the chief priest were ever on his track, and that his every movement was instantly reported to his arch enemy. He knew, too, that Topil, having become superstitious through the prophecy concerning Tlahuicol, and the two miraculous escapes of Tlahuicol's son from his clutches, thirsted for the blood of the young Toltec, with an eagerness that would have given anything short of life itself for his capture. Knowing all this, Tlalco still watched for Huetzin's departure from the palace, followed him to the place of his capture, allowed the guards to lead him for some distance, thus withdrawing themselves from the causeway, and then effected the prisoner›s release by stepping forward, and, in his capacity of priest, boldly denouncing their stupidity, and holding their attention by his words, until Huetzin had slipped away and disappeared.

Five minutes later, Tlalco was seized and dragged before Topil. "Ha, false priest! Have I discovered thee at last?" cried the latter in a voice well nigh choked with fury. "Long hast thou deceived me, but mine eyes are at length opened, and now shalt thou experience the wrath of the outraged gods, in a manner that will teach thee its possibilities as thou hast not dreamed of them."

From that moment the body of Tlalco was racked by a system of the most exquisite tortures that even the practiced ingenuity of Aztec priests could invent. For two weeks these had been prolonged, until, at the end of that time, the poor, agonized wreck of humanity lay where Huetzin discovered it, still conscious, but with the brave spirit just lingering on the threshold of its mortal home, before departing to the realms of immortality.

Heart-sick and filled with horror, at thus finding his friend and thrice preserver, the young Toltec knelt beside the hideous altar, and said: "Tlalco, my father, dost thou know me?"

The face of the dying man was lit with a glow of recognition, and in a whisper so feeble as to be barely heard, he answered:

"It is the son of Tlahuicol."

Then they severed the cruel bonds and lifted him tenderly into the open air, where the sightless face instinctively turned toward the glowing noonday sun. Here Huetzin moistened his blackened lips and bathed his face with water that was at the same time mingled with his own scalding tears of fierce indignation, love, and pity. While he was thus engaged, his white comrades, filled with a furious rage, tore the grinning wargod from his blood-soaked throne and rolled the senseless image out on the broad arena which had but just been the scene of so terrible a battle.

"The hour of the false God has come!" cried Huetzin in the Toltec tongue: "The white conquerors are about to hurl him from his loftiest temple! Now is thy victory gained, O Tlalco! for the power of Aztec priesthood is broken forever! Oh, that my father could have lived to see this day! Oh, that Tiata might have seen it! The gods of the Toltecs, thy gods and my gods, O Tlalco, be praised that thou and I are permitted to share in this their glorious triumph!"

As he uttered these words in a tongue understood only by the dying man, the face of the youth was transfigured, the wrath of battle passed from it and it shone with the light of an all-absorbing enthusiasm.

"Lift me in thy strong arms," whispered Tlalco, "and make for me the holy sign."

As Huetzin lifted him and gently touched him on forehead, breast, and each shoulder, there came an exultant shout from the soldiers, a sound of crashing, splintering, and rending, as the ponderous image of the god thundered down to the bottom of the vast pyramid and a great cry of terror and consternation rose from the multitudes below. At the same moment the tortured features of him whom Huetzin supported, became radiant with the glory of the immortal gods, to whom his glad spirit was already winging its triumphant flight.

30

MONTEZUMA'S SUCCESSOR DEFIES THE CONQUERORS

As HUETZIN ROSE to his feet, after laying gently down the lifeless body of the Toltec martyr, he beheld Sandoval patiently waiting to attract his attention. The young Spaniard stood with one mail-shod foot resting on the neck of a writhing Aztec priest, who strove in vain to free himself from its weight.

"Here is a vermin," spoke Sandoval, "who bears a certain look of familiarity and who, I imagine, must be accounted of some consequence among his own diabolical crew. Yet I cannot place him and have persuaded him to come to thee for recognition. I found him, squatted like a toad in a hole, after yon image was dragged from its pedestal. He seems not to be wounded, nor do I believe he appeared in the fight at all. Now, lift thy head, vermin, that a man may gaze on thy dev-il's face!"

Thus exclaiming, Sandoval caught at the matted hair of the priest and pulled up his head so that Huetz-in had a fair view of the fear-distorted features. As he glanced at them the young Toltec uttered a great cry and sprang forward.

"Aye, well do I know him!" he exclaimed. "He is the murderer of thousands, and thrice have I been in his clutches. From me has he taken father, mother, and sister! There (pointing to the mutilated body of Tlalco) is a specimen of his work. With his own hand did he slay Tlahuicol and Tiata! He is Topil, the chief-priest, the chief curse of Anahuac. Let me at him, that I may hurl him to everlasting damnation! Let me at him, I say! He is mine!"

"Gently, lad, gently!" interposed Sandoval, in a tone whose very softness intimated his rage. "To hurl him over the brink would be a kindness. 'Twould be too sweet a death for him. I have a better plan. Leave him to me, and I promise you thou shalt be satisfied."

With this he again grasped the long hair of Topil's head, and dragged the screaming wretch back into the shrine from which he had brought him. There, lifting him with a quick jerk to his feet, he drove him up the stairway to its top, hastening his movements with many a sword-prick in his bare legs. When Topil emerged on the roof, he was sixty feet above the platform where the combat had raged, and standing on the summit of a wooden tower. Sandoval bound his prisoner's wrists firmly together, behind him, and then fastened one of his ankles, by a copper censer chain that he had found in the temple, to a projecting timber, so that the priest, while allowed a certain freedom of motion, could by no possibility escape. There Sandoval left him, and, descending, closed the only avenue of escape behind him. Seizing a burning brand from an altar, he set fire to the woodwork of the temple in a dozen places. It was like tinder, and in a minute the red flames were greedily licking the slender tower on all sides. The screams of the miscreant, dancing in torment on its summit, attracted the attention of the multitudes below, and they, still trembling from the destruction of their god, were compelled to gaze helplessly upon the awful but well-merited fate of their chief-priest. Even after he was hidden from sight by a towering screen of flame and smoke, his voice could be heard in frantic appeals to the impotent gods.

When Cortes and the slender remnant of his victorious band descended from this memorable battle-field, the Aztec throngs shrunk from them as though they were plague-stricken, and they passed unmolested to their own quarters. That night the Spaniards again sallied forth, and, carrying blazing brands in every direction through the sleeping city, destroyed over three hundred houses.

On the following day, Cortes, thinking that by these reverses and by the overthrow of their principal god, the Aztecs must be sufficiently humbled to submit, called a parley. As the principal nobles and their followers assembled in the great square, he addressed them, through the voice of Marina, from the same turret on which Montezuma had received his death-wound.

"Men of Tenochtitlan," he said, "you have seen your gods trampled in the dust, their priests destroyed, your warriors slain by thousands, and your dwellings burned. All this you have brought upon yourselves. Yet, for the affection I bore the king whom you murdered, I am willing to forgive you, if you lay down your arms, renounce the hideous religion that offers no hope for your salvation, and resume the allegiance to his most Catholic majesty of Spain sworn by your king. If you refuse these things, then will I make your beautiful city a heap of smouldering ruins, as barren of human life as the fire-crowned summit of yon sky-piercing mountain. What say you? Shall it be peace with immunity from further suffering, or shall it be war to the death, and utter ruin?"

Then answered Cuitlahua, the newly crowned king: "It is true, O Malinche, that thou hast destroyed one of our temples, broken the image of a god, and slain many of my people. Many more will doubtless fall beneath thy terrible sword. But we are satisfied so long as for the blood of every hundred, we can shed that of one white man. Look on our roofs and terraces, our streets and squares. They are thronged with Aztec warriors, as far as thine eye can reach. Our numbers are scarcely diminished. Yours are lessening every hour! You are perishing with hunger, and thirst, and sickness! Your provisions are failing! We will see to it that you get no more. You have but little water! You must soon fall into our hands. The bridges are removed, and you cannot escape! Truly, O Malinche, is the vengeance of the outraged gods about to descend on thee."

At the conclusion of this bold speech, which well showed the temper of the newly made king, a flight of arrows compelled the Spaniards hastily to descend from the turret and seek the shelter of their defenses.

Cuitlahua's defiance filled the besieged with dismay. Of what use were all their fightings, their sufferings, and their brilliant victories? The enemy was more determined than ever, and a hundred fresh warriors stood ready to take the place of each one who was killed. A contest against such overwhelming odds was hopeless, and the sooner it was abandoned the better. Thus argued the Spanish soldiers, especially the recruits who had come with Narvaez. These, to a man, declared they would fight no longer, unless to preserve themselves in a retreat from the fatal city.

Against such a feeling among his followers, even the bold spirit of the commander was forced to yield. So, after a consultation with his officers, including the young chief of Tlascalans, he announced that preparations would at once be made for leaving Tenochtitlan. It was decided that the retreat should be by the causeway of Tlacopan, which, being but two miles in length, and thus much shorter than the one by which they had entered the city, would soonest lead them to the mainland, where they could fight to advantage.

In the meantime, as in their frequent sorties, the Spaniards had suffered their greatest annoyance through missiles showered down from the housetops, Cortes had designed and caused to be built three wooden towers that he termed mantas. These were of two stories, and were mounted on rude wheels by means of which it was proposed to roll them through the streets, with musketeers stationed in the upper stories, who should sweep the housetops of all enemies as they advanced. In each lower story, which was open to the ground, a force of brawny Tlascalans was to push and pull the movable fortress without being exposed to attack. It was now determined to test the efficacy of these rude machines in the sortie about to be made, to discover whether or not the avenue of Tlacopan was open and free from obstructions.

When all was in readiness the great gate of the fortress was thrown open, and, with much creaking, groaning, and rocking the manta issued forth. The Aztecs beheld its stately advance with bewildered astonishment. They could not conceive its purpose, nor understand by what power it was propelled. There was no sign of human agency and its progress filled them with awe. As they gazed in gaping wonder, it slowly crossed the square and entered the avenue of Tlacopan. Suddenly, as it halted before a building, the roof of which was thronged with armed men, a side of the upper story fell outward, and a volley of musketry was delivered with startling effect. A light, but strong, bridge was thrown to the housetop, and the Spaniards, crossing on it, quickly put its remaining occupants to flight with their swords. Then they retreated to their wooden fortress, pulled in the bridge, drew up their protecting shield and the engine of destruction proceeded on its ponderous way. But its purpose was no longer a mystery. The swarming occupants of the housetops withdrew to places of safety on its approach, or hurled down fire brands and coping-stones from such elevations as commanded it. Its utility had begun to appear doubtful when it came to a halt at the first canal. Here the bridge had been destroyed, and it could proceed no farther.

A tall building stood at this point, and from its roof an avalanche of heavy timbers and great stones was poured on the devoted manta, ere its progress could be reversed. One of these formidable missiles crushed in a side of the structure, causing it to sway alarmingly. Several others struck it together, a moment later, and, with a melancholy crash, it toppled to the ground burying its unfortunate defenders in the wreck, killing several of them, and injuring many more. With exulting yells the Aztecs rushed upon the prostrate tower, and, but for the prompt assistance of a troop of cavalry, whose fierce onset quickly cleared the street, not one of its struggling occupants would have escaped.

This experiment proved the uselessness of the mantas, on the construction of which so much time and labor had been expended. It also proved the truth of Cuitlahua's words. The bridges, over which the retreat must be conducted, were indeed removed, and seven open canals lay between the fortress and the causeway. These gaping chasms must be filled at all hazards.

After four days of incessant labor beneath a galling fire of arrows, darts, and stones, incessant fighting, incessant dying and suffering, the task was completed. The labor of tearing down buildings and filling the canals with their debris, devolved on the Tlascalans. The Spanish cavaliers charged up and down the avenue clearing it of the enemy who swarmed in behind them the moment they had passed, while the Spanish infantry guarded each bridge as it was finished. Many and fierce were the hand to hand struggles during those four days; and, at their conclusion, although their way of retreat was opened as far as the causeway, the white conquerors were in as sorry a plight as were ever any conquerors in all the world. But their present misfortunes were as nothing compared with those held in store for them by the immediate future.

31

THE RETREAT FROM TENOCHTITLAN

THE WAY OF ESCAPE was partially prepared by the filling up of the canals, but who could tell how long it would remain so? At any moment the forces guarding these all-important points might be overcome or driven back and the canals reopened. It was therefore decided, at a council of officers convened late on that fourth day of fighting, that the retreat should be undertaken that very night. Now began busy preparations for evacuating the palace-fortress occupied by the white conquerors for so many months. Litters for the transportation of the wounded were hastily constructed, and Huetzin was called upon to detail a body of warriors to carry and guard these helpless ones. The rich booty of the conquest was drawn from its hiding-places, and much of the gold was packed in stout bags for transportation on horse-back. Still a large portion of it must necessarily be abandoned. As it lay, scattered in shining heaps about the floor, the soldiers looked at it with longing eyes. It seemed to them that the wealth of the New World lay at their feet, waiting to be picked up.

"Take what you will of it!" exclaimed the commander, reading their thoughts in their faces, "but be careful not to overload yourselves. Remember that he travels best, who travels lightest."

With this permission the troops rushed at the glittering spoil like famishing men upon food, while the grim Tlascalans, indifferent to wealth of this description, watched the avaricious scramble with unconcealed contempt. The men of Narvaez, who had heard so much concerning Mexican gold without having thus far acquired any of it, greedily loaded themselves with as much as they could possibly carry, but the veteran followers of Cortes, taking heed to their leader's counsel, helped themselves sparingly, each selecting only a few objects of the greatest value. As for the piles of rich fabrics, jewel-studded weapons, feather mantles of inestimable value, delicate ware, and costly and curious articles of every description, the greater part of them was abandoned with hardly a regret, in the all-absorbing eagerness to escape from that sorrowful prison-house.

While these scenes were being enacted in one part of the palace, a party of workmen was busily engaged in another, constructing a stout portable-bridge. Although the canals intersecting the city streets had been so filled that they could be crossed, there still remained three that cut the causeway of Tlacopan. From there, as well as from the others, the bridges had been removed. As these three openings were of the same size, each being thirty feet in width, a single portable bridge, that could be taken up from the first opening after the army had passed, and carried to the next was deemed sufficient. It was placed in charge of a trusty officer named Margarino, who was given forty picked men, all pledged to defend it with their lives.

The night was intensely dark, and a drizzling rain fell steadily. At midnight all was in readiness for a start, and the great gate of the palace-fortress was swung open for the last time. The order of march had been carefully planned beforehand, and, according to it, Sandoval, mounted on Motilla, and commanding the advance guard was the first to ride forth. At his left hand rode the only mounted native of the New World, Huetzin, the young Toltec; for besides a score of cavaliers, and two hundred foot soldiers, the advance contained two thousand Tlascalan warriors. To these faithful mountaineers had been entrusted the object deemed most precious by the whole army, the covered litter in which was borne Marina, their well-loved interpreter. With the advance also marched Margarino and his forty men, bearing on their sturdy shoulders the heavy timbers of the portable bridge upon which the salvation of the army depended.

In the centre, or main division, were the prisoners, among whom were several of Montezuma's children, Cacama, Prince of Tezcuco, and a number of Aztec nobles held as hostages, the treasure, the baggage, the wounded, and the heavy guns. These were guarded by the veterans who had been with Cortes from the first, and a strong force of Tlascalans.

As these slowly defiled into the great square they were followed by the rear guard under command of Alvarado. It contained the bulk of the Spanish infantry who had been enlisted from the force of Narvaez, and a battery of light artillery in charge of Mesa and his well-tried gunners.

When the last man had passed through the gateway, the commander, who had waited motionless on his gray steed to assure himself that no stragglers were left behind, roused, as from a deep revery, gave a parting glance at the quarters that had been the scene of so stirring a chapter of his life's history, clapped spurs to his horse, and dashed down the long black line of his retreating army.

Although every precaution was taken to move silently, the passage of so large a body of troops through paved streets, could not be accomplished without noise. To the strained ears of the fugitives, expecting each moment to hear the exulting war-cries of their enemies, or to see their dark masses rushing from every cross street and alley, the heavy rumble of their own artillery, the sharp ring of iron-shod hoofs, the measured tramp of infantry, and the unavoidable rattle of weapons, seemed to create a volume of sound that must be heard in the remotest quarters of Tenochtitlan. Still the battle-wearied city slept on, nor did it betray, by a sign, its consciousness that the prey, it had deemed so surely its own, was slipping from its grasp.

On through the blackness, shrouding the long avenue of Tlacopan, moved the retreat. Here they stumbled over the corpse of some dead Aztec, there they could distinguish the dark heaps of slain marking some fiercely contested point of the recent fighting. To their excited imaginations it seemed as though these must rise up and betray them. The shadowy ruins of fire-scathed buildings seemed again peopled with flitting forms, and, as they crossed one after another of the canals, the ebon water seemed alive with swarming paddles. But they passed on as unmolested by the living as by the dead, until at length a lighter space between the buildings in front of them announced to the van-guard that the causeway was at hand. As they drew aside to allow the men of Margarino room in which to advance and place their bridge, they felt that the worst of the perilous retreat was over, and could hardly restrain the shouts that would have proclaimed their joy.

Suddenly a shrill cry, chilling the blood in their veins, rose from close beside them. There was a sound of flying footsteps, and the alarm was echoing and re-echoing through the wind-swept streets with an ever-increasing clamor. The priests, watching their fires on top of tall teocals, caught the cry of the flying sentinels and spread the alarm with sounding blasts upon their conch-shells. Now, from the desolated heights of Huitzil›s temple, the solemn booming of the great serpent drum, only sounded in times of gravest moment, vibrated through the remotest comers of the city and far out over the waters surrounding it. Red beacon flames sprang from the top of every temple, warning the whole valley that the time of the crisis had come.

"Tlacopan! Tlacopan!" was shouted in frenzied tones through every street and into every house of the sleeping city, and this single word named the rallying point.

With desperate haste Margarino and his men laid their bridge. No longer was there need of silence or concealment. Flight, instant and rapid, was the sole animating thought of the whole army. Sandoval, on prancing Motilla, was the first to test its strength, and after him streamed the eager troops. To the vanguard hastening forward without opposition, safety still seemed within reach; but to the rear, impatiently awaiting the movement of those before them, the night was filled with ominous rushings and sounds denoting the gathering of a mighty host. By the fitful glare of the lofty beacons, now streaming through the upper darkness from all parts of the city, they caught glimpses of hurrying forms and glintings of angry weapons. Mesa›s grim gunners blew the matches, kept dry beneath their cloaks, into brighter flame and chuckled hoarsely as they thought of the havoc their falconets would make when once turned loose.

The advanced guard had crossed the bridge and the dense squadrons of the centre, with the heavy guns, ammunition wagons, baggage, treasure, prisoners, and wounded, were passing it when the storm broke. First a few stones and arrows rattled on the mail of the cavaliers, or pricked the naked Tlascalans. Then the dark waters of the lake were smitten by the dip of ten thousand angry paddles, as though by the fierce breath of a whirlwind. The sprinkle of stones and arrows increased to a tempest of hissing missiles. The dark lines of on-rushing canoes dashed against the very rocks of the causeway, while their occupants, leaping out, threw themselves, with reckless ferocity, upon the retreating troops. The shrieks of wounded and dying men began to rise from the hurrying column and the despairing cries of others, overthrown and dragged to the canoes. Above all and drowning all, rose the shrill, exultant yell of "Tlacopan! Tlacopan!" made, for the time being, the Aztec war-cry and taken up by a myriad of fresh voices with each passing minute.

From the distant rear came the roar of Mesa's guns. There the cowardly enemy will be checked at any rate! But they are not. No longer do belching cannon nor leveled lances possess any terror for those whom the war-like Cuitlahua leads to battle.

As hundreds were mowed down by the storm of iron balls, thousands leaped into their places. So irresistibly furious was the Aztec advance that ere the deadly falconets could be reloaded, Mesa, his men, and his guns, were overwhelmed, and swept out of sight, as though beneath the overpowering mass of an alpine avalanche. Alvarado and his handful of cavaliers, who had charged again and again into the fiercely swelling tide of foemen, supporting the guns as long as any were left, now turned, and fled across the narrow bridge.

While these events were taking place with frightful rapidity in the rear, the advance had reached, and were halted by, the second opening in the causeway. Galled by the incessant attacks of their swarming adversaries, and with their own swords rendered well-nigh useless by the cramped space into which they were crowded, these sent back message after message imploring Margarino to hasten forward with the bridge. But the bridge would never be brought forward. Its timbers had become so wedged among the stones of the causeway, by the weight of ponderous guns and mail-clad troops, that not all the efforts of Margarino's sturdy men could move them. Desperately they tugged and strained, but in vain. The bridge was as immovable as the causeway itself. Even as they fulfilled their pledge never to move forward without the bridge, the exulting foe leaped upon them. For a few minutes there was a fierce conflict. Then the seething Aztec flood rolled on, sweeping over Margarino and his men, as it had over Mesa and his guns.

32

A NIGHT OF FIGHTING, DESPAIR, AND DEATH

THE DREADFUL NEWS that the bridge could not be moved, and that with its loss went their chief hope of escape, swept like wild fire from the rear where Alvarado and his gallant band were charging and momentarily holding in check the thronging masses of the enemy. Like a death-knell it sounded through the long line, beset on both lines by a myriad of assailants who seemed to rise from the very waters, to the distant front where Sandoval and his cavaliers fought, as best they might, and fretted at Margarino's delay. Everywhere the fatal message converted the orderly ranks into a panic-stricken mob. All subordination was at an end. Frenzied men flung away their weapons and sought only to save themselves. The wounded were abandoned and trampled under foot. The weak gave way before the strong.

In the very front, snugly nestled among the soft cushions of her litter, and surrounded by her faithful body guard, Marina hardly realized that anything more than a skirmish was taking place. Every now and then she heard the ringing voice of sturdy Sandoval, and more than once Huetzin parted the curtains to assure her that he was close at hand. She liked to see him on horseback, this noble cavalier of her own race, and, as she lay back in the litter, listening to the far-away roar of grim Mesa›s final volley, she saw a vision of a battle scene in which her hero led a glorious charge of cavalry, and the gallant horsemen were of her own people.

Suddenly she was startled by a swaying of her litter, as though by the advanced swell of a mighty tide. There came cries of terror and dismay, oaths, prayers, and a great surging to and fro. The panic-stricken fugitives in the rear were pressing tumultuously forward, and her Tlascalan body-guard were fighting savagely, against their own friends, in a desperate effort to stem the swelling flood, and keep from being swept off their narrow footing.

Already Sandoval and his cavaliers were dashing into the dark waters, and struggling to clear a way, in which the infantry might follow, through the close-packed canoes that blocked the passage.

Backward, step by step, were the Tlascalans pressed, until half of them had been forced to take the fatal plunge, and the litter containing the chiefest treasure of the Spanish army, hovered on the very brink of the black chasm. At this juncture the curtains were torn aside, and the terrified girl was lifted from her soft nest in a pair of strong arms. In a moment she found herself on horseback, in front of a cavalier who was saying, in reassuring tones: «Thou shalt yet be saved, dear one." In the next, the steed, bearing this double burden, had taken the leap, and all three were struggling in the cold waters.

Cocotin, though fleet of foot and brave of spirit, had not the body nor strength of Motilla, and quickly gave signs of being overweighted. As he realized this, Huetzin slipped from the saddle, pulled Marina back into its safer seat and swam beside her. The dark waters about them were filled with despairing men, fighting, struggling, and drowning each other in their frenzied efforts to escape the fate of which all seemed doomed. Among them dashed the Aztec canoes, their inmates dealing savage blows to right and left, and only striving to save lives that their gods might have the more victims. From one of these canoes Cocotin was wounded in the head by the blow of a maquahuitl, and unmanageable from pain, swerved toward the open lake. Huetzin let go his hold of the saddle to spring to her head. At that moment his feet were seized by some drowning wretch, and he was dragged beneath the blood-stained waters. It was a full minute before he could release himself from that death-clutch at the bottom of the lake. When with bursting temples, he again breathed the blessed air, the same awful struggle was going on about him, but Cocotin and her precious burden had disappeared.

In the meantime the gaping chasm was rapidly filling with the bodies of men and horses, guns and baggage wagons, ingots of gold that might ransom a prince, bales of rich fabrics, weapons and equipments of every description. It was a seething inferno from which frantic Aztec demons, plying war club and javelin, were reaping a goodly harvest of captives. The awful carnage that now raged along the length of the causeway, was nowhere so great as at this point. Finally, the ghastly opening was filled with the wreck of battle, until over the hideous bridge thus formed those in the rear passed dry-shod to the opposite side.

All this while Cortes, who had discovered, a little to one side, a passage that was fordable, was valiantly holding it with a handful of cavaliers, while vainly urging the troops to gain safety by coming that way. Through the storm-swept darkness, he could not be seen, nor could his voice be heard above the wild uproar. At length, swept onward by the human tide and forced to the opposite bank, he spurred forward to the third and last opening. Here he found Sandoval and a few followers engaged in another fierce conflict with the enemy, who had hurried a strong force to this point in canoes. At this place the exultant Aztecs hoped to complete the destruction of the shattered army, and but for the matchless bravery of Cortes and his cavaliers they would have succeeded.

Without a moment's hesitation the leader, close followed by Sandoval and the others, plunged into the
deadly waters, and, waging a hand-to-hand conflict
from canoe to canoe, finally forced the passage. All the
foot-soldiers, who were huddled like sheep on the brink
of this chasm, at which the dreadful scenes of the other seemed about to be repeated, now cast themselves
into the water. Many were drowned by the weight of
gold with which they had over-burdened themselves,
others grasped the manes or tails of swimming horses and so were helped across. Still others, having cast
away muskets, armor, gold, everything that might embarrass their flight, gained the opposite side by their
own unaided efforts. When all who were within hearing had scrambled, in one fashion or another, upon the
causeway the precipitate flight was continued, though
a distant din of battle showed some survivors to be still
waging the conflict of despair.

Cortes and the shattered remnant of his army had
hardly reached solid earth, when a breathless runner
overtook them, with the information that what was left
of the rear-guard had won its way to the farther side of
the last opening, where they were now battling against
such odds that, unless speedily relieved, not a man
would be left. Sandoval, utterly exhausted, had thrown
himself on the ground beside his dripping steed, as
had many of the others. At this despairing cry for help
the sturdy young soldier again sprang into his saddle,
exclaiming: "I, for one, am ready!" «And I!» «And I!»

shouted several more. With a grateful nod, Cortes put spurs to his own horse and galloped back over the fatal causeway followed by a dozen gallant gentlemen, who thus rode into the jaws of death as cheerfully as though to a friendly trial of arms.

For five hours had the battle raged, and in the gray light, now breaking, some of the hideous details of the night's disaster were made visible. As far as the eye could reach, the road of death swarmed with the victorious enemy, while on either side the lake was black with their canoes. The sight was fitted to appall even the stout hearts of the Spanish cavaliers; but near at hand was that which appealed to a feeling stronger than fear. On the opposite bank of the bloody gulf, which was fast filling with the dead, golden-bearded Alvarado, bare-headed, and bleeding from a dozen wounds, still fought with superhuman strength, and so animated his scant handful of troops, that, had they been fresh, instead of well-nigh fainting, their heroism must have been crowned with victory.

With a cheering shout that inspired new hope in the sinking hearts of Alvarado's men, the dozen cavaliers led by Cortes dashed once more into the water, swam to the opposite side, and plunged into the thick of the fray. For a moment the Aztecs fell back before their fierce onslaught, like a receding wave of the sea. In the respite thus afforded all but one of those who had fought with the «Tonatiah," cast themselves into the water, from which most of them emerged on the other side in safety. At that moment Alvarado›s horse, the faithful steed that had borne him so nobly amid a thousand dangers, fell, to rise no more, pinning her master to the ground as she did so. A Tlascalan warrior, who was so disfigured by wounds and covered with blood, that the Spanish cavalier had not recognized him, though they had fought side by side for the past hour, sprang to his relief. As he succeeded in disengaging the entangled man, the rescuing party was driven back upon them, with ranks sadly thinned, and unable longer to hold their own against the onrushing foe.

"Mount with me!" shouted Sandoval to his unhorsed comrade, "Motilla can bear us both!"

"I can care for myself! Take thou this youth, to whom I owe my life many times," answered Alvarado. Thus saying, he seized a long Chinantla pike, and planted one end in the wreck at the bottom of the canal. Then, gathering his strength for a prodigious effort, he vaulted clear across, and landed safely on the other side of the yawning chasm. Victors and vanquished, Aztecs, Spaniards, and Tlascalans, stood for a moment spellbound at the sight of this marvelous feat.

Sandoval was among the first to recover from his amazement, and turning to the youth whom Alvarado had recommended, he bade him mount behind him. They two, on the gallant Motilla were the last to leave; but it was not until the brave mare had borne them to the opposite side, and the young warrior leaped to the ground, that Sandoval recognized him. Then in joyful accents he cried out, «Praised be the blessed saints! Don Juan, that thou hast escaped yon hell in safety, for truly I had given thee up for dead."

"And I would that I were," answered the young Toltec, bitterly, "since I have lost that which, of all life, I held most dear. But I sought death in vain. It could come to all others, but not to me."

"What mean you?" cried Sandoval, bewildered by this strange speech.

"I mean that Marina lies somewhere in yon lake, and if I knew where, my body should lie beside hers."

Thus ended the dreadful night, called for all time the Noche Triste, or night of sadness.

33

MARINA IS LOST AND SAVED

As THE DARKNESS of the noche triste was dispelled by the rising sun, Cortes led the broken remnant of his army away from the fatal dike on which all had so nearly laid down their lives. The first march of the long anticipated retreat was an accomplished fact; but at what a fearful cost! Not a gun remained to the Spaniards, not a musket. Their banners and trumpets had disappeared. Of one hundred horses but a score were left, and all of these were wounded. There were no ammunition wagons, there was no baggage-train. Most of the treasure had been lost. Some of the soldiers had indeed clung to their gold, even while throwing away the muskets on which they relied to defend it; but, a few days later, even this, for which they had been willing to sacrifice all, became an intolerable burden, that was in turn flung aside.

All the prisoners had been slain in the mêlée by their own friends, and of the fate of the wounded no one dared to speak. Of the retreating Spaniards nearly one-half had been slain or captured on that two miles of causeway, while of the faithful Tlascalans over two thousand were missing. About the same time forty-five Spaniards, who had been sent by Cortes two months before to visit some distant mines, were captured and sacrificed by the Aztecs, at Zaltepec, while on their way back to Tenochtitlan, in total ignorance of the existing state of affairs.

Thus there were Christian victims for the altars of every Aztec city, while native nobles were armed with Spanish weapons, and wore odd pieces of Spanish armor. It was owing to the rich spoil abandoned by the well-nigh helpless survivors, that they owed their present safety. Had the Aztecs followed them as vigorously as they had attacked them on the causeway, not a soul could have escaped. But the victors were too busily engaged in gathering up such treasures as had never before fallen into Indian hands, in securing their prisoners, in making preparations for festivals of rejoicing, in cleansing their city and burying their dead, to concern themselves about the forlorn remnant of those who had been termed the "White Conquerors," but who would now quickly perish in the mountains, or be destroyed by the first of Cuitlahua's armies with which they should come into collision.

So the Spaniards, weak, weary, and wounded, disheartened, water-soaked, and ragged, defenseless save
for their swords, a score of lances, and as many disabled cross-bows, were allowed to straggle unmolested through the deserted streets of Tlacopan, and make
their way into the open country beyond. Here they
were halted by their leader, who endeavored to reform
the shattered battalions, and bring some sort of order
out of their confusion.

Near by rose the hill of Montezuma, crowned by an
extensive temple that offered a tempting place of shelter. But, as they could see, it was already occupied by a
force of the enemy, and at that moment the dispirited
Spaniards had no mind for further fighting. The cavaliers indeed were ready, but they were so few! And their
poor horses were completely used up. In this emergency, Huetzin, seizing a javelin from one of his Tlascalans,
sprang up the ascent. His mountain warriors followed
so promptly that, as he gained the outer wall of the
temple, they were also swarming over it, in face of the
shower of darts and arrows let fly by the garrison. Then
the defenders, amazed at so fierce an attack from those
whom they had deemed incapable of further fighting,
took to flight, and the place of refuge was secured.

In the temple were found a certain amount of provisions, and an ample supply of fuel, from which the
new occupants built great fires to dry their clothing
and warm their chilled bodies. Wounds were dressed
as best they might be, a hearty meal was eaten, and

then the weary troops sought to forget their sorrows in sleep. Not all slept, however. Sentries guarded the outer walls, and several small groups, gathered near the fires, conversed in low tones. In one of these the leader, planning for the future even in this his darkest hour of defeat, talked earnestly with Martin Lopez, his master ship-builder. Not far away Sandoval and Huetzin, drawn to a closer brotherhood by the similarity of their sorrows, talked of Marina, and the sturdy cavalier strove to comfort his stricken comrade with the tenderness that had come recently to him through his own irreparable loss.

Although no word of love had passed between Huetzin and Marina, each had known the heart of the other ever since those days of illness and nursing on the hill of Zampach. Many a time since would Huetzin have declared his passion for the Indian girl, but for a vow, that no word of love should pass his lips so long as an Aztec god reigned in Tenochtitlan. To their overthrow was his life devoted, and with the constancy of a crusading knight he had remained true to his pledge. When the image of the Aztec war-god was hurled from its pedestal, he had hoped that the period of his vow was nearly at an end; but with the ordering of a retreat from the city, he knew that it was indefinitely extended. Even when he held Marina in his arms as, on Cocotin's back, they plunged together into the lake, he had spoken no word of love, though indeed his tones had interpreted his feelings beyond a doubt of misunderstanding. Now that the life of his life was forever lost to him, he had no reason for concealment, and to his friend he laid open his heart.

Sadly enough, the litter in which Marina had been borne, and in which she had seemed in so great danger that Huetzin had snatched her from it, had been brought through in safety by its stout Tlascalan bearers, and now stood drying near the very fire beside which Huetzin and Sandoval sat. Until its emptiness was disclosed, the army had not known of Marina's disappearance; but the moment it was announced all other losses were lessened in comparison with this one, so generally was the Indian girl beloved. Even the leader, in planning his future operations, wondered if they could succeed without the almost indispensable aid of his brave girl interpreter.

To turn from this scene of a defeated Spanish army mourning its losses and sleeping the sleep of exhaustion in an Aztec temple, to the hut of a slave of Iztapalapan, is to make an abrupt transition. Still it is a necessary one, if the threads of our story are to be connected. Ever after it was learned that an alliance had been entered into between the mountain republic and the white conquerors, the lot of those Tlascalan slaves held by the Aztecs was of unusual hardship. They were everywhere regarded with suspicion and treated with cruelty. Even such faithful servants of their master as the aged couple who had dealt so kindly by Huetzin did not escape the harsh treatment accorded to their race. Double tasks were imposed, and not even their age, nor efforts to accomplish all that was required of them, saved them from the biting lash of the driver. They often dreamed, and even spoke in whispers, of escape. But how might it be accomplished? Whither should they fly? Not until long after the arrival of the Spaniards in Tenochtitlan did these questions find even the shadow of an answer.

In that country, and in those days, news, other than that borne by king's couriers, traveled slowly, and rare indeed were the items that reached the ears of slaves. So, although the aged Tlascalans knew something of the coming of the strange white beings, it was long before they heard that they were accompanied by a friendly Tlascalan army. It was longer still ere they learned that the leader of this army was none other than that son of Tlahuicol, who had been their guest in the time of his greatest danger.

With this bewildering news to consider, the aged couple glanced at each other meaningly, as they sat at night through a long silence, on the opposite sides of a tiny blaze, in their rude fireplace. Finally the old man said:

"If we could only get to him!" and the wife answered:

"He would be to us as an own son, for so he said."

Several nights later the old man asked, "When shall we make the attempt?" and the old woman answered, «Whenever thou art ready to lead, I am ready to follow."

"To be captured means a certain death!"

"But a free death is better than a living slavery."

"Thou art true and brave as always. On the first night of storm-clouded blackness will we set forth."

"On the first night of storm-clouded blackness," repeated the old woman, slowly, as though committing the words to memory.

Thus it happened that the very night selected by the Spaniards for their escape from Tenochtitlan was also the one chosen by the aged Tlascalan couple for their flight from slavery. After dark, and moving with the utmost caution, the old man secured the canoe in which they had been wont, though not for many months, to carry flowers to the city, and brought it to the beach near their hut. To it he conveyed their few poor treasures, some bits of rude pottery fashioned by himself, a bundle of gay feathers, a battered javelin such as he had used when a young man and a Tlascalan warrior, and the blanket woven of rabbit's fur, on which the old woman had spent the scant leisure of years. Then they set forth, guided by the faint altar fires of the distant city. They knew not how nor where they should find him whom they sought, but they had a simple faith that, once near him, they would be safe.

A long time they labored at the paddles, until at length they neared the city. Suddenly a startling clamor arose from it. There were shouts as of a mighty host, the discordant notes of priest-blown shells, and, above all, the dread booming of the great serpent drum. They rested on their paddles and listened in frightened bewilderment. Now red beacon flames blazed from every temple, and by this light they perceived a myriad of canoes sweeping past them, all hurrying toward the causeway of Tlacopan. To lessen the chances of being run down, the old man headed his canoe in the same direction, and drifted with the others.

Then came the sound of fighting, the terrifying roar of guns, the clashing of weapons, and the screams of those who fell; but, above all, they heard a sound that recalled their own youth and their own country, the shrill war-cry of the Tlascalans.

"Let us approach closer," urged the brave old wife. "Some of our own may be in the fight, and so sorely pressed that even our feeble aid may prove of value."

So they approached as close as they dared, to where the uproar was loudest. As they lingered, terrified but held by an awful fascination, there came a voice, seemingly that of a girl, to their ears.

"Save me, Huetzin! Save me, son of Tlahuicol!" it cried, shrilly. Then, in softer tones, "Steady, Cocotin! Dear Cocotin! Good Cocotin! If thou wouldst but turn thy poor bleeding head the other way! Oh! Holy Mother of the Christians! She is sinking! She is dying, and I am lost!"

Then a dark form struggled out of the blackness beside them; both the old man and the old woman reached out toward it; and in another minute Marina lay, hysterically sobbing, in the bottom of the canoe.

34

SORROW TURNED INTO JOY, AND DARKNESS INTO LIGHT

THE FIRST IMPULSE of Marina's preservers was to escape as quickly as possible from their awful surroundings. The spell that had held them in that vicinity was broken. They had snatched one victim from the jaws of death, and now they must remove her beyond reach of further danger. Instinctively they headed their canoe in the direction of the little hut, on the opposite side of the lake, that had for so long been their home. They had not gone far when, as though moved by a single impulse, both stopped paddling at the same instant.

"It is no longer possible that we should go back," said the old man.

"For we should be taking another into slavery,"

continued the old woman.

"Nor would we return to slavery for ourselves, even if there were no other."

"It is certain that we would not," agreed the wife.

"But whither shall we fly?" asked the old man, irresolutely.

"Ask the child; since she called on the son of Tlahuicol for aid she must be of our friends, and also she must be possessed of wisdom."

Marina, who had ceased to sob, and now lay quietly beneath the warm rabbit-hair blanket that the old woman had spread over her, listened to this conversation. Who could these people be? They did not talk like enemies bearing her to the altar of sacrifice. At any rate, a question could do no harm.

"Whither are you taking me?" she asked.

"Whither you would go," replied the gentle voice of the old woman.

"I would go to my friends. To Huetzin, and Sandoval, and Malinche, and the daughters of the king, who are captives."

"Where are they?"

"I know not, but I fear me they are dead. Who are you? You are not Aztecs."

"We are Tlascalans, and friends of the son of Tlahuicol, whom we seek," was the proud answer.

"I thought you were Tlascalans from your speech!" cried the girl, joyfully. "As such you must be my friends, and as friends of Huetzin you must be doubly my friends."

"Is he thy brother?" queried the old man, remembering that Huetzin had spoken of a sister.

"No."

"Thy husband?"

"No."

"What then——?"

"Hush, thou stupid!" exclaimed the old woman, "and waste not time in idle questionings. We be escaped Tlascalan slaves," she continued, speaking to Marina, "seeking the son of Tlahuicol, who has some knowledge of us, and who we trusted would aid us to freedom. Now we know not which way to turn, and would ask thy counsel."

"Will you in truth do as I advise?" asked Marina, who could scarcely credit her good fortune in falling into such friendly hands.

"In truth we will."

"Then," said the Indian girl. "I would advise that you seek no land before daybreak, but avoid all canoes. With daylight, if the fight be over, as ere then it must be, make thy way to Tlacopan, where we are almost certain to discover our friends—thy friends and my friends."

This advice was considered so sensible that it was acted upon, and the canoe lay motionless. After they had sat awhile in silence, listening to the distant din of battle, the old woman asked: "Were you not talking to some person, whom you called by name, just before we found you?"

"Yes," replied Marina, sadly. "I was speaking to poor, brave Cocotin, but she was not a person. She was a horse belonging to the son of Tlahuicol, and deeply will he grieve at her loss."

As these simple folk had never before heard of a horse, Marina found much difficulty in explaining its nature to them. When they finally comprehended, after a fashion, they returned to the name, Cocotin.

"It was the name of our little one," explained the old woman.

"Was she a babe but a year old, and left behind when you both were captured by the Aztecs?" inquired the Indian girl, with interest.

"Yes. But how knew you that?"

"Huetzin has told me of it, and his horse was named for that child; and you must be the brave Tlascalans who assisted his escape from the priests of Tenochtitlan!"

"That honor and joy were indeed ours," answered the old man; "but our part in his escape was so slight that he might readily have forgotten it."

"Indeed he has not!" cried Marina, "and his joy will be great when he again sets eyes on you, for his gratitude to you is like the love of an own son."

All this time Marina had not the least doubt of her

hero's safety, for it did not occur to her that serious harm could come to one who had escaped so often, and was so brave and skillful a warrior. Therefore, while he mourned her as dead, she was looking forward with confidence to the joyful meeting that would take place as soon as daylight permitted. Nor could she realize in the slightest what a terrible disaster had overtaken the army of the white conquerors. She had never known it as aught but victorious, and its defeat was something she did not for a moment consider possible. Thus, instead of being a prey to the feverish anxiety that would have absorbed every thought had she known the true state of affairs on the causeway, she entertained her new friends with an account of her own life up to that moment. Her auditors listened with eager interest, though saying but little in return. After awhile the girl also grew silent, and then fell asleep wrapped in her rabbit-fur blanket.

The old people were careful not to disturb her, and only occasionally moved their light craft when other canoes threatened to approach so close that there was danger of being discovered. This, however, happened infrequently, so great was the attraction at the causeway. Once the old woman said, musingly:

"Our own Cocotin would have been about her age."

"And by birth she is Tlascalan," replied the man, which showed that their thoughts tended in the same direction.

At length the night passed, and daylight came. By it they earnestly studied the features of the sleeping girl.

"She is the image of what thou wast when first I knew thee!" exclaimed the old man, in trembling tones.

"We will question her more closely when she wakes," answered the other, calmly, but with an intense longing in her voice. «Now let us to Tlacopan; the way looks open."

So they made for the town, and, as the canoe grated on the beach, the girl awoke. She was at first bewildered by her surroundings, but reassured by the kindly words of the old people, quickly recovered her usual presence of mind, and exclaimed, with decision, "Now must we find our friends!"

The old man gathered up their scanty property, and they entered one of the deserted streets. Most of the inhabitants had been drawn to Tenochtitlan. Stopping at a humble hut to ask for food and information, they found it empty. Entering without further ceremony, they found food, of which they did not hesitate to partake, and a fire by which the girl's wet clothing could be dried. Leaving the two women here, the old man went out to seek for information.

He was gone the best part of an hour, and when he returned his wife greeted him with tearful but joyous face. In trembling tones she exclaimed, "Husband, she is indeed our own Cocotin, lost to us these many years and now restored to our old age by the gods! The marks are unmistakable." And then Marina, also tearful with her new-found joy, threw her arms about his neck and called him "father."

There was so much to tell and explain and wonder at, that the day was well advanced ere they set out to follow the Spanish army. This, as the old man had learned, was camped, at no great distance, on the hill of Montezuma. He had also heard rumors of the strong Aztec force already gathering to descend on them and complete their destruction at that place. To this news Marina listened with eager attention and all of her wonted alertness.

"Let us hasten!" she cried, when he had finished, "for it may be that this information will prove of the greatest importance."

So they set forth, the childless woman who had so marvellously recovered a daughter, and the motherless girl who had found that she was still possessed of the greatest of earthly blessings, walking hand in hand.

With all their haste they made such slow progress, on account of their anxiety to avoid undesirable meetings, that the sun was in the western sky ere they climbed the hill of Montezuma, and received the challenge of a Spanish sentinel, from a wall of the temple. He was one of Cortes's veterans, and could hardly credit his senses when the challenge was answered in his own tongue, and in the voice of the girl whom all the army knew, loved, and was even now mourning as dead.

To Huetzin, roused out of a heavy sleep, she appeared like a vision from heaven, and her restoration to him like a miracle of the all-powerful gods. So over-powering was his happiness that it could find no ex-pression in words, and he was as dumb, in the pres-ence of her whom he worshipped, as might have been Sandoval himself.

To the White Conqueror this joyful coming again of her whom he had named his "right hand" seemed to render all things possible, and again the future glowed with the sunrise of hope. He and the others gathered in eager welcome, listened intently to her story, and, for her sake, the aged Tlascalans, whom she proudly claimed as father and mother, were treated with the courtesy due to princes.

When she told Cortes of the Aztec army gathering for the assault of his place of refuge, he exclaimed: "They shall have it and welcome, if they have the courage to take it; but, ere then, I trust we shall be far hence."

So, at midnight, the Spanish army, refreshed by its rest, and filled with a new hope inspired by Mari-na's restoration to them, marched silently away from the temple, to continue its retreat; but leaving behind them watch-fires that would burn until morning, for the misleading of the enemy.

35

THE DESPERATE BATTLE
OF OTAMPAN

IN THE RETREAT from the temple that had proved such a veritable haven to the shattered army of the invaders, Marina was borne in her own litter. Another was provided for her mother, but, never having been accustomed to such a luxury, she preferred to walk beside the conveyance of her newly recovered daughter. Guided by Huetzin, with a small body of Tlascalans who formed the vanguard, the little army made a great circuit among the rugged hills bounding the western and northern side of the Mexican Valley. Their progress was slow and painful, and they were at all times subjected to irritating attacks from the clouds of Aztecs who hovered about their line of march. These, constantly recruited from the surrounding country, assaulted them with sudden flights of darts and arrows, or by rolling great stones down among them.

At night they usually sought shelter in some hamlet, from which the inhabitants invariably carried away all provisions on their approach. Thus the Spaniards were soon brought to the point of starvation. For seven wretched days they had little to eat but wild cherries, the occasional unplucked ears of maize which they were so fortunate as to find, and the few rabbits and birds brought down by the darts of Huetzin and his Tlascalans. Many of the soldiers fell by the wayside from sheer exhaustion, while others, who had brought their treasure of gold through the perils of the noche triste and thus far in safety, now flung it away, as too great a burden to be longer borne. Always the enemy hovered in small parties on their flanks, or followed closely in the rear, eager to pounce upon stragglers in search of food, or those who had fallen from exhaustion.

In all this weary march, Cortes was the life of his fainting troops. With sturdy Sandoval at his side, he was ever at the point of greatest danger, driving back those adversaries who ventured within reach, helping the stragglers, cheering the wounded, sharing every hardship, refusing the few scant mouthfuls of rabbit-meat reserved for his table and distributing them among the sick or most feeble of his men. In one skirmish he was struck in the head by a splinter of rock and severely injured; but he made light of the wound, caused it to be bound up, and continued as before.

At the end of seven days the army was still less than thirty miles from Tenochtitlan, though owing to their circuitous march they had traversed thrice that distance. From an absolute necessity for rest, the last two nights were spent in the same camp. During the intervening day, while the greater part of the army lay sleeping about its camp-fires, the indefatigable Huetzin led a strong party of his Tlascalans on an extended scout.

Next to the undaunted leader himself, the young Toltec was the encouraging spirit of this weary retreat. Since Marina's return to him, life had assumed its brightest aspect, and not all the sufferings of the march could depress him. He animated his own warriors by telling them that now was the time to show the white soldiers, by their patient endurance and cheerful bravery, of what stuff Tlascalan mountaineers were made. In obedience to this suggestion his followers marched, day after day, with elastic steps and proud bearing, scouted to right and left, scattered hovering bands of the enemy with brisk charges, and in fact saved their white allies from despair and destruction. At night, whether there was food to be eaten or not, the Tlascalan camp-fires were centres of merry groups, whose songs and laughter exercised a cheering influence upon the whole army.

For the white men Huetzin painted glowing pictures of the welcome they would receive in the "land of bread" (Tlascala), of the feasting that should be theirs, and of the rest and safety to be found behind its impregnable mountain walls. It is certain that these pictures lost none of their attractiveness through the interpretation of Marina. Like him whose words she translated, she was light-hearted and joyous in spite of all hardships. And why should she not be? Was not the whole army devoted to her? Had she not a loving mother, like other girls? Was not her father a Tlascalan warrior, and captain of a hundred men (for so Huetzin had made him)? Above all, though her hero spoke not of love, could she not read his heart through his eyes? What more of happiness could a maiden of Anahuac ask?

On the day of the army's resting Huetzin extended his scout as far as the pyramids of Teotihuacan, two colossal monuments erected by his long-ago Toltec an-cestors. They were dedicated to the sun and moon, and were surrounded by a vast number of burial mounds, in which were laid to rest the most famous men of his race. These were symmetrically ranged beside avenues, all of which led to the pyramids, and the plain in which they stood was known to that day as "Micoatl," or Way of the Dead.

From the summit of the taller of the pyramids, on which in former ages stood a gigantic image of the sun, bearing a breast-plate of burnished gold that reflect-ed the earliest beams of the great luminary, Huetzin caught a glad sight of the blue Tlascalan hills rising on the farther side of the plain. They promised shelter and plenty; but, between him and them, he saw something else that filled him with dismay.

At several different points of the wide-spread land-scape, he could distinguish moving bodies of white-ar-mored Aztec troops, all converging toward a common centre. After an hour of watching, he located this as be-ing the village of Otampan, situated in the wide plain that must be crossed before the retreating army could reach the Tlascalan frontier. Here doubtless was the place selected by Cuitlahua for their destruction. With this melancholy news, and with but a scanty supply of provisions, Huetzin led his scouting party back to camp.

That night was one of deepest gloom and despon-dency. Even the Tlascalan warriors no longer main-tained their show of cheerfulness. Many times during its hours of darkness mysterious voices came to them from the surrounding hill-tops, crying:

"Hasten on, ye enemies of the gods! You will soon find yourselves where you can no longer escape their awful vengeance!"

In the morning there was naught to do but move on. Save in Tlascala alone, there was no place in which they might hope for safety. As the feeble army gained the crest of the intervening sierra, and gazed past the Toltec pyramids into the vale of Otampan, they were greeted by such a sight as assured them that their last hour had indeed come. As far as the eye could reach, the plain was so covered with the white of cotton-mailed warriors, that it was like a vast field of snow. By order of Montezuma's successor the full war strength of the Aztec nation was there assembled for the final overthrow of the invaders. From the mighty host came a volume of sound like the murmur of a wind-swept sea, while the morning sunlight was reflected from acres of shining bucklers and a forest of tossing spears.

Even the stout heart of the Conqueror failed him in the presence of this multitude of enemies. Noting this, sturdy Sandoval said: "We can die but once, and 'twill be much pleasanter for us, though not so amusing for them, if we die as soldiers rather than as sacrifices. Besides, it is not wholly certain that our time for dying has yet come. We have fought against odds before."

"Never such odds as these," replied the Commander. At the same time, the cool bravery of his young captain gave him new heart; and, as he formed his little army in order of battle, he strengthened the determination to fight as became brave men that he read in their faces, with stout words.

The women, the sick, and wounded were left behind in charge of the old Tlascalan and a half-dozen of warriors, instructed, in case of disaster, to kill them all rather than allow them to fall into priestly hands. From each of the grim warriors, Huetzin personally exacted the promise that these instructions should be implicitly obeyed. Thus, when he bade Marina a lingering farewell, it was with the hope of a speedy reunion, either on the field of an earthly victory or in the blissful realms of the sun.

So the scanty force of Spaniards and their Tlascalan allies, having neither artillery nor muskets, and supported by but a score of cavalry, of which half was posted on either flank, descended steadily to the plain to meet the on-rushing hosts of their enemies.

The air was rent with the fierce war-cries of the exultant Aztecs, and darkened by the tempest of missiles that they let fly the moment they came within range. The Spanish infantry received the shock on their leveled pikes, against which the human wave dashed itself as fruitlessly as those of the sea against some rocky pinnacle rising from a waste of waters. With lowered lances the cavalry charged in turn, opening broad lanes through the thick-set ranks. Into these sprang Huetzin's trained warriors, following close on the heels of the horsemen, and widening the lanes on either side, with javelin and maquahuitl. So stoutly did these and their white allies ply their deadly weapons, that the foremost ranks of the Aztecs, broken and dismayed, attempted to fly. The attempt was a vain one, for they were instantly overwhelmed by the crowding myriads behind them, who, sweeping forward with the irresistible power of uncounted numbers, completely surrounded the Christian army, making it the vortex of a seething maëlstrom of fiercely struggling humanity.

Bravely did the cavaliers fight that day, charging in parties of four or six, deep into the Indian ranks. Sandoval seemed to be on all sides at once, fighting with the practiced skill and deadly fury of a young war-god; while mail-fronted Motilla, screaming with the rage of battle, crashed through the Aztec files like a thunder-bolt.

Deeper and deeper did the Christian force work its way into this interminable host, ever meeting with fresh battalions and ever growing weaker from losses. Hundreds of the Tlascalans and scores of the Spaniards had fallen. All were wounded, including the gallant leader, who had received another cut on the head. The noon-day sun beat pitilessly and with a fierce fervor on the steel-capped soldiers. Dying of heat, thirst, and wounds, panting, praying, and cursing, their blows falling slower and more feebly with each moment. What hope was there for them but that death would put an end to their sufferings as quickly as might be? Like a horrid vision, the faces of fresh foes ever danced before them. A score would fall, and a score of others, so similar that they appeared the same, were instantly in their places.

"Holy Mother!" cried Sandoval, reining in Motilla beside the steed of Cortes, "is there no end to these infidels? I have killed until I can kill no more, and their legions are as at the beginning! Methinks, General, the end of all things has come for us. Our brave troops can hold out no longer. They have fought as never mortals fought before; but now they are giving way on all sides. Does it please you that we make one more charge and die as becomes Christian soldiers, with our lances in our hands?"

36

VICTORY SNATCHED
FROM DEFEAT

Before answering Sandoval, the White Conqueror,
like a stag at bay who tosses his mighty head aloft in
search of an opening through which he may escape ere
gathering himself for the death-struggle, raised high in
his stirrups and surveyed the field. In all directions, as
far as he could see, tossed the plumes and waved the
banners of the Aztec host. The battle raging at his side
disturbed but a portion of it. His own men were falling fast. The exhaustion of their recent hardships, combined with the present heat and four hours of incessant
fighting, was doing more to deplete their numbers than
even Aztec weapons. He had no reserves to call up, no
guns to fall back upon. Of the hundred trusty knights
on whom he could have depended a week since, four
score had left him on that most sorrowful of noches

triste. Never again would they answer the call of the trumpets, nor charge with leveled lances and cheery shouts. "If they cannot rejoin us, we can at least join them!"

With this last sigh of a breaking heart, the leader was sinking back into his saddle, when his eye was caught by a more dazzling object, a richer gleam than any seen elsewhere in all that bedizened host. It was the sunlight reflected from the gold and silver armor, the gorgeous feather mantle, and the glittering escort of a Cacique, borne in a golden-plated litter. He was the Aztec general, the commander of all these myriads of warriors. Without his guiding orders the mighty army would be as helpless as a ship bereft of its rudder. With the gleam of his armor a ray of hope flashed into the breast of the Christian leader.

"Yes, gentlemen," he answered, dropping into his saddle and gripping his ponderous battle-ax with a fiercer clutch. "It pleases me to make one more charge. One more! Sandoval, Alvavado, Olid, Avila, cavaliers all! One more for victory or death! Forward! And may Christ and St. James go with us!"

Thus crying, the White Conqueror gave spurs to his steed, and, with whirling battle-ax clearing all obstacles from his pathway, he again plunged into the dense ranks of the Aztec host. At his side rode Sandoval and one other; behind them came three more. Six against ten thousand! But so terrible was the thrust of their lances, the swing of their axes, and the whistling sweep of their good swords, so frightful the screaming and tearing and crushing of their mail-clad chargers, that while its impetus lasted the death-dealing progress of this little group could no more be checked than that of a bomb-shell just started on its shrieking flight. The thick-set Aztec ranks reeled before them, and crowded to either side to give them passage. The earth behind them was cumbered with dead and dying. Their audacity paralyzed resistance, and their mission was accomplished ere its purport was suspected.

Straight as an arrow to a mark, rode Cortes to the spot where the proud Aztec leader lay indolently back in his cushioned litter. He was too certain of the fortunes of that battle to take much further interest in it. Already he was planning his triumphal entry into Tenochtitlan, and hoping that Malinche might be taken alive to grace it. All at once his pleasing reflections were interrupted by some unusual commotion near at hand.

As he raised himself to learn its cause, shrill screams of terror greeted him, and he saw what appeared to his startled vision a mighty war engine, fire-breathing, steel-armored, and death dealing, rushing toward him. In an instant more it was upon him. There came a crashing blow, a death shriek, and the Aztec leader would dream no more of triumphant entries into Tenochtitlan. Scattered like chaff were his body-guard of gay young nobles; and as they fled, terror-stricken, they spread on all sides the dread news that the chief had fallen.

Who, now, will give commands? No one. Who would obey them if given? None. Consternation seizes upon the mighty host. A wave of panic sweeps over it. No longer will it fight. To fly is its only thought. The strong trample whom they may; the front ranks flee in terror from those behind, fancying them the enemy. They fling away weapons, banners, everything. They fill the air with their cries of terror. Over all ring out the exultant shouts of Christians and Tlascalans, their hopeless death-struggle changed in a moment to an amazing, unheard-of victory. Forgotten are thirst, wounds, and exhaustion, as they pursue their flying enemies, and drink draughts, long and deep, of vengeance to compensate for la noche triste.

Thus was fought and won the desperate battle of Otampan, one of the most notable of all the world's battles, when the disparity of the engaged forces and the results of its issue are considered. So thoroughly panic-stricken were the defeated Aztecs, that one Spaniard or Tlascalan could put a hundred of them to headlong flight. Their losses were terrible, though they would have been much greater, but that the victors were too exhausted to push the pursuit. As they returned from it, they gathered up the rich spoils of weapons, armor, gold, jewels, and blazoned banners scattered over the field.

Among the first to weary of slaughter was the young Tlascalan chief. When there was no longer a show of resistance, he turned his steps toward the place in which the helpless ones of the army had been left. For long hours had they noted the varying fortunes of the battle, with straining eyes and sick hearts. From their distance they could not distinguish its details. Many times they so completely lost sight of their friends in the white-armored sea surrounding them, that they gave up all for lost, and expected the grim Tlascalan guard to execute its dread instructions. As time passed, and no enemy appeared to molest them, they gained new courage, and, hoping against hope, watched eagerly for further indications.

When the amazing rout of the mighty host began, they could not credit their senses, nor were they convinced that a glorious victory had been won by their friends, until Huetzin, blood-stained and disheveled, but radiant with triumph, appeared among them with the marvelous tidings. As he told the wonderful story, the men, wild with excitement, crowded about him craving every word of detail. The women, with over-strained feelings finding relief in joyful tears, caressed him, and bathed his wounds, and questioned one another with their eyes, as to how they could have doubted that this their hero would be victorious.

After a while he conducted them to the appointed rendezvous, a fortified but desolate temple on the outskirts of Otampan. Here the army of the white conquerors, now indeed worthy the name, were to pass the night of their victory, a night of as profound gratitude and heartfelt joy, as that other had been of defeat, humiliation, and heart-breaking sorrows.

On the following day they passed the rude fortifications marking a boundary of Tlascala, the brave mountain republic, to which, next to their own indomitable courage and incredible powers of endurance, the Christians owed everything, including their lives. Here at a little frontier town they rested, doubtful of the reception to be accorded them by those who had suffered such losses in their behalf; while Huetzin, attended by a small body of his own warriors, hastened to the capital. In this city of his birth the young warrior received the welcome reserved for victors, and amid joyous acclamations from the populace, made his way to where the venerable councilors of the nation awaited him. The disaster in Tenochtitlan, the noche triste, and the retreat, were all forgotten for the time being, and only the glorious victory of Otampan was remembered. The aged chieftain of Titcala fell on the young man's neck, with grateful tears in his sightless eyes, and blessed him. All voices sounded his praises, and proclaimed unwavering allegiance to the Christians. Only one was silent, and it was that of the envious Xicoten.

The next day, again clad as became his rank, Huetzin returned to the anxious army accompanied by the noble chieftain of his house, and many of the most prominent citizens of Tlascala. These bore messages and tokens of a generous welcome to Cortes, and offers of the hospitality of their city, to him and his followers, for as long as they would accept of it.

With a glad gratitude was this offer accepted, and in the hospitable city the weary army rested until its wounds were healed and its strength restored. In the palace of Titcala, Cortes himself, succumbing to his hurts and the mental strain that had been upon him for so long, lay many days in the weakness and delirium of a fever. As soon as the active brain began again to work, and while he still lay helpless as an infant on his bed of convalescence, the undaunted soldier planned for the future. Never for a moment had he relinquished his purpose to conquer Tenochtitlan, and supplant its hideous religion with that of the Cross.

With his first strength he undertook a brilliant campaign against a number of Aztec cities, situated within striking distance of Tlascala, whose inhabitants had cut off and sacrificed to their gods small parties of Spaniards. At the end of four months he had reconquered the whole of the vast Puebla table-land, had received reinforcements of men, horses, guns, and ammunition, and was again ready to march back over the frowning western Cordilleras, which he had already traversed four times, under extraordinary circumstances.

37

ONCE MORE IN THE MEXICAN VALLEY

DURING THE FOUR months occupied by Cortes in re-conquering the eastern half of the Aztec kingdom, so that when he was ready to proceed against its capital city he might leave no enemy behind him, events of importance were taking place elsewhere. One of these was the death of Cuitlahua, Montezuma's brother and successor. He fell before a dread scourge now sweeping over the land, and reaping such a harvest of dead as even that warlike country had never known. It was the small-pox, introduced to the Western World by a negro, the first of his race to set foot on the American continent, who had been one of the followers of Narvaez. Breaking out at Cempoalla, it swept over the land with the virulence of a plague, seizing alike upon hut and palace. In Tlascala, the blind chieftain of Titcala was among its victims. Huetzin, hastily summoned from a distant battle-field, stood at the bedside of his dying grandsire, and as the old man breathed his last under the holy sign of the Cross, the son of Tlahuicol was proclaimed head of the proud house of Titcala, and ruled in his place.

At nearly the same time and in the same city, Marina closed forever the eyes of her parents, who expired within a few minutes of each other, of the same fatal disease. Thus the young chieftain and the orphaned Indian girl became companions in sorrow, as they had been in seasons of rejoicing.

In the proud city of Tenochtitlan the dead king was succeeded by his nephew, Guatamotzin, a young man of twenty-five, well instructed in the art of native warfare, fierce, energetic, and shrewd, hating the white men and their religion with a bitter hatred, fanatically devoted to the bloodthirsty gods of his own land, and influenced in all his actions by their priests. In him the white conquerors were to encounter their most formidable opponent.

But they were not to encounter him unprepared, and their most important preparation was in progress during the four months of their military activity. All that time Martin Lopez, the ship-builder, aided by a few Spanish carpenters and a great force of natives, was hewing down timber in the forests of Tlascala, and converting it into a fleet of thirteen brigantines. These were to be completely set up and launched for trial on a small lake near the city. Then they were to be taken to pieces, transported on the shoulders of tamanes across the mountains to Tezcuco, where they were to be again put together, and finally launched on the great salt lake washing Tenochtitlan. Their rigging, sails, iron-work, and anchors were transported on the backs of tamanes from the distant port of Vera Cruz, where this material had been stored ever since the destruction of the ships that had brought the conquerors to the country.

When Cortes returned to Tlascala from the subjugation of the neighboring provinces, he found this fleet well on its way toward completion. Several of the brigantines with which he proposed to conquer the distant island city were already floating bravely on the tiny lake, beside which they were built, to the wonder and delight of all Tlascala.

As the Christian leader and his companions entered the city, they completely won the hearts of its inhabitants, by wearing badges of deep mourning in honor of the late chieftain of Titcala. After causing a solemn mass to be performed in memory of the dead, Cortes, in the presence of the whole city, conferred the degree of knighthood upon the aged chieftain's successor, who, with the accolade, formally received the christian name of "Juan." Thus, for his own noble qualities and unswerving loyalty to the faith of his fathers, even to the point of death, Huetzin, the son of Tlahuicol, became a Knight of Castile, and the first native of the New World to receive that honor.

By the Christmas of 1520, all preparations for again advancing on Tenochtitlan were completed, and on the following day the Spanish army, together with an allied force of ten thousand warriors under command of Huetzin, marched forth from the friendly city of Tlascala. As on former occasions, it was accompanied for miles by half the population, who mingled their acclamations with tears and prayers to the gods for its safety and success. Besides the Tlascalans, the present army contained nearly six hundred Spaniards, forty of whom were cavaliers, and eighty bore muskets. The rest were armed with swords and Chinantla pikes. In addition to all this, Cortes had nine small cannon, and a fair supply of powder, manufactured by himself with sulphur obtained at fearful risk from the smoking crater of lofty Popocatepetl.

In two days this army had scaled the western Cordilleras, and were again gazing, with mingled feelings and memories, into the fair valley of Mexico that, bathed in its golden sunshine, lay outspread at their feet.

In spite of the ominous beacon flames streaming from the tower-like temples of every city in the valley, they marched at once to the city of Tezcuco, from which the Prince, who had succeeded Cacama, and many of the inhabitants fled at their approach. They entered the city, the name of which is interpreted to mean "place of rest," on the last day of the year that had been so filled with stirring events, and in which defeat and victory, disaster and triumph, had succeeded each other with such rapidity.

From Tezcuco as a base of operations, Cortes proposed to reduce, in succession, every city of the valley, before proceeding to the attack of Tenochtitlan. Many of these, and conspicuous among them Chalco, on the fresh-water lake of the same name, he found heartily ready to throw off the hated Aztec yoke, and enter into an alliance with the whites. Others, such as the royal city of Iztapalapan, he assaulted and captured.

Wishing to test the temper of the new king, and to avoid further bloodshed if possible, Cortes liberated several Aztec nobles made prisoners in Iztapalapan, and sent them with a message to the capital. They were instructed to say that, if the city would return to the allegiance sworn to by Montezuma, and renounce human sacrifices to its gods, the authority of Guatamotzin should be confirmed, and the persons and property of his subjects respected by the Christians.

To this message no direct answer was received, but a royal proclamation was made, commanding that every Spaniard or Tlascalan captured within the kingdom should be immediately sent to Tenochtitlan for sacrifice. It also offered tempting rewards for every one thus taken, or for his dead body.

Then Cortes knew that the war must be fought out to its bitter end, and immediately set forth with another expedition for the reduction of the surrounding country. This time he advanced as far as Tlacopan, where, in his mind and in those of his veterans, sad memories of the terrible night, the noche triste, were revived. Two well-fought battles were necessary for the reduction of this city, and after its capture Cortes occupied it for several days, during which he made sorties into the neighborhood.

In one of these he, with a small body of troops, pursued a flying party of Aztecs out over the fatal causeway. The enemy fled as far as the first bridge, and there, suddenly opening to either side, displayed to the astonished Spaniard a large and well-appointed force advancing rapidly toward them. At the same time a great fleet of canoes appeared, and directly Cortes found himself engaged in another desperate struggle on this sadly remembered battle-ground. Ere they could make good their retreat, a dozen of the Spaniards and twice that number of Tlascalans had been killed or borne off to a more horrible fate in the canoes, and all were more or less wounded. It was a severe lesson in the tactics of Guatamotzin, and the Conqueror meditated it deeply, as he led his force back to Tezcuco.

At this place he received word from Tlascala that his brigantines were finished and ready for transportation across the mountains. Thereupon, he immediately dispatched Sandoval and Huetzin, with two hundred Spanish foot, fifteen horsemen, and two thousand Tlascalan warriors, to convoy them to the scene of their intended usefulness. On their way these passed through the little town of Zaltepec, the place in which

the five-and-forty Spanish explorers had been treacher-
ously captured and sacrificed.

The inhabitants fled at Sandoval's approach; but
in their deserted temples he found many traces of his
unfortunate countrymen. Not only were their armor
and clothing hung about the walls as trophies, but their
heads were found embalmed and suspended before the
altars. Here, too, were the skins of their horses, so skilfully mounted that for a moment the Spaniards stared
at them in amazement, thinking them live animals. As
a punishment for this crime Sandoval ordered that the
town be destroyed by fire, and that such of its inhabitants as might be captured should be branded as slaves.

From Zaltepec, Sandoval and Huetzin rapidly
crossed the mountains; but before they reached Tlascala they met the advanced guard of an immense army,
headed by Xicoten, and threading its sinuous way
through the narrow defiles of the sierra. Old Martin
Lopez, having finished his vessels, tested them, and
taken them to pieces again, was impatient to see them
in action. So he persuaded the Tlascalan councilors to
furnish him with a convoy to Tezcuco. Xicoten, the
war-chief, refused to march at the head of less than fifty
thousand men. Consequently this number of warriors
had to be gathered and placed under his command. His
instructions were to join his forces with those already at
Tezcuco, and place them at the disposal of Cortes, for
the capture of Tenochtitlan.

Sandoval, knowing that it would be almost impossible to feed such an army at Tezcuco, kindly but firmly dismissed two-thirds of Xicoten's force as soon as he met it; the remainder, still under Xicoten's lead, he allowed to act as a vanguard. With his Spaniards he protected the flanks of the army of Cortes bearing the precious brigantines, and to Huetzin he entrusted the responsibility of the rear.

For twenty leagues was this inland-built fleet of war-ships thus transported over rugged mountains. The thousands of tamanes bearing its timbers, spars, sails, rigging, anchors, and, in fact, its entire equipment, formed a compact line of over six miles in length; and as, on the fifth day after leaving Tlascala, this unique procession filed into the streets of Tezcuco, joyfully welcomed by Cortes and his entire army, it occupied six hours in passing a given point. On this great occasion Sandoval had insisted that to Huetzin and his tried warriors should be accorded the honor of heading the brilliant train. This so filled Xicoten with mortification and jealous rage, that from that moment he plotted, not only the overthrow of his rival, but of the Christian army.

That very night he caused Huetzin to be seized in his own quarters and hurried away toward the mountains. At the same time he ordered the secret departure of the entire Tlascalan army. In the morning he was the first to report to Cortes this defection of the allied force. He attributed it to Huetzin, who, he declared he had reason to know, had deserted to the enemy.

To his confusion, even while he was making this statement, the young Toltec, who by the aid of some of his own faithful followers, had succeeded in making his escape, returned and confronted the Tlascalan war-chief. Greatly incensed at this baseness, and at the same time desirous of making an example that should impress his allies as well as his enemies, Cortes caused Xicoten to be tried by court-martial. By it he was without hesitation condemned to death, and that same evening he was publicly executed, in the presence of the entire army.

38

LAUNCHING THE FIRST AMERICAN WARSHIPS

THERE WAS NO harbor at Tezcuco where vessels the size of the brigantines, which had been so skilfully brought thus far over leagues of rugged mountain trails, could be put together and launched. Indeed, the only place fitted for such work was half a league distant from the lake shore. Here, therefore, was the shipyard located, and while the vessels were being rebuilt, a force of eight thousand laborers were set to work to construct a canal from it to the deep waters of the lake. This canal, which when finished was twelve feet deep and twenty wide, was provided with gates, and had its banks strengthened by wooden palisades or, as was in some places necessary, by walls of masonry. The labor of constructing it was so great that, even with the immense force of workmen engaged, it occupied two months.

During this time, Cortes, with three hundred Spaniards and Huetzin's entire force of Tlascalans, swept entirely around the valley, and even penetrated into the mountains on the southeast, dispersing Aztec armies and capturing or conciliating Aztec cities, until only the capital remained unsubdued.

While thus engaged in cutting off the enemy's sources of supply, not a day passed without its fighting or deeds of heroism. One of the last cities to be thus attacked was Zochimilco, on the border of the salt lake. After a stout resistance the enemy gave way and fled through the city streets, pursued by almost the entire force of Christians and their allies. Cortes, being weary, remained with but two servants near the principal gate, to which the troops had been ordered to return.

Huetzin, who, as usual, tired of slaughter long before the vengeance of his fierce followers was satisfied, was the first to make his way back to the place of rendezvous. As he approached it, he was dismayed to see a fresh body of Aztecs rush out of a neighboring lane and make a furious attack upon the general. He defended himself valiantly, but was quickly overpowered by numbers. His horse was thrown down, and Cortes himself received a severe blow on the head. Ere he could rise, he was seized by his exulting foes. As they were dragging him away Huetzin reached the spot and sprang at them with the fury of a tiger. Almost before the astonished Aztecs knew they were attacked, three of their number lay dead, pierced or cut down by the young Knight's good Toledo blade. With this timely aid, and that of his servants, the general regained his feet, tore loose from those who still held him, vaulted again into the saddle, and, in less time than it takes to write it, was scattering the foes who had so nearly dragged him to the altar of sacrifice. It was the narrowest escape of the Conqueror's career up to that moment; and, had the Aztecs been content to kill him instead of being fanatically determined to deliver him to their priests, Guatamotzin might have reigned for years undisturbed.

When next the General and Huetzin met, the former dismounted to greet the young Knight, and grasping his hand, said, earnestly:

"I am well aware of my indebtedness to thee Don Juan, and to my dying day will I not forget it. Still, see thou to it that thy vigilance makes me not over-confident. With such quick blades as that of thine and of trusty Sandoval ever at hand, I am apt to lose sight of all need for care."

At the end of this expedition, during which there was enough of desperate fighting, hair-breadth escapes and rescues, sacking of cities, and romantic adventures, to fill a volume of knight-errantry, Cortes led his spoil-laden troops once more into Tezcuco, where he heard, at once, three items of good news. His brigantines were ready for launching; the canal was finished; and strong reinforcements, for which he had sent to Hispaniola six months before, had arrived.

As, to his mind, the launching of his little navy would

mark the beginning of the end, he determined to inaugurate the event with due pomp. Accordingly, on the 28th day of April, 1521, after attending the celebration of high mass, the entire army, with sounding trumpets, rolling drums, and waving banners, marched to the shipyard. Here the thirteen vessels, with masts stepped, sails bent, and colors flying, sat on their well-greased ways, awaiting the signal that should consign them to the element for which they were intended.

At the firing of a cannon the first slid gracefully into the water. Then came another gun and another launch; and so on, until, with the thirteenth gun, the thirteenth brigantine entered the water, and the first American-built navy was afloat. Now, amid a roar of artillery and musketry, the acclamations of tens of thousands of dusky spectators, and the sound of martial music, with the banner of Castile flying from every mast-head, and their own guns answering the glad salute from the shore, the fleet dropped down the canal, and spreading its white wings to a brisk breeze, stood proudly out over the broad waters of the lake.

It was a novel spectacle to the simple natives, and a glad one to the white conquerors; for, with the combined forces of an army and a navy opposed to it, they felt assured that the bloody priesthood of Tenochtitlan was destined to a speedy overthrow. So inspired were they by these feelings, that, led by their commander, the entire Christian army raised its voice in a grand Te Deum.

At this time, exclusive of their allies, the besieging army consisted of eight hundred and eighteen foot soldiers, and eighty-seven cavalry. For weapons they had one hundred and eighteen muskets and crossbows, three heavy iron guns, and fifteen falconets of brass, half a ton of powder, fifty thousand copper-headed arrows, and a thousand long Chinantla pikes, besides their swords and the lances of the cavaliers. To each of the brigantines was allotted a falconet, and three hundred of the troops were detailed to man the fleet. The remainder of the Spaniards, together with one hundred thousand warriors from Tlascala and other allied cities, all eager for the downfall of Tenochtitlan, the stronghold of the oppressor, were divided into three armies, commanded by Sandoval, Alvarado, and Olid.

By the end of May, everything being in readiness, these armies were dispatched to their stations at the ends of the three great causeways leading to the city, while Cortes took temporary command of the fleet. He set sail from Tezcuco; but before he reached Istapalapan the breeze failed, and his vessels lay becalmed. While thus helpless, they were approached by an immense flotilla of Aztec canoes and periaguas, sent out by Guatamotzin for their destruction. These came on boldly until within pistol shot of the drifting fleet, and then halted, irresolute as to how they should attack such monsters.

Just then, a light air springing up, the brigantines bore directly down on the gathered canoes, which greeted them with a dense, but ineffective, flight of arrows and stones. Gathering headway as they advanced, the vessels crashed into the massed flotilla with frightful effect, at the same time letting fly their falconets to right and left. The rippling waters were instantly covered with the wreckage of shattered canoes and struggling human forms. The few survivors fled, with all speed, back to their city, and thus ended the first naval engagement in American waters.

Continuing his way to the great dike, by which he had made his first entry into Tenochtitlan, Cortes assaulted and captured the fort of Xoloc, by which it was defended, midway between the mainland and the city. Here he planted his heavy guns, and this place he made his headquarters during the siege.

In the meantime Alvarado had succeeded, after a stubborn battle, in cutting the aqueduct by which fresh water reached the city from Chapultepec. He next attempted to gain possession of the fatal causeway of Tlacopan, but was driven back, with heavy losses, after several hours of fighting.

After a week spent in the comparative inactivity of perfecting the blockade, the Commander resolved upon a general assault on the city by the three armies. As Huetzin had no longer a separate command, he asked and obtained permission to devote himself to the especial destruction of the Aztec gods. For this purpose he carefully selected one hundred of his most valiant warriors, and attached himself to the division led by the General over the causeway of Iztapalapan.

Its several openings were guarded by strong barricades, behind which the enemy made resolute stands. By the aid of the brigantines, which attacked them on each side, these were successfully carried, one after another, and at length the conquerors trod once more the familiar streets of the city.

How different now was this reception from that of their first entry! Then, myriads of eager and welcoming spectators, men, women, and children, were gathered on the flower-roofed houses. Now, most of the women and children had been sent from the city, and the house-tops were thronged only with grim warriors, who showered down a continuous storm of arrows, darts, and great stones, that stretched many a bold Spaniard and swarthy Tlascalan in the dust.

At every canal in place of a bridge was a rampart, that must be battered down by the heavy guns. Still, doggedly fighting, the besiegers made their slow way to the square, on one side of which stood the quarters they had evacuated on the noche triste, and on the other the great temple of Huitzil. As the Spaniards cleared the courtyard of the temple, Huetzin and his agile followers dashed up the long flights of steps to its top. Here they found only a few frantic priests, whom they pitched headlong from the lofty platform. In the shrine was a new image of the war-god, more hideous and more lavishly covered with gold than its predecessor. This they dragged from its pedestal, and, with an exulting heart, the young Toltec saw it, too, go thundering and crashing to the base of the great teocal.

Outraged and infuriated by this sacrilege, the Aztec warriors gathered about the temple in such overwhelming numbers, that the besiegers were forced back, down the avenue up which they had come; and only by the most determined fighting did Huetzin and his followers escape from being cut off, and rejoin their friends.

Although on this occasion the besiegers were driven from the city on all sides, Huetzin at least felt that the day's fighting and losses had not been in vain. He knew that his time for triumph was at hand, and that, with this overthrow of their war-god, the power of the Aztec priests had received a blow from which it would never recover.

39

ALDERETE'S
FATAL ERROR

THE NEXT DAY another assault was made that penetrated, as before, to the square of the temple. On this occasion the Spaniards, filled with hatred against the ancient palace in which they had suffered so much, set fire to it in a hundred places, and soon had the satisfaction of seeing it in ruins. As on the previous occasion, the retreat to their own camp was so bitterly assailed that few reached it without bearing on their bodies smarting tokens of the fight. These assaults were continued for many days, though with but slight results; for, wherever the besiegers filled canal openings during the day, the Aztecs cleared them out again at night. They also, contrary to their usual custom, made constant night attacks upon the Christian camps, so that the Spaniards were allowed no rest.

At this stage of the siege, Guatamotzin succeeded in capturing and destroying two of the brigantines, by luring them into a trap of stout stakes, driven just below the surface of the water. Thus, with varying fortunes did the days and weeks of the siege pass, until July came, and still the city made no sign of surrender. Famine was beginning to stalk through its streets, and its hardy defenders were sickening of the brackish water with which they eked out the scanty supplies nightly smuggled to them in canoes from the mainland; but the priests still promised ultimate victory, and were still believed.

At length another concerted attack was planned, by which two armies should advance from opposite sides of the city, and endeavor to force their way to a meeting in the great market-place of Tlateloco. Alderete, the royal treasurer, one of the late arrivals, was particularly anxious to have the market-place captured and occupied as a base of operations against the rest of the city. Reluctantly yielding to his importunities, Cortes ordered the assault to be made. From one side were to advance the combined forces of Sandoval and Alvarado, and from the other his own troops were to make their way, in three divisions, up three parallel streets, all of which led to the tinguez. One of these divisions was entrusted to Alderete, one to a younger Alvarado, while Cortes himself commanded the third. With this division went Huetzin, in command of the Tlascalans.

To each commander the General's last and most

implicit instruction was, to be sure and fill the canal openings as he advanced, so as to provide a way of retreat. Then, dismounting and advancing on foot, he led his own division to the assault. The Aztecs fell back after offering less resistance than usual, and the division carried barricade after barricade with comparative ease, carefully filling each canal with rubbish ere they left it. On either side of the street, Huetzin and his active warriors scaled the house-tops, engaging in hand-to-hand conflict with the defenders, and ever driving them from their positions. Nor did the young Toltec neglect the teocallis, several of which were encountered on the way. In every case these were deserted of their priests, and Huetzin caused them to be quickly deserted of their gods as well. From one of these tall observatories he descended with the information that the other divisions were so far in advance of that led by Cortes, that they were actually entering the great market-place while he was still but half way to it.

"Then," exclaimed the commander, "they cannot have stopped to fill the canals, and I fear me greatly are being decoyed into some trap!"

Halting his own division, he ordered Quinones, the captain of his guard, to maintain it in that place at all hazards, until hearing from him. Then, accompanied by Huetzin, Olea, and several other cavaliers, Cortes hastened through a narrow street connecting with the broad avenue up which Alderete had passed. The roadway of this was bordered by canals on either side, so

that the Spaniards had been able to bring a fleet of canoes with them. In these they had been ferried across
a wide gap, connecting the two canals, from which the
bridge had been removed. In the exciting rivalry and
ease of their advance, they forgot the commander›s
instructions, and neglected to fill this gap. Thus they
pressed exultingly forward, without a thought of disaster or of making provision for a hurried retreat.

Cortes had hardly reached the avenue before he
discovered this yawning chasm in the roadway, and realized the deadly error committed by Alderete. He and
those with him attempted to remedy it by casting in
rubbish with their own hands. They had scarcely begun, when the distant roar of conflict grew louder, and
in another minute a torrent of panic-stricken humanity
came rolling back, down the avenue to where the fatal
opening awaited its victims.

Alderete had made his way to the market-place
with such ease as to inspire him with a contempt for
his adversaries, and fill him with the idea that he was
about to conquer the city at a blow.

Suddenly, from the lofty summit of a neighboring
temple sounded, loud and clear, the thrilling tones of
the horn of Guatamotzin. It was a summons rarely issued, and, as the Spaniards had learned to their cost,
was invariably followed by a struggle to the death. On
this occasion its long-drawn, piercing notes had not
died away, when the Aztecs, who had fled before the
advance of Alderete, turned on him with the utmost

fury. At the same moment swarms of ambushed warriors poured out from every cross street and lane, rending the air with their savage cries, and springing upon the flanks of his straggling column.

Bewildered and staggered by the force and unexpected nature of the onset, the Spaniards paused, listened in vain for the accustomed rallying-cry of their great leader, wavered, and broke into a mad flight back over the way they had just come. In the frenzied rush friends and foes, Spaniards, Tlascalans, and Aztecs, were mingled in inextricable confusion; so that many of the terrified fugitives were struck down by those beside them, and snatched into waiting canoes by unseen hands.

Blinded by terror, the fierce human wave rolled on toward the gulf, on the opposite side of which Cortes and half a dozen companions shuddered at the impending horror. There was no pause at the awful brink. The leading files were forced to the leap by those pressing from behind, and in a moment the most hideous feature of the noche triste was being re-enacted. In this case there were no horses nor guns to plunge with wretched humanity into the chasm, nor did darkness multiply the confusion. Still it was a fearful sight, and Cortes, extending helping hands to whom he could, groaned aloud to behold his soldiers disappear by scores beneath the choking waters, or dragged into waiting Aztec canoes.

As he thus stood in the edge of the water, striving

to save some victims of this terrible disaster, a large canoe containing six athletic Aztec warriors dashed up to
him, and with wild yells of "Malinche! Malinche!" its
occupants made a determined effort to drag him into
their boat. A spear-thrust in the leg partially disabled
him, and though he struggled with the almost superhuman strength supplied by a vision of the sacrificial altar,
his assailants would have accomplished their purpose
had not Olea on one side, and Huetzin on the other,
sprung to his rescue with flashing swords. After killing
two of the Aztecs, Olea fell mortally wounded. Another
cavalier named Lerma was instantly in his vacant place,
and for several minutes he and the Tlascalan Knight,
bestriding the prostrate body of their leader, held the
whole swarming mob of assailants in check. The cool
bravery and expert skill of the two were a match for the
reckless ferocity of an untrained score.

Meantime the report carried to the General's own
division that he was slain, spread such dismay through
the ranks that, but for the prompt action of the captain of the guard and a few others, they would have
joined in the senseless flight of Alderete's men. Those
who prevented this, refusing to believe that their leader
was dead, rushed to his rescue, and with a fierce charge
pulled him from the very edge of the water, into which
the Aztecs, despite the efforts of Huetzin and Lerma,
had succeeded in dragging him.

The body of brave Olea was borne away in triumph
by the enemy, as was that of a page, pierced through

the neck by a javelin, as he came up with the General's horse. As the lifeless hand of the page dropped from the bridle this was instantly seized by Guzman, the chamberlain; but ere Cortes gained his saddle, this faithful attendant was also snatched away and dragged into an Aztec canoe, vainly screaming for help.

The continued retreat along the canal-bordered roadway was marked by death and disaster to its very end. The Aztec attack was bold and incessant, while the press was so great that many an unfortunate was forced from his footing and slipped into the fatal waters. From these he was only rescued by Aztec canoes, that would bear him to a fate far worse than instant death.

The dismay and terror of the fugitives was heightened by the display, on the uplifted ends of Aztec spears, of two bloody Spanish heads. This dismal spectacle was accompanied by savage cries of "Sandoval! Sandoval! Tonatiah! Tonatiah!" intimating that the other army had also been routed, and its leaders slain. At the same time that army, barely holding its own against a most determined attack, was horrified at seeing a bloody Spanish head tossed, with wildest glee, from hand to hand of their assailants, who greeted it with exulting shouts of «Malinche! Malinche!" thus striving to convey the idea that the great leader had fallen.

The disastrous retreat of Alderete and his men was not stayed until they reached a place where the light battery and a body of cavalry, sent to their succor, could operate. Even then the Aztecs did not give way, until, in return for the losses inflicted upon them by the artillery, they had captured several troopers and killed their horses.

Next to the noche triste, this affair was more disastrous to the whites than any in which they had been engaged since entering that land of battle and death. Besides their long list of killed and wounded, sixty-two Spanish and a multitude of Tlascalan prisoners had been captured by the triumphant Aztecs. These had also killed seven horses, and gained possession of two pieces of artillery.

As the sun was setting that evening, the penetrating vibration of the great serpent drum, from the lofty but dismantled temple of the war-god, attracted all eyes in that direction. A long procession of priests wound slowly up and around the sides of the vast teocal. As it reached the summit, the Spaniards recognized with horror, in the figures of several men stripped to their waists, the white skins of their compatriots. These, urged on by cruel blows, were compelled to dance in front of the altar, before submitting to the itzitli blade of sacrifice. For eighteen successive evenings was this awful scene repeated, and on the last of them, Guzman, the General's devoted attendant, met the cruel fate that had already overtaken his companions, whose number he had seen dwindle, day by day, until he alone was left.

The Aztec priests caused it to be proclaimed throughout the valley, that within eight days from the date of their terrible defeat, every Spaniard would be either dead or a prisoner, for so the gods had decreed. At the same time they warned all allies of the Spaniards, who did not wish to share their fate, to desert the Christian cause, and retire to their own places.

This prophecy had such an effect upon the allies, that by thousands and ten of thousands they left the camps of the besiegers, until only a few hundred faithful Tlascalans remained. But when the eight days were passed, and, in spite of repeated attacks from the city, the white men still held their ground, their shame-faced allies began to return in such numbers that the besieging army was soon as strong as before.

40

FINAL OVERTHROW OF THE AZTEC GODS

THE SIEGE OF Tenochtitlan had now been going on for nearly three months. Still the besieged, animated by the heroism of their young king, and the fatal superstition that caused them to believe in the promises and tremble at the threats of their false priests, held out. Famine, sickness, and death stalked abroad through the city; but it would not surrender, nor would it so long as every house was a fortress and every canal a barricade. Guatamotzin steadily refused to treat with embassies, or grant a personal interview to the Christian leader. Scores of Spaniards and hundreds of Huetzin's brave warriors had been sacrificed by priestly knives, and their blood cried out for vengeance. In view of these facts, Cortes came reluctantly to the conclusion that the beautiful city must be destroyed, its buildings leveled to the earth to afford a clear sweep for his guns, and its canals, filled with their debris, converted into solid ground for the unimpeded movements of his cavalry.

So the fatal order was given, and a hundred thousand natives of Anahuac, who had suffered too bitterly from the oppression of the Aztec to feel pity for him in the hour of his distress, seized their heavy coas (picks), and sprang cheerfully to the work of destruction. First, the openings in the causeways were so solidly filled that they were never again opened. Then the frail tenements of the suburbs were demolished, and a broad belt, encircling the more substantially built portions of the city, was presented for the movement of the troops. The defenders of Tenochtitlan did not view these measures with indifference; but, sallying forth on all sides, maintained an incessant warfare with the besiegers.

At this stage of the proceedings a message was sent to Guatamotzin, offering honorable terms of peace, and he called a great council to consider it. His nobles advised its acceptance, but the priests, foreseeing their own downfall if its terms were agreed to, forbade him to submit. Their councils prevailed; and thus, in obedience to priestly selfishness, was this queenly city of the New World doomed to annihilation.

For two days the besiegers quietly awaited an answer to their message. At length it came in the shape of a furious sortie, from every city street, of host after host of desperate Aztecs. Like swollen mountain torrents bursting their confining flood-gates, they swept in wave after wave, across the causeways, to the very entrenchments of their enemy, threatening to overwhelm him by sheer force of numbers. But the besiegers were too strongly fortified, and too well armed, to be dislodged. Into the very faces of the dense Aztec ranks was poured a withering fire from the land batteries, while their flanks were enfiladed by the guns of the fleet. Finally, hidden beneath clouds of sulphurous smoke, their shattered columns wavered, and then rolled slowly back into the city. It was their last great effort, and from this time on, the proud city seemed to await its doom in sullen apathy.

Now the work of destruction was pressed with the utmost vigor. Day after day witnessed the demolition of dwellings, palaces, and temples, the filling of canals, and the penetrating of the besiegers, from two sides at once, further and further toward the heart of the Aztec capital. Fiercely did its starving defenders contest each foot of progress, fighting from house to house, darting out in small parties from side streets to slay a score or so of workmen, and then as suddenly disappearing, charging after the retreating forces at each nightfall, and at all times battling with the ferocity of despair.

From the six hundred temples of the city Huetzin and his band of picked warriors hurled the idols, one after another, until at length, in all Tenochtitlan, only one abiding-place remained to the Aztec gods. This was the lofty teocal overlooking the market-place of

Tlateloco, which was second only in size and importance to the mighty structure from which the war-god
had long since been driven.

Three-fourths of the beautiful city, including the
stately palace of its king, lay in ruins, when near the
close of a day of destruction, the two attacking armies,
doggedly fighting their way through the still innumerable host of Aztecs, came in sight of each other on opposite sides of the market-place. Suddenly, from the
teocal overlooking it, a bright blaze shot high in the
air, reddening the eastern sky with a glow like that of
the western sunset. So ominous was the signal, that for
a moment all combatants paused to regard it. As they
gazed upward, a small body of men appeared on the
verge of the lofty platform, and the next instant a huge,
shapeless mass, came crashing and thundering down
the steep declivity. During the momentary silence that
followed, a single figure stood boldly outlined, on the
point from which the image had come, and, in the ringing tones of Huetzin the Toltec, were heard the words:

"Thus perishes the last of the Aztec gods!"

Then, making in mid-air the holy sign of his faith,
he disappeared.

With joyous shouts the Christian soldiers sprang
forward to complete their victory; but it was completed. Guatamotzin was already a fugitive, and, without
king or gods, the Aztecs would fight no more.

That very evening Sandoval, who had been made
admiral of the fleet, chased with his swiftest vessel

a large periagua that was endeavoring to escape from the city. As he drew near to it, and was about to open fire, a stately figure sprang up, and proclaimed:

"I am the king! Slay me if you will, but spare these helpless ones."

On hearing this, Sandoval ordered his men to lower their weapons, and received Guatamotzin with courtesy and honor on board his vessel.

Thus ended the bitter siege of Tenochtitlan, a siege unsurpassed in the annals of war for the heroic fortitude, bravery, and persistence shown on both sides.

That night the fall of the Aztec capital, and the overthrow of its gods, was signalized by one of the most fearful storms ever known in the Mexican valley. For hours the rain descended in torrents, the heavens were rent by incessant flashes of blinding lightning, and the continuous crash of thunder shook the encircling mountain-walls to their foundation. It was a fitting requiem over the death of a brave and powerful, but at the same time cruel and superstitious, nation.

On the following morning began an exodus, from the devastated city, of its remaining inhabitants; and so great was the number who had survived the horrors of battle, pestilence, and famine, that the sorrowful processions occupied three days in defiling across the causeways to the mainland. As they had for many days been unable to bury their dead, the deserted city was now but a vast charnel-house in which no human being could exist. As soon after this as was practicable, Cortes set to work, with the aid of the conquered citizens and immense levies drawn from the surrounding country, to rebuild what he had destroyed. The first building to be erected was a magnificent Christian cathedral, which, dedicated to St. Francis, was made to occupy the very site on which formerly stood the temple of the Aztec war-god. So actively was the work of reconstruction pushed, that in less than four years' time the new city of Mexico, in many respects more splendid than its predecessor on the same site, had arisen from the ashes of Tenochtitlan.

With the fall of the Aztec capital, and the final overthrow of its cruel gods, Huetzin, the Knight of Castile and head chief of the free republic of Tlascala, was absolved from his vow. Thus the moment his military duties would permit, he sought the brave and beautiful Indian girl, to win whom had for so long been the hope of his life. He found her in the royal gardens of Tezcuco; where, above the grave of Tiata, he declared to Marina the love which had been hers, and had been reciprocated by her, from the time of their first meeting. A few days later they were married by the good Father Olmedo, the Christian priest who had accompanied the white conquerors through all their weary marches and battles.

Thus when the Lord of Titcala returned to his mountain home, at the head of his army of victorious warriors, all other causes for happiness seemed to him insignificant as compared with that of taking with

him, as his wife, the maiden whose services as interpreter to the white conquerors were no longer needed.

The fall of Tenochtitlan occurred in August, 1521,
and for seven years longer did Cortes remain in Mexico,
founding new cities, rebuilding many of those that had
been destroyed, extending the dominion of the Spanish
king, and in all ways perfecting his glorious conquest.
At the end of that time, or in the early summer of 1528,
two fine ships, laden with the rarest products of Anahuac, sailed from Vera Cruz, and, after a prosperous
voyage across the Atlantic, entered the port of Palos,
in Spain. On the deck of one of them, eagerly gazing
at the land which some of them had not seen in many
years, and others were now viewing for the first time,
stood a group, most of whom would be recognized
by those familiar with the Mexico of that day. Chief
among them was Hernando Cortes, the leader. Beside
him stood Gonzalo de Sandoval, his beloved and well-
tried Captain, and several other cavaliers, all heroes of
the Mexican wars. Near at hand were Huetzin, Lord of
Titcala, his beautiful wife, a son of Montezuma, and a
number of other Tlascalan and Aztec nobles.

Immediately on their arrival these repaired to the
convent of La Rabida, long since inseparably connected with the immortal name of Columbus, to offer up
thanks for their safe voyage.

Here, on the threshold of his native land, sturdy
Sandoval took sick of a mysterious malady, which, it
was quickly evident, was about to terminate his earthly

career of glory and usefulness.

About the dying bed of the soldier were gathered his commander and his best-loved friends. With the same composure and undaunted courage with which he had faced death on a hundred battle-fields, he faced it now. With a lingering hand-clasp to each, he bade farewell to the comrades who had fought those battles beside him.

"To thy gentle care, Marina, I commend Motilla. From thee, Juan, my brother, I will bear a message to Tiata."

Very faint were these words, but with the mention of her name, to whom his loyal troth had been plighted years before in the royal gardens of fair Tenochtitlan, a smile of ineffable glory illumined his rugged features. In another moment his soldier spirit was answering the glad trumpet-call of the Immortals, while above its earthly habitation, Huetzin the Toltec was making the holy sign of the peace-loving but all-powerful God of the Four Winds.